TAYLOR'S THREE

IN A RACE

AGAINST TIME

An Adventure Story For Grown-Ups

Rosie Chapple

For Liz Davies and Alison Woodeson
with love and thanks.

CONTENTS

ACKNOWLEDGMENTS

Arvon

Writers HQ

Lauren Nicholls

Stephen May

Isobel Pearce

Hilary Lane

Liz Tuckwell

Ian Saunders

Michael Munday

Madeleine Bradbury

20% of royalties to go to Ovarian Cancer Action.

8-12 Camden High Street, London, NW1 0JH

Registered charity no. 1109743 (England & Wales) and SC043478 (Scotland). Company Limited by guarantee no. 5403443.

Prelude

October 2007

In a cloud of exhaust fumes, with her windscreen wipers faltering, April draws up outside her flat. At work the manager thinks she has gone out to a doctor's appointment: 'woman's problems', April whispered, backing away with a mournful shake of her head. She turns off the engine but keeps the radio going whilst 'Big Girls Don't Cry' finishes (an irony not lost on her) and meanwhile adjusts the rear-view mirror to see her face. Her hair is a mess, she hasn't looked at it since getting up so late and now she sees it is tangled over her head and flattened on one side. Time is too short to bother looking for a brush, so she combs her fingers roughly through it. She must try to look organised and cheerful, not 'deranged mother'.

Whilst driving here she has decided to try out the helpful and supportive role. Maybe this time it will work. She picks up the fairy cakes she has pinched from work (someone's birthday again) to give her a vague reason for being here mid-morning, 'in case you were hungry, darling'. Ahead of her the kitchen windows of the flat reflect the glare of headlights as a juggernaut roars out of the industrial estate behind her. The white plastic slatted blinds are still tightly closed. She's lived in worse places and used to think she was going up in the world, yet this place is a steep dive downwards again. How can such a nondescript flat look dismal even from the outside?

April knows Kate won't be up and will be annoyed at being woken. Even bringing the cakes is too obviously an excuse, they both know the reason for April being there when she ought to be at work. But Kate should be up and about preparing herself for that interview. She'll be angry. She's always angry these days.

April has made the mistake of finally gathering up her courage and opening her bank statement at work this morning. What she saw in black and white (and red) was not unexpected but ripped into her mind through her eyes. The rent has left her account and they only have £20 to survive on until the end of the month. What can she possibly buy with £20 that will last them three weeks? How will she even get to and from work? They won't do it, can't do it. Kate must get a job. But the harder April pushes the more Kate resists. But if April stops pushing Kate will just sleep and go out as usual and never try to get work and, worse, not feel guilty about it.

She gets out of the car. She strides to the front door. She waits for a moment with her key poised, trying to fix a smile and hears nothing. Drizzle falls on her, one large drop falls on her raised hand. Everything she does is wrong, has always been wrong, even things she thought were right have turned out badly.

This will not end well.

Can she face another argument? Such anger directed at her. So much to bear. Today? Now? And what for? She'll lose again. Kate won't go to the interview anyway.

Kate is impervious to her mother's pleadings; she has returned home from London with an invisible personal shield as seen in

2

Science Fiction movies. It leaves her out of reach, and any ray guns of need ping off her and rebound on April. She pauses, her hand wavers, tightens, relaxes, tightens, yet after a second she swivels and plods back to the car. She drives away, leaving only a black cloud of petrol fumes hovering over the empty crisp packets on the tarmac.

*

Trish finds some bread and a piece of old cheese that are just edible at the back of the fridge and makes herself a sandwich which she eats whilst dancing around the messy kitchen to Black Sabbath. There is some boring household stuff that she should be dealing with, but she goes out to see Stu and ends up smoking a joint and watching her son try to fix the problem with his motorbike. From the old sofa in one corner of the garage, lying with her feet on Stu's lap and blowing smoke into the air, she issues her solutions to what is wrong with it and is greeted by raised eyebrows and cries of 'leave off, let it go ma', which have no effect on her comments at all. Eventually she returns to the kitchen, chooses a mug from the pile of unwashed crockery lying in and around the sink, but has to abandon any idea of a hot drink because the kettle has stopped working again. She shakes it, hopefully, for a second, looks inside it to detect any bubbles, but it stays dead. Catching sight of the clock she gasps and runs upstairs to collect a towel, hoping she can get a shower before starting work. She strips off her jeans and t-shirt, removes her shoes, catches sight of herself in the mirror, stops for a moment, poses, and smiles and is on her way to the bathroom when the telephone rings. She pauses on the landing, jostling her feet on the torn lino and dropping her remaining underwear whilst listening as the answerphone kicks in. Her mother's familiar plummy tones sound out.

"Patricia! Patricia! I know you're there. In that awful council place. Your father and I are still expecting you for our diamond wedding anniversary celebration tomorrow. Everyone will be here. Anthony's eldest is coming all the way from Aberdeen, Geoffrey's family has flown in from Japan and America. I'm TRUSTING you will, just for ONCE make an EFFORT for your family. Your father's old school friend Sir Moresby is making one speech, and Geoffrey is making another. So sweet of them. Don't you dare pretend you forgot. I'll never ever forgive you. Patricia! You're so bloody annoying. I've told everyone that ALL the family will be there and that means YOU."

Trish, busy grimacing, does not notice the door behind her opening quietly until she hears the patient voice of her youngest daughter pleading with her to make herself decent.

"Oh come on now, darlin'," she complains, "what's wrong with a naked body?" and, evading the response, she swoops into the bathroom, only to find the water is cold.

*

Sam goes up the stripped oak stairs to her attic studio and closes the door behind her. She switches on the player so she can continue listening to Joni Mitchell's latest album that Michael has sent her from LA, she's really enjoying it. Turning, she sees her working space and exhales, feeling her shoulders drop and going to her workbench she picks up the silver brooch she has been enamelling. She holds it up and adjusts the light, examining it minutely, planning how she is going to get the exact shades of blue and grey needed. A familiar noise downstairs makes her pause, listen and tense, but, hoping she is wrong, she tightens the straps of the cotton apron and bends forward again. A voice calls her, "Mum? Are you in your studio? Mum? Where are you? Mum?"

"I'm coming down, dearest," and her fingers place the brooch carefully back on the workbench and fold a cloth to cover it. Opening the door, she practices a smile as she steps down towards the kitchen whilst the screeching sound grows louder. In the kitchen her daughter is wrestling with a toddler who turns and stiffens in her arms, emitting supersonic shrieks. The minute the door is fully open her daughter turns and pushes the fighting mass into Sam's arms. "There you are. At last."

Sam looks down and sees a puckered mouth and pink watery eyes, the small fists lift and hit her on her chest. She winces and attempts to lift the bulk higher, but Salome leans backwards away from her and wails.

"Jeremy and I really need some time off this evening, we've both had a hell of a week, so we thought you could look after Salome tonight. And you might as well start now, I have to go shopping and you know how she screams in shops." Sam opens her mouth to reply, but Salome pitches forward and grabs hold of her hair with sticky fingers and tugs. By the time Sam has carefully prised open each hand and lowered Salome to the table the front door has closed, and she is alone with her granddaughter who promptly vomits onto the tiled floor.

One

October 2007 – Saturday morning

The doorbell rings. April grunts, turns over, presses the pillow to her head. It rings again. April removes the pillow and listens. It sounds again, longer, louder. April rolls out of her bed groaning with irritation, pushes her feet into the monster claw fluffy slippers and grabs the bright yellow wrap from behind her bedroom door. The bell shrieks once more in a continuous stream of ear-battering clanging as she thuds her way over the magazines and mugs strewn on the floor of the living area. The insistence of the bell pulls her forwards but the door crashes open before she gets there.

In front of her, inside her flat, across her doorway, are two men, both looking directly at her, one is pointing as if he's going to speak. Her heart beats faster, her breath stops. They are both strangers. She stretches the wrap around her stout body and leaves her arms firmly crossed. She cannot move, she thinks of running but her legs seem frozen. Her mouth is open, her hands clench at the flexible material. Time waits. Nothing happens.

They look at her, step forward and one of them gently closes the door. She's now imprisoned in here with them, she wants to take a step away, but her legs are shaking. They are flashily dressed: buffed leather shoes, grey suits, clean white shirts, large watches. The younger one with a tattoo on his neck keeps rubbing his clenched hands, his nails are clean and filed sharply. The older man is taller and broad with a pale round face and a crooked nose. He looks burnished.

"Mrs Roberts?" asks the tallest man, his soft voice with its London accent is more threatening than a shout. She looks at his pointed finger, cannot find her voice, and nods. 'We'll only be a minute. Sit down." He points to the stool behind her. This is not a request. April leans back onto it, grabbing a stray tea towel and laying it protectively across her thighs. She waits. She sees a bread knife just out of reach and her phone on the table beside the sofa. She is conscious that the younger man has crossed the floor and is opening and shutting doors and going into the other rooms. Oh God, she is going to be burgled. This thought is almost a relief until she wonders why her, and what happens afterwards?

"What do you want?" she gasps, adding, "how do you know my name?" The second man comes back and shakes his head in response to the tallest man's questioning glance. Then they both stare at her in silence. April looks back, very aware of their ominous unity. The coldness in their eyes is frightening, and the way they hold their hands and stand, delicately balanced, shows that they are ready for violence. Outside her control her lips quiver and her hands shake. She feels tears beginning and curses her weakness. She grips herself more tightly and tries an appeasing smile that gets no response. The tallest one glares at her through red-rimmed washed blue eyes and appears to be thinking. The second one, who has examined every part of the flat, shifts on his feet and picks up some chopsticks. He beats a little rhythm with them on the draining board but stops when the leader frowns. He catches April's eye and stares at her whilst continuing to turn and bend the cheap plastic sticks almost to breaking point.

"We don't like these sorts of visits, Mrs Roberts, but sometimes they 'ave to be made." The leader looks down at her as she shivers on her stool and shakes his head with regret. "Sometimes people are stupid, know what I mean? Like Kate. We really wanted to speak to Kate, but she ain't 'ere. So we 'ave to speak to you." April sits up a little with shock, both when her daughter's name is mentioned and then with the further news that she isn't in the flat. April opened the door for her at three that very morning, drunk, lost her key, they'd quarrelled as usual, the second or third time that day. Kate had shouted and flung herself into her bedroom with the door slamming so loudly that it must've been heard throughout all the flats. She swallows. "Where's Kate, Mrs Roberts?"

"Kate?" she says feebly, "Kate?"

"Yes, Kate, Mrs Roberts. She owes our boss money."

"Kate? Kate owes you money?" She is suddenly relieved. Bailiffs! They are bailiffs, of course. She will pay them and then they will go away. "How much does she owe you?" she says, looking round for her cheque book, remembering and reaching across to get it from where it lies in her handbag on the worktop.

"Thirty-five grand." There is a silence, her hand stops.

"How much?"

"Thirty-five thousand."

"Thirty? Five? Thousand?"

"Yeah, yeah. Thirty-five thousand quid, Mrs Roberts. An' we don't take cheques before you ask." There is absolutely no way that she can pay them thirty-five thousand pounds. She rents this flat. She is overdrawn as usual. She has no savings at all, her credit cards have been taken away. She has nothing to sell. Even her car is so old and mechanically unsound that she would have to pay to have it taken away. It's a ridiculous amount of money.

"There must be some mistake." The leader nods to the younger man who puts his hand in his pocket and produces several squares of paper. He holds them out to her. They are copies of notes written in Kate's small neat handwriting and they are all IOUs on paper headed 'Gametime'. One of them has a note written by Kate on it 'Double or Quits'. She catches a glimpse of one for £1,200 and another for £7,000. Suddenly, April is furious. Gambling! The stupid idiot has been gambling. Thirty-five thousand fucking pounds! What a waste! Thirty-five thousand thrown away. So much money. Lost. Gone. For nothing. She turns the bits of paper over and wants to tear them, burn them, see them disappear in a flash of fire. Her eyes scan without seeing. She thinks of all the unopened bills festering in the drawer, the credit card she could've paid off, the food she could buy, the clothes, the car, the flat she should now be living in. A sob starts in her throat and cannot be stopped.

"What happens if I don't pay?" she says, letting the bills crumple and fall from her hands. "Supposing I, say, take her to court, I don't care…" The tallest man becomes even more confidential and leans forward.

"Oh, but you must pay. You really must. I'm 'ere to collect the money. My boss never uses courts. And unpaid bills now, 'e really can't let punters get away with that. I'm sure you see. 'e has a reputation, a business to protect. I don't 'ave to spell out for you what would 'appen to Kate? Or to this flat?" The chopsticks break with an emphatic crack and the young man jumps back with an expression of mock repentance. He turns and with a sharp arm movement sweeps the crockery off her draining board, picks up a carving knife and stabs it into the worktop, leaving his fist clenched on its handle. The plates and mugs collide and crash, spattering broken pieces across the floor. She crouches back on her stool and puts a hand over her mouth; she knows better than to say anything. The other man does nothing except look at her, but she stays very still. It seems to her they are waiting, almost wanting, some response from her, any excuse for a further attack. She thinks of Kate, scarred and in a hospital bed and the blood on her face.

"So how are we going to pay you then?" her voice seems to come from someone else. Both of the strangers move back a little and relax.

"We'll collect the cash, from you 'ere, next Saturday. That'll give you lots a time to get the money. We're reasonable. But we want all the thirty-five grand. In cash." April nods. She has no choice. She tries to look as if she has a plan, a secret source of money, but her mind is racing round looking for a solution like a rat in a cage. They begin to leave, but the leader turns back to her suddenly,

"I don't 'ave to tell you not to speak to anyone official, do I? After all, we've only been 'ere to talk about 'ow your daughter is going to pay 'er dues, 'aven't we?" April nods once more. Then as she sees his back and knows that he is going she suddenly panics.

"But how can we contact you? What happens if something goes wrong and we can't get the money that quickly?" They stop and turn and she takes a step away from them.

"We'll be 'ere Saturday next week, Mrs Roberts. Kate knows where we are. As for not 'aving the money... I really don't think that's very clever." He pauses and leans forwards; she smells a whiff of acid aftershave and sees that he has a razor burn on his chin. "I really don't. Not much protection around 'ere is there? I mean if a fire started? Terrible what fires can do to 'omes. I've seen quite a few.

So best to pay up. Easier in the long run. Know what I mean?" April nods. "So, we'll be back next week. Make sure you 'ave all of the money. Every bit. Or else."

She hears the front door closing and then they have gone. She cannot move, she cannot think, she starts to sob but hears her grandfather's voice in her head telling her to pull herself together. Picking up the phone with shaking hands she dials Sam.

Two

Saturday afternoon

April parks her car on the gravel drive in front of Sam's double-fronted house and gets out into a knee-high cloud of exhaust fumes and looks into the garage, noting with relief that Hugh's car isn't there. She rings the doorbell and waits in the porch, shifting from foot to foot in order to warm up. Soon there is the sound of running footsteps and April makes out Sam's slim shape mottled through the patterned glass, hurrying towards the front door. She snatches it open.

"Ah April dear one, there you are. Come in, come in…." Sam calls back to her, leaving the door open as she runs away again across the parquet and into the passageway that leads towards the kitchen. Undeterred, April follows her, hearing the sound of a child crying and knowing immediately what she will find.

In the airy kitchen, Sam is trying to persuade her eighteen-month-old granddaughter to sit in the highchair and drink some apple juice. Salome lies wailing on the kitchen floor surrounded by a chaos of paper and pens. Any attempt to pick her up makes her rigid with rage and emit violent screeches.

"Gin! Gin!" calls Sam to April. April, who has stepped over Salome to put the kettle on, stops and diverts to the drinks' cupboard. Soon she has two large gin and tonics in her hand.

"Step away from the child!" she calls to Sam, and giving her the gin, makes her sit down in a chair she's pulled out from the pine kitchen table, then sits down herself. Sam swigs back the gin and gazes at Salome, who is now tearing up the paper and throwing it and the pens around the room.

"Helen just dumped her on me again! I was in the studio, working on this new idea when the key went in the lock."

"Change the locks," interrupts April, knowing full well that this repeated advice will never be acted upon. Sam, who is usually cool and elegant, runs a hand through her short dark hair with its red streaks and looks at April pleadingly over the top of a large cotton apron smeared with what looks like chocolate and pen marks.

"I really should be able to cope. And there was Helen, saying that she and Jeremy needed some time to deepen their human connection. I just hope I'm not having her for the full weekend again." Sam speaks in a desperate whisper, in between mouthfuls of gin and with her brown eyes persistently returning to Salome who is now colouring the terracotta tiled kitchen floor.

"Will it clean off?" asks April softly.

"God knows! But at least she's quiet," breathes Sam and leans back in the chair and finally looks and smiles at April, then frowns.

"I'm so sorry," she says, reaching out to April and putting an arm round her. "I'm moaning on about me and you are far more important. I couldn't believe it when you rang me. How horrible for you! What a shock! Are you OK? Are you really?" April slowly shakes her head. "At least you're here now. I was so worried for you. Have you double-locked that front door?" April looks down and shakes her head again and then gives in and leans into Sam and really sobs. Sam's arms wrap around her and they rock for a while, forming a solid comforting mass with Sam stroking April's back. They separate with a laugh and Sam passes the tissues. "I'm so proud of you! You didn't buckle under on your own, you kept your cool."

"It didn't feel like it. I was just so scared!"

"Bloody Kate! Have you found her? I can't believe it. And her an accountant! What was she thinking?" April replies automatically that Kate is qualified as an auditor, a difference Kate has been keen for everyone to recognise. She mops her cheeks and relays all the places she has looked for Kate, her favourite haunts, all the old friends' mothers she has called and finally the hospitals. No-one has seen her. April has left her phone number with all of them but holds out little hope.

"I don't know where she is, if she's coming back, if she's OK." Sam makes soothing noises as April continues, "she's really dropped me in it."

"No, no," protests Sam, "I can't believe she'd leave you in the lurch like this, it seems out of character somehow. She was so good as a child, so caring, so willing and always worked so hard. Your golden girl, your gift. Getting that first-class degree! Then landing that amazing job in London. How proud we all were of her. Then this. This just doesn't seem like her." Sam has been secretly angry with Kate since she got back. It's so cruel of Kate, considering the very real sacrifices April made to ensure that she had stability and a dependable maternal presence. How April changed from a carefree, freewheeling, dope-smoking woman to a serious conforming single mother, holding down mundane jobs with difficulty, always on the edge financially, never breaking free. A life of continual scrimping and saving. All for Kate. Then Kate grew up, went to uni, qualified, got that dream job and moved to London. And April moved to a better flat, started going out, buying real first-hand clothes. Back to her old self: naughty, fun, carefree. But then Kate returned and April was forced backwards, she had to give up her nice new flat and get the miserable one that she lives in now, in order to accommodate Kate. It was so unfair of Kate not to explain, and to treat April like shit, as if she had caused it all. 'We none of us get the life we deserve,' thinks Sam, 'or the children.'

"Did anyone know why she lost her job in London?"

"Well it was shocking how few of her old close friends she'd seen. Some of them didn't know so I kept shtum, but those that did know said she hadn't said why. And the fact is," continues April, "the stupid, bloody truth of the matter is that I don't know either. I can remember collecting her from the station after that awful phone call, she just stood there looking lost. Not knowing where she was. In shock. I had never seen her look so drained, as if all her strings had been cut. She couldn't speak, just said she'd blown it. Lost it. FIVE months now. Five fucking months she's been back. I never found out. She just wouldn't talk. I should've found out. I should've made her talk. Maybe if I'd made her talk this wouldn't have happened."

April flicks back in her memories to the good times, when Kate and she were companions, cooking together, sharing jokes, doing homework. This is the Kate she misses: her close ally, the one that kept her on track, in reality the Kate who disappeared when university and a new life claimed her. Then reappeared horribly changed.

"Did I cause it? Do you think in some way I made it happen?" April can scarcely say the words as guilt catches in her throat. "I missed her so much when she left for uni and then that London job. I was pleased, really pleased, don't get me wrong, that she'd made it.

Become independent. But…."

"You were lost for a while without her. I know, dearest." Sam refrains from adding, 'but later so much happier…'

"So when she came home suddenly, I didn't ask in case she left again?"

"Stop the guilt trip. Whatever reason she came back had nothing to do with you. It doesn't really matter does it? I mean, what she did in London?" continues Sam. "How she lost her job? She's been back for a while. Done nothing, and now she's gone. With no explanation." They take a swig of gin and simultaneously realise that there is silence. They look under the table to where Salome is stretched out flat on her back, asleep. Sam smiles. "Peace at last! Thank God for underfloor heating eh?" She goes to fetch a child's blanket and comes back with Trish. "Just caught her at the front door about to ring the bell, stopped her just in time," Sam says, drooping the blanket over Salome and showing Trish what she might've woken. Trish grimaces and raises her eyebrows at April.

"Hello, you old tart," says April standing on tiptoe to hug Trish, "left the Harley lowering the tone on the driveway?"

"Hi there, fat-arse! You can talk! So many bloody holes in your old jalopy you might as well be on my Betty. I came the minute I could get away. I'm so shocked, but not really surprised if truth be told. Her behaviour recently… well……you know what I think." Sam responds to April's defensive shrug by asking Trish if she wants a gin which Trish brusquely refuses as she's just come from her session at the pub and will be going back there in a couple of hours. As they talk Sam makes sandwiches, setting them out on earthenware platters.

"OK," says Trish, "Let's get down to it. Taylor's Three on task."

"Of course," grins April, "I'd almost forgotten that's what we were called."

"That awful squat," smiles Sam.

"We had some good times there," says Trish, "it was rent-free in London, near Clapham Common and the station, you finished your art degree from there, Sam."

"Taylor's Court," says Sam with a sigh, "I understand it's an exclusive care home now."

"We got raided…" chips in April with a smile. They all laugh.

Trish leans towards April, "So, are you going to try to find the lucre or forget it and hope fucking Kate gets home with the money?"

"She might come back," waivers April.

"Bloody unlikely," continues Trish, ignoring Sam's warning glances. "She's been absolutely vile since she got back. I think she's fled and can't face the consequences of gambling away all those tens of thousands. Bloody hell. YOU will have to face up to HER mess." Trish and Kate used to get on well until recently when Trish, in irritation at the pressure April was facing, tried talking to Kate one afternoon when April was at work. It ended badly with Kate swearing at Trish to mind her own business and Trish telling Kate to get a fucking grip. "Do you have a plan?" she asks suddenly in a kinder tone. "We're here to help. You're not on your own." April shakes her head. "I know you said they were bloody threatening, but can you just let them do their worst?"

"They said about setting fire to the flat."

"Well what's in it?"

"It was unfurnished, so everything in it is mine. There's all my mother's and grandparents' stuff and my cooking equipment." Trish and Sam both nod: April's one relaxation is food, both making it and eating it and she excels at both, creating dishes for all those near to her. "There's Kate's stuff. There's my clothes. I know it doesn't seem much to you, or even to me, but it's all I have. They said about 'accidents' happening to people. That must mean me or Kate. He held a knife …" April's voice falters. Sam stops and leans over and puts an arm round her shoulders.

"I could hide you," says Trish, "really well. Stu has contacts."

"How long can I hide for? Anyway, I need to stay in the flat for when Kate comes back. She might have a plan. Maybe she's doing something now as we speak. I still need to go to work. It's the only steady income I've got. I can't take any time off: I've used up all my holidays. I must look for Kate some more, I need to make sure she's OK. I have to face this. I can't see any other way out. I must just get on and try to get the money." Her speech tumbles out of her; she is repeating a now-familiar scattered thought process. "I need at least some plan to get the money."

"OK then darlin'. Let's start," says Trish. "We need a serious plan with loads of dosh at the end. How much can we rake up between us?" Trish and April both look at Sam expectantly, who turns to get some milk from the fridge.

"I will pay it back," says April, "or Kate will. I promise. Though it may take a little time." Sam now fetches a bowl and starts making a salad. April and Trish look at each other.

"What's going on then?" asks Trish, "Come on, Sam. What's up?" Sam, apparently absorbed slicing tomatoes, does not appear to hear the question. "Come on now. Sam?" Sam continues looking for the dressing. "Sam, stop it! Sam, turn round." Sam faces them and slams the salad bowl on the table and thuds onto a chair.

"OK. OK. I know you both think I'm rich 'cause I live in this," she waves her hands loosely in the air, "and can afford this," she gestures to the piles of food on the table, "but the fact of the matter, the truth is that Hugh manages everything. Everything! And there's been a little trouble lately. You know the bank stuff that's going on? I don't pay it any attention. But he's begun to go on about money. Saving it where we can. Cutting back a bit. Taking care. I wouldn't have told you, 'cause I know you both have REAL financial problems. We have this house, we can downsize. We're not destitute just 'a little trouble with cash flow'. But it does mean I can't fucking help out like I want to. I really can't. And it's so pathetic." She angrily turns and fills up the cafetière. Trish leans back and snorts, April stands and puts an arm round Sam's waist, reassuring her that it doesn't matter whilst secretly feeling another safety line has been cut.

"Welcome to the real world!" says Trish. April and Sam turn and glare at her.

"Shut up, Trish," says April, "that's just not helpful. We all live in the real world. What other world is there?" Unabashed, Trish picks up a sandwich, takes a bite and looks inside.

"Darlin', shouldn't this be fish paste now rather than prawns?" There is quiet for a moment then Sam chuckles and it gathers depth and soon they all laugh, falling forwards onto the table and taking the food, April scoffing two sandwiches and biscuits in great mouthfuls, Trish eating half of everything, Sam passing the napkins and lemon wedges. They discuss the money.

"Oh darlin'!' says Trish, 'if only I had a spare bob or two but you know that the only way I've ever managed to get any cash was by borrowing it from my vile parents. And my mother has wised up to it and whenever I get my father alone for a second she's there like one of those bloody yappy terrier-things." Trish has regaled Sam and April often with tales of her family (her father is the grandson of a baronet). 'And, as you know, I've almost had the bailiffs round about my credit cards, which I'm just paying off with the minimum per month. I know you're in the same boat there." Trish nods at April, 'But I have been commanded to go to their diamond wedding anniversary celebration tomorrow. I wasn't going to go. I hate the hypocrisy of it all. Everyone making toasts…. to what? To surviving 60 years of each other, to six decades of fucking misery. And that bloody awful house, I was only really free when I was away from it.'

"Well no-one could accuse you of hypocrisy!" says April.

"True enough! I won't behave as my mother wants, it drives her mad." She grins for a moment. "But what I was going to say is … for you, only for you darlin', I will go to their nasty anniversary celebration, and if I get a chance I'll see if I can cadge some money off them. It's a slim chance but I might be able to pull it off."

"I'll ask Hugh," promises Sam, "see if he says we can afford anything. But I don't hold out much hope."

They discuss other ways of getting money. Sam rushes to get a pen and paper, they make a list for April to follow up and then for each of them. They are just discussing this enthusiastically and putting down priorities and adding points when there is a sound and Sam's daughter appears, like Banquo's ghost, in the kitchen. Sam jumps up as Trish and April say hello flatly: greetings that are not acknowledged by the slight stiff figure. April offers her a coffee in a tone that expects refusal.

"Where's Salome?" asks Helen. Sam nervously looks under the table where Salome is still asleep, a peaceful bundle of softness. Helen gives a gasp and crawling under the table snatches Salome up. "Mum. How could you?" Salome opens her mouth and blinks. "Your own granddaughter! On the floor, like a dog." Sam starts to say that there is underfloor heating, when Helen bursts out again, "AND you haven't changed her! I'm taking her home, immediately. Bring all her things out, whilst I buckle her into the car seat. I could hardly park my Audi for strange vehicles littering the driveway." She leaves, carrying a now crying child, followed by Sam toting bags, jars of food and feeding bottles. Once she's gone, April and Trish fall to sniggering and mocking, 'littering the driveway' 'like a dog' 'strange vehicles'. April tells Trish about seeing Helen in town ordering a soya de-caff latte. When Sam returns looking tired and guilty, they both chorus out,

"There is underfloor heating!"

"But there is. She was perfectly warm," says Sam and then notices Trish and April's expressions and begins to giggle. "She accused me of partying! Partying! I can't remember the last time I partied." Laughingly they all continue the planning, Sam quietly making notes. Top of her list for April is: FIND KATE.

*

April drives up the one-way street a couple of times, trying to recall the house and remembers it being on the same side as the post box. They all look so similar: Victorian, tall, terraced with steep steps leading up to the front door and down to a basement. She looks at the Entryphones and only one house has not been made into flats. That must be it! The father was an extremely big wig in some insurance or finance company. She parks the car haphazardly and runs up the steps and presses the lone doorbell which makes the familiar pinging hi-lo chime. A sleek young woman that April has never seen before answers the door with a small boy holding onto her leg gazing upwards at April who smiles at his stoic stare.

"Yes?" the young woman asks, her hand resting on the boy's head.

"Is Martina Chowdhury in?" asks April. "Does she live here still?" The woman raises her defined eyebrows and looks April up and down.

"And you are?"

"April Roberts, Kate Roberts' mother. Martina was Kate's best friend at school. I just wanted a word with her about Kate." The woman opens the door, but only to point to the basement with a beautifully manicured fingernail.

"She's down there, you will have to knock hard, the bell's not working," and she closes the door sharply. April descends the slimy stairs, past what would have been the coal hole and an old bicycle, and raps on the corrugated glass door under the steps. She bangs her feet together, blows on her hands and tries to push back her hair, realising that, once again, she hasn't brushed it. After a short while the door opens to show a dark corridor lined with boxes and Martina's cheeky triangular face under a cropped haircut peering out from behind the door. She is having some trouble opening it and curses until she recognises April.

"Mrs Roberts!" she says, forcing the rucked carpet under the opened door with her running shoes.

"April please. You're too old for all that Mrs stuff. Anyway, you know I'm Miss."

"OK April. Come in. You should've, like, come down the internal stairs. It's easier. I, like, don't open this door too much." She steps back so April sees her more clearly; lithe and wearing a black training outfit that looks both funky and functional, as if she's ready for a workout at the gym but could afterwards go out partying. Martina arrived defiantly at the local comprehensive, having been thrown out of a couple of expensive private schools, but she and Kate hit it off immediately. They became virtually inseparable for a time. She's still erupting with energy. April remembers her and Kate endlessly bouncing on beds, dancing along to music videos, doing backflips on the trampoline, chasing Trish's dog round the park.

"A woman upstairs told me to come down this way."

"Oh, her. Her with the blonde hair and big tits?"

"Yes."

"My stepmother."

"Ah."

"Yeah. Ah. Would you like a cup of tea? Come in, like, mind the boxes. I'm still moving stuff." They go along the corridor and into the small galley kitchen as Martina informs April that this used to be the au pair's quarters, then her brother's den and now she is renting it, "for a nominal rent. Though she, like, thinks I should be paying more." She speaks with the modern upward questioning lilt at the end of all her sentences yet despite this, anger flows out of her petite dark form and joins the musty smell in the gloom. April remembers that Martina once talked Kate into getting into people's houses by the cat flaps 'just for fun.' April collected them from the police station, the only time Kate has got into trouble. Before now.

"Is Kate OK?" Martina asks.

"I was about to ask you that."

"What do you mean?"

"She's disappeared. I can't find her."

"Oh," says Martina, leading the way into a small front room with a random pile of old furniture from the 80s and a sticky brown carpet. She arranges herself easily cross-legged in a saggy chair. April remembers she was adept in one particular sport but can't recall which one it was… running? long jump? trampolining?

"I was afraid of that."

"Martina please tell me what you know. I must find her."

But Martina is unwilling to snitch on a friend. It's only after April tells her of her threatening visitors that she reluctantly agrees to tell April what she knows.

"I was, like, sitting here chilling with a few friends. Last night. Well, like, early this morning. Really early. Thinking of going to bed. Getting light. You know. Anyway, she almost breaks down the door.

I had to answer it before her upstairs got the hump. Kate was, like, drunk and crying." Apparently, Kate sobbed that she owed a huge amount of money for gambling to some thugs who were threatening her. She said she was going away. She thought that if they couldn't find her, then they may give up totally, or at least back off for a while. She just needed time to think. Martina offered her a bed here but she refused and left suddenly whilst Martina was making some coffee. Martina has been texting her with no reply and is shocked when April tells her that Kate left her phone behind. April tries to make herself comfortable on the lumpy sofa, by padding herself round with dubious-looking cushions, and asks what Martina knows about Kate losing her job in London.

Martina settles down for a while and talks with genuine concern. Kate spoke to Martina when she first got back from the London job; she called round and they got drunk on Martina's father's champagne. Kate apologised for being out of touch for a while, but Martina was just so pleased to see her. Over time Kate told her story. "Not in one go, like, bits and pieces. She was ashamed." Kate's first job after graduating was the one she always wanted: a trainee auditor with a large international company. She was so excited by it. Couldn't believe her luck. Her, a girl whose grandfather had been a miner, where no-one owned anything of value, was now living in the centre of London in a flat with a view of the Thames. She was mixing with people from public school, making elegant friends, eating out, going to the opera. The international financial services company adored her, a first-class honours graduate from the LSE. They gave her extras, she passed all the exams with flying colours, worked long hours, threw herself into it, learnt so much. Loved it, loved it, loved it.

She began an affair with someone high up in the organization. He was dishy as well as rich and took her to fancy restaurants, clubs, holidays, weekends away. At work she was offered auditing trips abroad alongside him, pay rises; she went to Switzerland, South America, travelled business class. She was having an unbelievable time. Then something happened on one of these trips. She wouldn't say what. It was important enough to make her angry but worried her too. She tried to talk about it with the man but they quarrelled, badly. He finished it. She was devastated. She left to come back and speak to her boss in London.

When she got back, her dismissal notice was waiting for her. She couldn't even get into the building; her assistant came down in tears carrying a cardboard box containing her belongings. She never got to see her boss; no-one would speak to her. All those work friends disappeared overnight. "That's it," said Martina "and she swore me to secrecy. Wouldn't, like, tell me the name of the company they were auditing. Or, like, anything. But I know the man she was with, warned her about him."

"Who was he?"

"My brother actually."

"What, 'wanker William'?" Martina nods sadly. "The nasty prick that teased you both mercilessly and actually beat you up at one time?" Martina puts her hands up.

"She knew, she knew. I, like, don't know why, it began. He'd been there for a few years, knew his way around, like, everyone seemed to respect him."

"He tore the head off her favourite doll, said she was too old for it and threw it to a dog." April is outraged.

"She said he'd changed; he was nice to her."

"He pushed her off her bike."

"What can I say?" Martina obviously is as bemused as April and shakes her head sadly.

"So what about the gambling?"

"Well, like, I better fess up. That was my fault." Martina went on to explain how she found out that you could register for this casino for only £5 and then go in and get free sandwiches and sometimes drinks. It sounded like a classy but cheap night out. It was upmarket; they both needed a bit of glamour. They went once and had a great time. They got glammed up beforehand, flirted with lots of older men, only lost £10, got pissed and ate all the bar snacks. Kate made friends with the barman. "I think she, like, went back to see him, I think he took her to other places, like, late night places, members only, for gambling. She wanted someone, like, different from William, a bit rough and earthy. Really bad at choosing men, isn't she?"

"The one area she's not bright in," sighs April and shifts on the sofa removing a framed photograph with cracked glass from under the cushions.

"My brother's den, like I said. Not been used for years. I think there's mice. More tea?"

"I should be looking for Kate, or for money. I have a list," and April roots in her handbag failing to find the paper. "I must've left it in the car somewhere. Do you really truly think she's OK?"

"Yes, I do, April. I think she's fine. She's not here for a start. That's good. I think she, like, believes she's protecting you by going away or something. Like, she must have old uni friends in London. Maybe she's gone to them."

"I'm glad Kate has you as a friend still, give me a hug. Let me know if you think of anything or hear anything. Here's my number." Martina escorts her to the door whilst putting the number on her phone, and on being asked how she's going to spend the evening replies, "SHE thinks I'm going out. SHE is planning a romantic evening in with my father. She's bought the oysters and is chilling the champagne. I've, like, invited a few friends round. One of them is, like, practicing to be a DJ. He's bringing his decks."

Three

Sunday morning

April parks at the front of her mother's care home and sits for a moment looking at the large gabled 1930s house. It is easy to see the modifications that have made it suitable as a rest and nursing home: the ramps that make wheelchair access easy, the self-opening doors and the car port in front of the modern nursing home extension. She gets out and stands for a while wondering whether she is being sensible. She is making her minimal weekly visit now with the additional motive of seeing if her mother has any spare money around; Sam and Trish have insisted, "With her history she may have an old flame somewhere she can tap for dosh," said Trish.

Even though she knows her mother would have tapped any old flame for money years ago, April has reluctantly agreed to ask. She rings the doorbell. The manager opens the heavy door after a little while. She is a tall, stout, commanding woman with piercing eyes and a functional and distant manner, who always makes herself visible around the home. The hot air drifts outwards, bringing with it the usual waft of disinfectant, institutional cookery and air freshener.

"Hello Mrs Weekes,' April says, 'Is my mother, Dorothy Roberts, downstairs or up?'

"She's in the front room at the moment. I saw her sitting there with the others and having her morning tea." Mrs Weekes brushes an imaginary speck from her trouser suit and inspects April's usual eccentric charity-shop wear with a slight twist of her mouth.

"How's she getting on?"

"Not too bad. Though her incontinence problems seem to be worsening. But her disability from the stroke is stable, the carers think it's even getting better and she's started to take part in the activities we provide here. This week she joined in the singing and dancing classes. Not that she can do much dancing now, but she keeps the fitness trainer amused. Kicks her legs up off the chair, makes us all laugh."

"Ah," says April, "the old Tiller Girl trick. Still got it in her!"

April walks into the vinyl-floored front room and looks around the group of elderly residents, all of whom she now recognises. There is the ex-butcher who laughs at her mother's jokes, but is now slouched dozing in his high-backed chair, the retired nurse who often shouts for no reason is drooling and slumped over to one side, three others in various stages of consciousness. It looks like a scene out of an elderly zombie apocalypse movie. The urine smell is unmistakable, forcing its way through the air fresheners and detergents. Everyone in nappies, April thinks. Her mother is sitting half asleep in the best chair in the room, next to the window overlooking the back garden.

Her mother, in startling contrast to April, is a thin woman with excellent legs, tiny feet and a flirtatious manner. April watches her for a moment as she sits slightly skewed to one side. Her mother has always inhabited a distant maternal zone that April cannot reach, does not now want to reach, but still, annoyingly pulls on her. She is wearing powder and her lopsided mouth is coated carefully in lipstick and so April knows that she is OK and gives her a little tap on the shoulder to wake her. Her mother looks up and smiles back at April, sits more upright, automatically straightens her cardigan, pats her hair and turns to look at the day and date that are written on a board on one of the walls. "Did you tell me you war comin?"

April bends down, gives her a perfunctory kiss and drops a packet of small cakes into her lap.

"No, just called on the off-chance. I've made you those chocolate bites that you liked so much. I made them soft so you can eat them without taking your teeth out."

"I dunna want those," replies her mother, speaking with the slight slur left over from two strokes and pushing them off her lap. "And what are you wearing?" April is wearing a thick wool dress in mauve and cream check with a wide belt, it does nothing for her, but she thinks it looks cheerful.

"It is real wool," she says defensively, loosening the belt that is cutting into her belly. "How are you, mum?" April picks the cakes off the floor and puts them into her own bag with a sigh.

"In fine fettle. 'cept I'm 'ere."

"I need to talk to you in private," says April, refusing to enter into the usual argument, "can we just go upstairs for a moment?"

"Do we have to? I'm comfy here." April insists, refusing to explain until finally her mother agrees. Her mother leans heavily on her as she eases her from the chair and they go to the lift moving slowly, arm in arm. Her mother does not say much and moves with a limping gait, her left foot making a slight sideways kick as she steps carefully in her heels, and her left elbow slightly raised and less in her control. April asks her about what she did yesterday, but her mother only shrugs and tells her not to be so daft, she did nowt yesterday, as ever.

Once upstairs April takes her mother straight to the poky shared back bedroom that is the only place that can be afforded on her mother's state pension. April sits on the bed and her mother gets herself settled in the one armchair as April gazes around the room and reflects on the many wrong decisions that have led her mother to this final gloomy place. April is well aware that she is facing a similar future despite all her efforts.

Four framed photographs are on the walls above her single bed; their contents are difficult to make out in the low light, but April knows them well. One of her mother in a Tiller Girls line-up. One of the stage cast of 'My Fair Lady' that includes her mother in the back row of the chorus. One of her last husband (the escapologist and drunk that committed suicide and left her financially destitute). Finally, one of April about 15 years ago when she was going through a thin phase; the almost-teen small girl beside her, clutching her hand and smiling unreservedly is Kate.

On a shelf there are five other photograph albums, and in one of them is the only picture April has seen of her father. He is dressed in naval uniform with two other ratings, leaning on a balustrade of a ship and all looking as if they are laughing at the person taking the photograph. The sun hit the lens and her father's features are hard to make out, yet he had April's stoutness and her smile. In all the albums there is just one photo of her grandfather standing in a cultivated space with her mother looking very small, both holding Indian clubs and smiling. There is a copy of it on Kate's wall, she loved the cheerfulness on both their faces and the grimness of the municipal park background. In the same album there is only one of April as a small child, curtseying coyly at the door of her grandparent's back-to-back in Leeds, dressed in a shiny party dress. It must have been when she was about seven, on one of her mother's rare visits to see her, most probably bringing the dress. April can remember the tornado of glamour and excitement she caused, and how her grandmother wept when she left, mourning her as a lost soul, and how her grandfather prayed for the sheep who was astray; how April wondered each time what she had done wrong to be left behind. But worse was later, when she was taken away by her mother to some new boyfriend, a new school, a new 'daddy'. Her mother promising her a better life, a promise that was never fulfilled and always ended abruptly with her being sent back to her grandparents.

She looks up and finds her mother's eyes fixed on her with a knowing intelligence in them.

"So why did you make me come up here?" her mother slurs. April is once again surprised when the knowing mother reappears unexpectedly from amongst the remains of this feeble old woman. "What do you want?"

"I don't know if you can help, it's such a long shot."

"For God's sake stop faffin."

"I need £35,000. I don't suppose you've got it?"

"Are you in some bother?" This reply is unexpected, it hints at a chance, it's far from an immediate exclamation of impossibility.

"No, well yes, well maybe. Not me, not directly. It's complicated. I really must get £35,000 and quickly." She hesitates to tell her mother about Kate, remembering one of her mother's many lovers who gambled her savings and then disappeared. April was living with them at the time, in a flat over an off-licence in Streatham. They opened the door one day to an echo of deserted rooms, with not one single item remaining. They slept on the floor, her mother weeping and outraged. The next day, alone, she was put on the train back to her grandparents.

Her mother leans back, seems to think for a moment and then

leans forward slightly at an angle and tries to speak clearly, "Look, I might have a way of getting some money. I don't know whether I can get £35,000 though."

"£10,000 would do," interrupts April "Or anything actually."

"Any road," continues her mother, "I need to know what it's for. I'm not troublin' myself less I think it's important. Right important!"

So April, opening the discarded cakes and eating three of them, tells her mother the story. She consciously makes it sound as casual and mundane as possible, rather as if it is an overdue parking fine. Her mother, however, shows some understanding and is not at all shocked, but is cross. April sees her struggling to come to terms with the news, predictably blaming April for not handling Kate properly, saying she must have been led astray and asking how April could've let it happen. April, who feels unjustly accused but guilty nevertheless, asks her roughly whether she has the money or not and eats another cake.

"I may," says her mother, to April's surprise. "I've allus had a soft spot for Kate as you know, and she is my granddaughter. Let's get the money and then deal with her, eh? I'll see what I can do, but I must talk to someone and it might teck a while. Give me an hour and then come back. It canna be cash."

"I'd better write down what I want," says April, digging in her bag and tearing a page out of her diary. She knows that her mother's memory is faulty at the best of times. She digs again, finds a pen and starts writing, telling her mother to make sure the cheque is made out to A. Roberts. Her mother demands her help in getting out of the chair and struggles upright clutching the paper tightly.

Giving April a little push and commanding her to go away she makes her way out of the room. She waits, watching April leaving by the stairs and says that she's 'not promising anything mind'.

Sitting in her car in the cold and wondering what her mother is up to, April shivers and is about to start the car when her mobile rings and she sees the caller's name flash up.

"Martina," she gasps, "have you heard from Kate?"

"No," says Martina, "Sorry, no news there."

"Any more ideas?" April means, as to where Kate is, how she can be found, but Martina interrupts her.

"Look, actually I have an offer to make you. It might suit us both. When can I talk to you?" April asks her what it is about but Martina will not say, insisting that April comes to her place. Finally, April agrees to call on her later this afternoon, after she's finished with her mother.

*

Sam hears Hugh opening the front door and her gut clenches instinctively as she turns slowly on the stool and puts down the brooch as his voice calls out her name. She trudges down the stairs and is taking off the apron by the time Hugh appears in the bedroom doorway. He kisses the top of her head as he begins loosening his tie, the usual prelude to him taking off his suit.

"How was your work?" asks Sam. He has gone in even though it is Sunday, but he is back earlier than she expected.

"Oh chaotic as usual. Opening that branch in Krakow has certainly made business boom. It's just what's needed. These Poles are a joy to work with and so easy to place, employers are over the moon. It's our poor old Brits whom we struggle with. They seem so unmotivated by comparison." He continues his usual diatribe about his recruitment agency, the lacklustre British and the feckless youth of today, continuing to talk whilst changing into jeans and a T-shirt while Sam brushes her hair and thinks about the day ahead. Is it just going to be her and Hugh? Hugh busily engaged on his computer again, doing accounts, sending emails to Krakow, speaking at her, not expecting a response. Is that all there is these days?

"Helen left Salome with me yet again and I've spent most of the morning trying to entertain her. I've only just managed to get down to some work."

"Oh yes?" says Hugh automatically.

"Why don't we go out?" Sam asks. But she has interrupted him halfway through his thoughts and sees that he is discomfited.

"Out?" he sounds shocked as if she has suggested that they go for a naked swim in an icy sea.

"Yes, let's go to that new Italian restaurant that's opened in town. I think it has a jazz band on Sunday lunchtimes. It'll be fun."

'It won't be fun if I can't hear myself think. Anyway, I have work to do." He looks tired and Sam knows that all he has to do is stop for a second and relax. She doesn't understand why he can't give himself a break. He looks at her momentarily and some expression that she can't quite interpret goes across his face, is it disappointment? "I must get on with my work. I'm sorry, dear," and he stops looking at her and picks up his case full of papers and goes into the study.

She follows him and watches for a moment as he starts the computer and logs on. "Dearest, is there no time for fun anymore?" she asks him.

"Fun!" Hugh snorted, "You had lunch with the girls yesterday, wasn't that fun enough? Anyway, we do have fun but in a simpler way. Once I've done this, we can have a nice quiet meal together and a bottle of wine." Sam grimaces to herself as he taps away. She hasn't stopped thinking about April. She has put off asking him, hoping for a suitable time when he would be relaxed. But last night he came home late and tired and now he's still distracted. She has to ask. There is a pause and she speaks into it.

"April talked to me yesterday."

"Yes?"

"Bit of an emergency."

"Mmmh yes..." he stays looking at the screen, his back towards her.

"She needs some money badly..." Hugh does not look up and is already sending an email.

"Got herself into financial trouble again eh?"

"Well it's Kate..."

"Bloody Kate. She should get herself a job. She got a first-class honours degree and has just wasted her chances. Can you remember when she first came back from London? April begged me to help." He swivels round in the executive chair to speak more directly to Sam, "I got Kate the offer of a job in a bank and phoned her myself. She was furious, acted as if I'd offered her a job sweeping the streets. I didn't bother after that." He twirls back to the computer screen and continues typing.

"Could we lend her some money do you think?"

"You mean could I give her some money?"

"Well yes, I suppose that would be nice but..."

"Oh Sam, dear. I know you mean well. But you're such a pushover for a sob story. Whatever money I lend will be soon gone. It'll never be paid back. Kate needs to learn (and I'm afraid so does April) to manage her finances. Anyway, whatever I lend she'll need more, they always do."

"I don't know what you mean by that. April isn't 'they'. April has never asked for money before. She's only ever been a good friend to me. A really good friend." Sam stops. She wants to say that April is the main person that has seen her through the cancer and mastectomy, has visited and phoned her almost every day, has sat with her watching crap DVDs, handed her tissues when she cried, bought her the naff Amazonian statuette that has pride of place on top of Sam's bookcase. All this and the treatment happened whilst Hugh opened his office in Poland and went away a lot. But now Hugh is tapping his keyboard again, seemingly oblivious to her and any protests she might make.

"Well I don't have any spare cash around to just give away to anyone at the moment as you know. Opening that branch in Krakow has really stretched my finances. And you're not cheap yourself, dear, I noticed that last bill for silver for your jewellery-making. It's lucky I've got a bit of savings or you wouldn't have anything at all for housekeeping. Anyway, April will get over it. She always manages somehow. It might teach Kate a useful lesson." And he continues tapping and staring at the screen. "You haven't promised her anything, have you?" he asks suddenly as she is leaving. Sam shakes her head. "Thank goodness! We only need your brother back here begging as well and our bank account will be totally emptied." He returns to his computer.

Sam has so much she wants to say. This is depressingly familiar ground for disagreement between them. But her stomach clenches again and she has promised herself that each day will be a blessing. She has to go carefully still. She decides to take out as much money as possible from the cashpoint each day without Hugh's knowledge. She can save it and give it to April at the end of the week. She looks at his back and walks slowly towards the kitchen.

*

When April returns to the care home, her mother is sitting in the front room again, looking tired but awake. There is the smell of soup and overcooked mince in the air and the other residents, she knows, are in the back room eating their meal. Her mother though, waits here for her. She holds a folded cheque in one hand and April bends down and takes it gently from her grip. She reads it; £5,000 addressed to A Roberts in a tiny, elderly shaky hand. But she can't read the signature.

"Bloody hell!" exclaims April looking at the cheque. "Is this real?"

"Expect so," says her mother quietly.

"Hurray, hurray!" calls out April and dances around the room waving the cheque and gives her mother a kiss on the forehead. "Brilliant! Hurray. Well done."

"That's grand," is all her mother can say, watching her daughter with a tired smile and resting further back into the chair. Finally, April stops her skipping and looks at the cheque again.

"But who is this from?" she asks her mother.

"Philip Henderson," replies her mother, "not that it matters to you!"

"At least let me thank him. Where is he?"

"Don't bother," her mother replies, "He's got so much brass he won't notice this at all. Go off, and get it cashed for Pete's sake!"

"But why should he do this for me?"

"He didn't do it for you," her mother replies bluntly, "he did it for me. He and I are old, old friends. I did him a favour." She stops her daughter's further questions by trying to stand up. "Help me up. I want summat to eat. Then I'm gonna take 40 winks. I'm tired, right tired. Now go!"

April makes her way to the front door but hears her mother's weary voice calling her name, so goes back. "Best start thinking how you're gonna get that other thirty thousand quid!"

Four

Sunday afternoon

Trish notes the house, in its fold of hills, as she goes up the motorway. The glimpse of the familiar slant of roofs and the weather-vaned chimney pot, that the family calls The Cottage, bring a sourness to her mouth. She swallows and takes the next turning, making her Harley Fat Boy slow to its familiar uneven rumble, passing the row of farm terraces that they used to call 'the slums'. She smiles, remembering standing in a mass of children with the large mother slavering peanut butter on white sliced bread and passing it out indiscriminately to the squabbling laughing crowd. Later, her own mother explained to her exactly why she shouldn't play with them.

"The whole point of your going to that expensive private school is to make friends there so that you don't have to mix with those sort. They don't speak proper English and have no manners at all. You really must try to make friends of our own class," she said, going on to ask why Trish didn't invite anyone from her boarding school home for the weekend. Trish could hardly say that the other girls took the piss out of her because she was deeply unhappy and hated the rules and confinement of the all-girls' school. One group in particular picked on her until she followed her brother's advice and slapped the ringleader. Hard.

After that no one spoke to her at all.

Trish stops, gets off and leans against her bike, Betty, in the layby and rolls a cigarette waiting for Stu. Betty is warm and her heat soothes, making the rattles of the journey disappear. She loved the ride, the uneven roar, the weighted feeling as she goes around curves controlling the flow of movement. On her bike everything is vibrant and near and once more she feels in touch with life and the world. But now the muddy path to The Cottage winds through the trees and the house and its inhabitants loom ahead unseen beyond the bare branches of the orchard. She has never felt she belonged here. She never became the young lady her mother wanted her to be. She is not alone in bearing the weight of unsaid disappointment; none of her children are coming. This is their choice, she believes. She tries never to interfere with their preferences, she wants them to make their own decisions and stand by them. As she has done.

Stuart drives up. "Tailed by the police," he says through his helmet and swears.

"All OK?" asks Trish and when Stuart nods, she drops the remains of her cigarette, swings her leg over Betty, kicks back and starts the engine.

They soon reach the driveway, which is already filled with cars of every variety. She parks up, hangs her helmet and picks her change of clothes out of the saddlebag. Stuart stops beside her and rolls a cigarette, obviously not overeager to get inside. Trish takes a deep breath and shivers and leaves him placidly smoking. She last lived in this place when she was 16, just before she ran off with her first love, the emotions that drove her then are still alive and squirming.

"Bloody April ... Bloody Kate..." she mutters and goes through the portico. Ahead of her is the hallway with its wooden panelling and carved staircase with the sitting room and drawing room to either side. Many guests have already arrived, and welcoming a few newcomers is a thin older woman dressed immaculately in a green cashmere suit and low heels. Her naturally streaked hair, subtle make-up and distinctive jewellery set off the whole ensemble to perfection. Born the only daughter of solid working-class stock she has camouflaged herself totally and become, to all outward appearances, the perfect wife for a blue-blooded aristocrat. She is talking to a group of guests when she glances up and catches sight of Trish. She excuses herself and comes forward with an overloud exclamation of delight to greet her daughter, her lips tight.

"Patricia darling, how lovely to see you. Always so eccentrically dressed!" she clutches her, air-kisses her ear and whispers, "What are you wearing? Couldn't you have made the slightest effort for once?" Trish steps back and waves to her father's sister Mildred, tottering past, wearing a gabardine dress covered in dog hairs, its hem held up by safety pins. Her mother turns at the gesture, sees Mildred and smiles coldly. Trish grits her teeth and shows the carrier bag,

"Lovely to see you too, mater. Beautifully clad as ever I see. Came up on the bike but I have bought a change." Showing her mother the carrier bag she skips sideways, goes up the stairs and into the smallest back bedroom, closes the door and sits on the bed rolling a cigarette. The door opens and an elderly man peers round. Trish sags as she recognises her father's old school friend, Sir Henry Moresby. He comes slowly into the room and holds out his hand, the fingers twitching.

"Well, well, Patricia ... looking splendid I must say." She takes the grasping hand offered and shakes it gingerly, wriggling her fingers free and lights her cigarette. Her siblings have christened him 'Hands' due to both his German ancestry and his inability to stop himself from stroking and squeezing any female that takes his eye. "Caught sight of you, had to say hello. Don't see you that much, you know." His lips are glistening wet, as if he's drooling. Trish sighs, he always has made a beeline for her, and now she is in her leathers, well, she is irresistible.

"I'm sorry. I don't keep in touch with the family a lot. You know how it is."

"Always were the black sheep," and he steps further into the room. Trish eyes the door he is blocking and wonders if she is actually going to have to slap him off. "Lovely black sheep," he continues. Trish blows smoke at him as he advances towards her, making him stop, blink and cough, so giving her an opportunity to skip out behind him.

"So sorry Uncle Henry, must go." She opens the door and almost bumps into a large woman of about her own age wearing a frilly pink dress.

"Have you seen daddy?" she asks. Trish remembers her: Hands' daughter Felicity who one year ratted on Trish after seeing her kissing the apprentice gardener. The gardener lost his job and Trish was locked in her bedroom for a week. Trish swore at 14 that she would never speak to Felicity again, a pledge she has kept, so she just opens the door behind and goes into the hallway brushing past Felicity who rolls her eyes and shakes her head.

This whole trip has been a mistake. Once again, she has been exposed to the pretence of her mother's adopted lifestyle: manners without heart. Going downstairs to find her father, she ditches the idea of changing clothes and resolves to get the money immediately and escape.

She sees her mother going towards the conservatory and hears the sound of a string quartet playing there. She heads in the opposite direction, stashing her carrier bag under the hall table. She looks into the sitting room and sees her two older brothers and their wives bellowing at each other in vaunting upper class tones.

"Jamie's just finishing at Magdalen ..."

"Got into a bit of a barney with some vile chav..."

"We've set up a Trust Fund ..."

She reels back and opens the door opposite into the drawing room and through a small group of people she sees her father sitting on the sofa sipping a glass of champagne that a waiter has just given him. Grabbing a glass from the tray as she goes past, she lurches at her father who looks surprised.

"Hiya pater!" and she kisses his cheek before sitting beside him. He is at least a head taller than her.

"Ah hello there, Patricia, you made it I see." And he puts an arm round her shoulder.

"How's my little girl then?"

"Oh not so bad..."

"I don't see much of you, you know... can't remember the last time we met, was it at Easter?" He pats her knee and looks down at her with pale grey eyes, his long face seems pinched around the temples and mouth.

"No, not at Easter," and she shivers at the thought of what Easter could have been like, "It was Anthony's daughter's wedding, actually, papa, in June this year."

"Really? I remember now, you bought your latest man along. Nice chap. Biker of course." This is typical of her father, distant but pleasant.

"We've been to all the recent weddings, papa. Surely you

remember?" Bloody awful they were too; she and Stu were always sat at the lowest table with the vicar, someone with a speech impediment and usually a child with behavioural problems.

"Well goodness me, weddings … doesn't time fly..." he looks unbothered as ever. He was always one-step removed from the family, leaving all the day-to-day decision-making to her mother. Charming to all, well-mannered but never thinking that the usual rules of conduct applied to him, so blatantly unfaithful. Bloody Kate, she thinks, and decides to get to the point.

"Papa I need some money badly." He raises an eyebrow.

"Again? Haven't we given you some just recently?"

"You haven't given me any for ages," she says, "and you know I wouldn't ask you unless it was absolutely necessary."

"You'd better ask your mother," he responds in a tired tone and turns his head to look around the room. Trish can feel her anger rising, how often has she heard that phrase?

"It is your money, papa, you know. Come on now, get out your cheque book and cough up." And she tickles and prods him, so he chuckles. "I am your only daughter." He laughs and pats her hand, asks her what she's doing now. She encourages him to get up and go to his study where she knows he keeps his cheque book. Her father laughs and putting an arm over her shoulder walks out into the hallway towards his study. But coming towards them is Trish's mother, who the minute she sees Trish escorting her father cannot contain herself. She strides up abruptly, physically separates them and sends her husband off with a small push in his back.

"Off you go now, dear. Just mingle with the guests. I'm having a quiet word with Patricia." Trish does not resist as her mother pulls her towards the front door and addresses her in a low furious tone.

"I know exactly what you're up to, my lady! I'm watching you, let me tell you. You and that dreadful man you've brought along."

"Really mama. Whatever's wrong with Stu?"

"I've had about as much as I can take from you. I know you're trying to get some money. I don't know how often we've bailed you out over the years ..."

"I don't know why you're making such a fuss," says Trish, "you've helped Geoffrey buy his house, you've paid for Anthony's daughter's wedding. Why am I different?"

"Look what you've done with your life! Nothing! Look at who you mix with! Look at where you live. Look at how you dress."

"And, apart from marrying my father, what have you done that's been so useful?"

"I suppose that roadying in a band and marrying junkies is useful? Hanging out with bikers, slobs and dropouts? Working in a pub is useful?"

"Better than this!" says Trish, gesturing roun. "Much better than hiding away in this." Her mother looks round and sees that a little cluster of guests including Hands has gathered in the nearest doorway. She turns, pats her hair and gives a little pout of apology to them and a low laugh.

"Really," she says to her audience, "you'd think she had something better to wear to her parents' 60th anniversary party, wouldn't you?" Trish is by now obviously so enraged that anyone who knows her well would've known trouble was ahead. She brushes past her mother, walks towards Hands and takes his arm.

"Oh but Uncle Henry loves my outfit. Don't you, Uncle Henry?" and she pats his hand as he smiles at her. "Let's go into the conservatory, shall we?" She grins at him, snuggles up, barely flinches as he pats her bum and leads him smiling down the hallway away from her mother. She scoops a couple of champagne glasses off a waiter's tray as she passes and gives one to Hands.

"Anyone wanting to learn a bit of our family history follow me," she calls out and notices a couple of nieces dropping behind her and beckoning to their husbands. There is a string quartet playing in the conservatory when they get there. Some palms in large pots have been pushed to one side and wrought-iron chairs have been placed in small intimate groups. She turns to a back wall where there are a couple of old framed pictures, hard to see.

"This is my parents' wedding portrait," exclaims Trish, pointing to the first photograph of her mother poised on a love seat leaning forwards, with her father alongside holding her hand. Both look young, groomed and elegant and the portrait is obviously staged in a studio. "This went to the Tatler of course."

"What a spectacular dress!" exclaims a niece, edging forwards to look at it more clearly.

"Yes, it rather dominates the photo, doesn't it? Made by a hardworking cockney seamstress. My grandmother. My mother's mother in case you are in any doubt, who worked in the East End of London. Worked for a Jewish tailor and was a brilliant dressmaker. He gave her the material for the gown and veil as a wedding present for her daughter. Lovely man. Not invited to the wedding of course." There is a silence.

Trish moves on to the next picture which is further back. The string quartet decides to take a break. There is a huddle of people round Trish now, Hands has slipped in behind her and is pressing rather closely, Trish moves an elbow backwards and he gives a gasp.

"And this is the full wedding photo!" She steps back so they can all gather round it. "Rather cleverly positioned, don't you think? Meant to be the full family, only it's rather lopsided. My mother's parents are almost hidden, they're squashed behind mater who has pulled herself up to her full height, but my father's family are out in full force and all over the place." Aunt Mildred has pushed her way to the front of the group and is holding a cigarette that she points at the photo.

"That's me!" she exclaims, "I was a bridesmaid. Bloody awful headdress!" She blows out a cloud of smoke. "Gosh, they even roped in Great Uncle Archibald to swell the crowd. Never married, had a close friend who lived with him, rather dishy, the friend I mean."

"My mother's parents had a sweet shop," continues Trish.

"Your mother always says he was a businessman," blurts out a teenager at the back. She blushes as everyone turns to stare at her.

"But at the time of this wedding he was working in a factory, making saucepans," Trish pauses theatrically.

"Jolly nice man, actually," says Mildred, "he and I had a good laugh and he danced with me. War damaged of course. Loved dogs. Mother hated him. And loathed your mother."

"Let's dance," says Trish to Hands, "to celebrate this anniversary." She steps back, leaving the group looking at the photo and asking Mildred questions. Trish is in the process of spinning Hands around, who is now decidedly wobbly on his feet, when his daughter and her mother separate them and Felicity leads him, protesting, away.

"Have fun, Hands!" she calls to his departing back and blows him a kiss. His daughter glares at her. Her mother quietly and coldly suggests that Trish leave.

Trish strides into the hallway, picks up her bag and stamps out of the front door. There is no sign of Stuart, so she is in the process of buckling up the saddlebag when she hears a scuttling sound behind her and then her mother is in front of her, absolutely puce with rage.

"You think you're so free spirited, you think you're still young and with-it. Let me tell you. You're old. You're old. You look ancient in your motorbike outfit and rather sad. And your free lifestyle is just sordid and pathetic. You're going nowhere. You never have and you never will. When I think what we've done for you over the years..." Trish puts on her helmet to block the noise and starts her Harley. She makes the engine roar, then releases the clutch and rumbles loudly round the drive, passing a gathering group of young people outside the front door. She finally speeds up a little, and circles her mother, creating muddy wheel marks in the grass. She stops, bids her mother have a good pretend life, lowers her visor and accelerates away.

Once at home, which is, unusually, deserted, she makes herself a cup of tea and sits down to try to get some focus on the afternoon. Stuart's mobile is off, she's no idea where he is, but presumes he'll be home soon. She stands up and gazes at herself in the hall mirror for a long time, noting the crows' feet around her eyes, turning sideways and seeing the seat of her leathers drooping slightly to match her buttocks. She rubs her aching thighs and back, her body protests at such drives these days: she doesn't make as many as she used to. Maybe her mother is right and she is old, but she still feels young inside, she's not yet 60, she's still attractive, isn't she? Yet catching sight of herself again in the mirror she turns away. Her mother has got to her again and Trish feels defeated.

She is about to pick up the phone to call Sam when she hears a motorbike and knows it is Stuart's. She starts to form a spliff and waits as he comes in through the door. He walks quickly towards her and scoops her out of her chair, making her knock over her tea and the half-formed joint. He hugs her hard and laughs uproariously. He swings her round and throws his head back and falls backwards with her on top of him. He can hardly speak for laughing and Trish, looking at his face, smiles at first then chuckles and soon is roaring with laughter and wiping tears from her eyes.

"My God. My God. That was brilliant," Stuart sobs, "if you could've seen your mother's face." He breaks down once more. "Priceless." After they both calm down, they sit, share the joint and a can of beer chuckling, whilst making half sentences.

"The lawn..."

"Hands' daughter."

"Your mother's face..."

Then they kiss and soon are making love. But in the middle Stuart leaps away and rummages amongst his discarded clothing, cheers, and comes back waving a small piece of paper which he drops on Trish. "Before I forget," he says.

Trish looks at it and sees it is a cheque for £5,000 written to her and signed by her father. She stares at it in astonishment and then gazes questioningly back at Stuart.

"Piece of piss really. Whilst you were having fun in the conservatory, I cornered your father in the study and he wrote this, I insisted on this amount. I don't know that I could've got any more." Trish merely stares at him and the cheque. "Then I pocketed it, heard part of the speeches, stayed for a while chatting to someone about Harleys and then came back here."

"Come here, you lovely man you," says Trish and Stuart obliges.

*

April knocks on the door at the bottom of the steps and through the glass sees a light at the end of the corridor. Martina forces the door back and leaves it ajar, she puts her fingers to her lips, beckons April inside and then whispers to her,

"Go outside as if you've, like, left something in your car and when you get back look up above the front door," she pushes April away. April does as she's told and glancing up at the front door as she comes back sees nothing except shuttered windows, the usual security camera pointing down and a burglar alarm. She descends to the basement where Martina is pointing upwards.

Looking again, the only thing April can see is the security camera, its lens positioned to cover all the steps into the house. Martina closes the door with difficulty and, without saying anything, leads her along the corridor and opens the back door. She takes April by the hand and they go up some steps and across a small garden, beautifully laid out, with low decorative hedges, a water feature and seating area. Then she opens a gate and gestures, so April looks out of it. There is a thin dark public alleyway. Martina pulls April back in, turns the key in the lock and then silently directs her across the garden, down the steps and into the basement. April is so mystified by now that she is totally silent even when they get inside. Martina makes her a cup of tea, April, who has eaten all the cakes she made for her mother, asks Martina if she has any biscuits and is handed a bag of nuts. The flat looks completely trashed, there are new spills on the carpet, bin bags full of cans and bottles in the corridor, and a strong smell of alcohol, smoke and dope. April, crunching absent-mindedly, asks how last night went and Martina says it couldn't have been better.

"Really wicked. Lots of people. Kept everyone awake. Even I was, like, well tired by the end, I had to, like, put in earplugs, went to bed, left them to it. Come in here." They went into the front room that seemed even dirtier than before with suspicious looking stains over both the carpet and the furniture. April, who is not usually squeamish, has difficulty choosing where to sit. "Like, I've tried washing it out," apologises Martina.

"What am I here for, Martina?" says April finally, "and what was I looking at?"

"What do you think about theft? I mean, is it, like, ever ok?"

Martina sits on the sofa and bends her legs easily underneath her.

"I don't know what you're talking about." April turns a cushion over and puts it behind her, to cover a stain that is still damp.

"But, like, suppose it isn't theft. Suppose it's, like, just taking back what's yours?" Martina shifts again, bends forward and rises up smoothly to stomp around on the sofa as if pressing grapes. April is puzzled by her whole behaviour since she arrived. "Just suppose someone, like a stepmother, has stolen some jewellery that, like, actually belongs to the real daughter." Martina puts her hands on her hips and stares at April who has to tilt backwards to see her.

"Will you stop saying 'like'!"

"OK. OK. But suppose the daughter whose jewellery it is wants it back…" She drops onto the sofa again, making a compact pile of her legs.

"Martina, for fuck's sake, speak straight. I'm tired and I don't understand. Just explain what you want in words of one syllable."

"I need to know you're not going to tell anyone about what I'm going to say." Martina places herself in front of April and examines her face. This is important to her.

"Cross my heart and hope to die. For God's sake get on with it."

"I want you to do a heist for me." As April coughs up her tea Martina slaps her on the back and explains, whilst sitting on the arm of April's chair.

"The problem is that I've asked her often for my mother's jewellery. Well not even my mother's. My grandmother's. It was coming to me, it's mine. But she up there's got it now. My stupid mother left. Just went when the shit hit the fan. No fight in her. Didn't take anything. Nothing. Left everything. Everything. Left for India. Went back to her roots. Now has joined some ashram, says she doesn't care. Well I do. I don't see why shitface should have what's mine. She got him, she got the home, she saw my mother off. And my fucking ballsup of a father just smiles and says not to worry. Well I want it. I've seen her wearing it. I know she won't let it go. But it's mine. Mine. She can't have everything." She is up and pacing round the room now, April puts down her mug.

"I don't see why you want me to do anything. Just go upstairs and get it. What's the problem?" Martina moves round the room again, stepping from sofa to chair to chair to beanbag.

"That's it. The minute it goes, she'll know it's me and all hell will break out. My father will be down and insist on me giving it back. If I refuse, I'll be out. I need this place. Anyway, it's MY HOME. I know I'm driving them mad. My father came down this morning. Told me that if there's one more 'happening' I'm out. He really means it. She's pregnant again, a girl this time. He's so excited. SHE needs rest and calm. I'm a grown up. I can take care of myself." She stops and pushes her fists into her eyes. "I don't want to leave. I want to stay here. It's my home. I grew up here. I want my home and my family back. But big tits is having a bloody girl! That means she'll, for sure, want the jewellery and he says that he doesn't see what the problem is. He says that he hasn't got it. But I've seen her up there wearing it. Then he says my mother gave it up. She didn't, she forgot it. That's all. I don't see why bouncy boobs should have it. Why should she win everything? This is my home. And here I am in the fucking cellar!"

"It's so easy, just take it and then act innocent."

"They'll know. He'll know. Absolutely. I made a bit of a scene about it this morning. Lost it a bit. Said she's stolen it, which she has. Called her names. He was furious. Says I'm out at the first sign of any more trouble. SHE now comes first. I want what's mine. So, it has to look like an outside job. A passing burglary. Nothing to do with me. I have a fool proof plan. Dead easy."

"I don't get it."

"Let me tell you."

"OK. Spit it out." Martina sits forward on the arm of another chair and speaks eagerly, her hands gesturing.

"I, like, go with them and have a meal out. So, I have an alibi. You saw the front door and the steps down here are covered by a security camera. I showed you the back-way in. No cameras there. All someone has to do, is, like, go down the alley, I'll leave the gate open, go through the garden. I can, like, leave the back door here open too so you can get into the house. Go up the stairs. Go into her bedroom. Get the jewellery. And leave. Simple!" April looks at her in amazement.

"It has to be done this Thursday evening. It's dad's birthday. We're going out. I'll have to smooth things over till then."

"Why should I even consider it?"

"Money!"

"I thought you didn't have any money."

"I have my mother's credit card and pin number. I have access to all her savings in an emergency. I'll get you cash on Friday when you hand over the goods."

"How much?"

"You tell me."

"£35,000?"

"Too much."

"What then?"

"£25,000?"

"Let me think."

"Thursday evening. Last chance. Don't take too long."

Five

Monday morning

"As we can see, this cool new program enables us to compile those vital government statistics," says Becki, April's manager, looking down to adjust her PowerPoint presentation. The slide switches on the screen. April almost screams with boredom on seeing the title 'Essential Software Checklist' and a list that is over 30 items long. She takes a packet of peppermints out of her bag, and passes one to the people on either side, then spends some time unpicking the wrapping. She looks up, having finally freed the last mint, to find Becki glaring at her.

"In terms of the database, as I've shown you today, we cannot be entrenched in old ways of inputting but must transform our thinking along the lines of the Eezi-Sync software ..." Becki continues flowingly with terminology that sets April's teeth on edge. The meeting is due to finish at midday, yet Becki is far from summing up. She is a tall woman in her thirties, slim, suited and with a sleek dark geometrical haircut that frames her pinched white face. Newly appointed and over-anxious, she speaks briskly with sharp gestures to emphasize her remarks, and her eyes alert to her audience. Becki was, according to staff rumour, removed from her previous position in another city for some problem over a member of her team. She has come with the whispered nickname of 'The Black Widow' which has created much speculation and joking. On the very first day, being introduced to all the staff, Becki, hearing April's name, looked at a list and made a comment, saying she 'knew about April' in an ominous tone.

Whenever April looks up from her desk in the open-plan office Becki is always regarding her with a predatory gaze, like a tiger in the long grass, stalking a wildebeest.

Now all the staff are seated in a circle on a variety of chairs in the meeting room, this is ostensibly in order to 'lower barriers' between them all. But the real reason for the arrangement, April knows, is so anyone dropping off will be immediately visible. This public exposure ensures all attendees attempt to stay awake despite the tedium of the presentations.

Downland Town Council is committed to its staff's development. What this means in practice is at least one morning a month the staff are 'informed and involved about ongoing developments critical to the Council's success'. And that is what April is undergoing at the moment. The topic for today is 'Software Quality Ensurement'. April is almost certain that the word 'ensurement' will not be found in a dictionary. Becki, as the manager of the Downland Journey Enhancement Support Service, is delivering the information session with enthusiastic flourishes. April, with the rest of her colleagues, has been stuck here in an overheated room with no natural light for over two hours. All damp, all past bored and approaching inert, they slump, keeping their eyes open only by stalwart concentration and fear of a disciplinary. In the corridor behind Becki, the department head, Toby, strolls past the glass doors. Off to lunch.

"You are measured by what is on the computer," Becki continues, "unless you put full information correctly on the database your work does not exist. We need to prove the value of our vital services that enhance the lives of the residents of this city. No data field can be forgotten." April, sucking on her mint, looks around at the blank faces and starts doing her pelvic floor exercises. She counts 10 tighten and 10 hold, then relax, she has done these so often at work recently she should have pelvic floor muscles with the suction power of a vacuum cleaner. Not that she needs the muscles for sex (that activity seems to have disappeared altogether and she has no interest in pursuing it), but in the hope of staving off her mother's kind of incontinence problems. She's starting a difficult age in the genital area, getting too old for Tampax, too young for incontinence pads, but at least it's momentarily less expensive in 'feminine hygiene' products.

Finally, the meeting comes to an end and April dashes to her desk, grinning at work colleagues as she goes and stifling any conversational openings. She dumps her papers, picks up her bag and coat and runs downstairs, waving to her friend behind the reception desk,

"If The Black Widow asks about me if I'm late back, Doug, say I was looking pale and unwell, will you?"

Doug, an older plump man with a lined and lived-in face, nods at her from his wheelchair and waves, "OK darlin'. You're fine though?"

"Course, especially now I'm out of that. See you later," and she sweeps through the swing doors, just avoiding Becki who is coming back inside.

The building where she works, being part of the town hall, is right in the centre of town, and so she is immediately in amongst shops, cafes and banks. She loves the feel of busyness and just being amongst the action, it is one of the reasons why she sticks with the job: the regular pay comes first of course. Ever since Kate was seven, she has forced herself to take reliable Monday to Friday jobs; the consequent boredom has enabled her to raise Kate on her own and see her through university. She has forgotten if she ever had other ambitions. At one time she worked in a school as a dinner lady, a position she enjoyed, until all that was privatized. She should be grateful to the council for her employment, but what she would really like is an income and not to have to work at all, just be able to cook whenever and whatever she wanted. An impossible dream. She draws her bag more tightly to herself, closes her coat collar against the cold wind that has suddenly blown up and makes her way first towards her building society in order to deposit her mother's friend's cheque. Afterwards, she goes to her bank. Trish and Sam have told her to apply for a loan.

The bank is surprisingly busy when she gets there, and she has to wait a few tense minutes until the customer adviser is free. She sits down opposite a man who looks about twenty and says she's come about getting credit. April can almost hear the clogs turning as the customer training kicks in and he immediately smiles.

"I'm sure that can be arranged with no problem." She grins back, trying to look confident and sane and pushes her hair behind her ears. "I'll just take your account details. You do have an account with us?" April nods and then gives him the details and waits as he taps the details into his computer. He looks at the numbers appearing on the screen, looks back at her, straight-faced this time, scrutinizes the screen again, glances at her once more and smirks.

"I'll just have a word with my manager," he says and abruptly leaves his seat and goes through the number-coded door behind him. April looks around uneasily and considers making a run for it. But the door opens silently and an older face, another male, enters the room. She feels suddenly cold.

"Mrs Roberts?" he asks. She nods, everyone calls her Mrs and she's given up insisting on Miss or Ms. "Would you come in here where it's a bit quieter?" She stands up and gazes for one moment at the exit, noticing that the sun is now lighting the shop fronts in the high street. Sighing, she picks up her bag and follows him into a small bland soundproofed room containing an empty desk and three plastic chairs and the inevitable computer. All lit by fluorescent bulbs. She puts her bag on the table with a thump. "My name is Robert Seymour." He says and extends his hand. His skin is the pallid white that comes from sitting inside a lot, sorting his stamp collection, April suspects, or watching pornography. She shakes his hand rather grudgingly, noticing its dampness and resisting the urge to wipe her own afterwards. "Please take a seat, and won't you take off your coat?" His face is set without a possibility of a smile. So she is in for a grilling. All memories of her school days come back to her. Standing endlessly outside various heads' doors, being told repeatedly to change her attitude and never quite clear why she was there. She knows that her first reaction to anyone in authority is indignation and that her lifestyle has led her frequently into headlong conflict with autocrats and bureaucrats. But over the years she has watched others in action and realises that sometimes there are better routes to getting your way. She smiles at him sharply, then unbuttons her coat with a flourish and sits down. He blinks as he sees her colourful outfit.

"I see that you are wanting another loan," he begins, sitting down opposite her, facing the computer, "can I ask what for?"

April feels her cheeks redden and prays that she is not going to get one of her hot flushes at this time, but her neck glows and heat seeps out from her cleavage. She tries to concentrate.

"For replacing my car," April replies quickly. "I need it for my work." There is a moment's silence and April, now a startling crimson, bares her teeth again as he looks at her. She tries to look middle-aged, matronly and respectable and not at all like some flighty old thing that will abscond to some unobtainable part of the British Commonwealth. A drop of sweat trickles down from an eyebrow and she brushes it casually away, looking straight at him. He appears puzzled.

"Only, you see," Mr Seymour continues, "you already have three loans outstanding with us. One for consolidating some other loans from various lenders taken out in 2005 with another four years to run. One for helping you move to a new place when your daughter returned, taken out in June this year and one last December for…" he coughs slightly as if he is going to say a rude word, "a new car for your work." 'Shit!' thinks April, her bloody memory has let her down again, she should have said a computer. But how is she going to get the money if the bank won't help? The sweat congeals on her skin.

"You are also rather seriously overdrawn. You seem to be having problems with existing loans as it is. So, I wondered where you are going to get the money to reimburse any loan that we may give you?" April stays silent and shivers. She hates his patronising tone; does he really think that she is such an idiot? Of course she has no way of repaying the money. Why else would she be asking for a loan?

"Giving blow jobs," she mutters, buttoning up her coat as coldness hits her again. Now that it is clear that he isn't going to give her a loan she just wants to leave as soon as possible

"Pardon?"

"Just so, Bob," she says rather more loudly and then has an afterthought "Actually, I could wait on a car, but I do need some extension on my overdraft?" There is a pause, and he looks at her with obvious surprise.

"As far as I can see, Mrs Roberts, you have a rather generous overdraft facility that you seem to have consistently disregarded for the last five months, despite our agreement in June. You are now overdrawn to the tune of…" he looks at the screen, "£2,212.65p!"

"Are you sure about the 65p?" says April before she can stop herself. Mr Seymour looks back at the screen again and is calculating the figures. April knows the battle is lost.

*

Going up into her studio, Sam lays her yoga mat on the polished oak floor in order to do her exercises. She stands for a moment 'centring herself' as her yoga instructor, Cara, says. She lifts her hands and bends backwards to start the salutation to the sun. Her neck makes a slight popping sound. Is that good? Or bad? She decides to begin with a softer opening exercise that Cara has taught them. She keeps her back straight and bends her knees, which emit a crackling sound, like someone scrunching cellophane. She hopes this is a sign of her joints easing open. She straightens again and turns to the left and then right. Or is it the right and then left? She pauses trying to recall what happens next and adopts a few poses erratically. Two of them make her grunt with effort.

She finally decides to collapse into 'child' asana, curled up, face down in a foetal position. As she puts her head on the floor, some muscle at the front of her knee aches and another at the base of her skull. She never knew she had muscles in her head. Cara says you have to breathe into the discomfort and let go. So Sam tries breathing deeply and finds that the knee pain gets worse, so sits up. She practices a few of the easy arm and neck exercises but decides to skip the more rigorous ones and lies down on her back. She breathes in the peace of the empty house and sees, through the velux window, the clouds scudding across a grey autumn sky.

Small daily realities have come to mean so much to her because at one time she thought that everything was going to end. She remembers the clarity of feeling 'this may be the last time'. How amazing and precious the small things then became. The feel of air on her face on a walk to the shops, the taste of a cup of tea, the sight of a bird in a tree; all were miraculous gifts. The morning after her diagnosis with cancer she drew back the bedroom curtain and, looking out over the garden, was struck with a searing love for this planet, this Earth, seeing it as beautiful beyond compare. She was momentarily overwhelmed and struck into stillness. The sky stretched upwards and away, the trees rooted into the soil, all creation pulled at her heart with a sadness that has never quite left her. Each day she inhales the world anew. Begging for it not to fade, to be there in all its glory eternally. But she is the one who is dying, who can never shake off this monster, who can only aim for remission.

She carefully feels her breasts. She is used to the lack of mass where her right one was and is familiar with just having the scar cutting across its flatness and no nipple. She regards its loss as a toll she has to pay in order to continue to enjoy these small moments of existence. She decided not to go for reconstructive surgery, being exhausted by hospitals and treatments and others taking over her body. She just wanted to get on with living. Yet as time passes that feeling of being lucky every moment is fading, though she feels positive now, with a full day all to herself ahead of her.

She hears footsteps and banging sounds downstairs and knows once more that Helen has arrived with Salome. She stands up slowly and plods downstairs.

"Hello dearest, I wasn't expecting you," says Sam, putting some fresh water in the kettle.

"I don't need to make an appointment, do I?"

"Of course not, only it would be nice to know if you're coming round."

"Why? Most grandmothers are only too pleased to spend time with their ONLY grandchild. What else have you got to do? I didn't come up to your studio," says Helen defensively, "even though Salome really wanted to. You made such a fuss last time." The last time was last week and resulted in a broken picture, two torn sketches and a large urine stain on her Turkish kilim. Helen seems to have forgotten this and keeps talking about 'not stifling Salome's exploratory instincts' repeating that Sam must be prepared for some 'mishaps' in the process. "Nothing is as important as Salome," Helen said to Sam last week when she demurred about looking after Salome yet again. "Nothing. You should be delighted to spend time with your granddaughter," as she went off to her girls' luncheon book club.

Helen is sitting down whilst Salome is busy emptying pots and pans from a cupboard, they crash onto the tiles and roll around, making a cracking sound that makes Sam's eardrums vibrate.

"You know I don't mind spending time with Salome. It's just …." Salome takes this moment to start banging two pans together, killing any possibility of speech. Sam looks at Helen, expecting her to remonstrate, but instead she just turns away.

"You always say you're busy," says Helen, "I never see what you're doing. You just go up there and shut the door."

"I thought I showed you."

"You haven't shown me stuff for ages."

"I didn't think you'd be interested. You're so busy with Salome."

"Are you still working on your bits of jewellery? Is that all?" This is such a condemnation of her art and so in line with Hugh's unsaid estimation of her work that Sam walks away from the kettle, stepping over Salome who is denting a small pan by banging it hard on the floor. Sam does not know where to begin explaining to Helen how she feels about her work.

"I've never made what I really wanted to," she says. She means she's never had the time to fully concentrate on her work, throw herself into it. Her mother would say she is playing at being an artist, so maybe Helen and Hugh are right.

"It was so lovely going down to Bowhouse," says Helen suddenly, "grannie was sweet. So relaxed and loving." Sam remembers the chaos of the artistic commune where she grew up with a shudder. One June she was wandering round the large rambling house in Cornwall, looking for her homework book, when she found her father asleep in the summerhouse wrapped round her 'aunt' Doris. This was not unusual, so she kept searching and disturbed her mother sketching quietly in the workshop wearing a distant expression and few clothes. The door crashed open and uncle Leopold (Doris's husband) stood there, a bottle of vodka in his hand and his beard streaked with tears, "She doesn't love me any longer," he wailed. Her mother put down her pencil and went to speak to him, but Aunt Doris and her father appeared suddenly, and pleas and accusations were hurled round the room. Sam was told to leave, which she did, gratefully. This was just one of many similar highly-charged scenes. Everyone was too highly-strung, too over-dramatic, too busy experiencing their own lives to provide the mundane basics for a young girl.

With Hugh she revelled in providing the stability she never had: cooking, shopping, tending two growing children. But now he never notices her; she's become a background service industry.

"My mother was beautiful," says Sam wistfully, remembering her warm Greek–born mother and wondering if Helen has decided to be hurtful today. She is quite capable of being vindictive in a way that

Sam has never understood; she remembers her deliberately and calmly emptying a pot of ink over a sketch her brother Michael was doing. Michael is now working for a graphics company in LA and he and Helen have never got on. Sam misses him terribly, everyday. The noise of the dented pans is now deafening, so any nuances are lost, as Sam and Helen shout their conversation.

"She would've loved Salome." Sam is doubtful whether anyone can love Salome at the moment but gives her response cheerfully.

"She would. And I do, dearest." Salome bangs the pans on the floor and throws one across the kitchen. "Can you hear what I'm saying?"

"Do you want to stop her playing?"

"Is that what she's doing?" Helen suddenly snatches up Salome, making her cry out and stiffen.

"Nasty mean old grannie," she says, "leave her precious kitchenware alone!" There is a moment of quiet whilst Salome gathers herself for a screaming fit, and Sam picks up the pots and pans, noticing the dents in them and the chips in the tiles. She puts them on the countertops and wonders if a piece of kitchen roll will defend her ears. Helen pulls up her blouse, sits down and after a little while is breast-feeding a quiet Salome.

"It was weird bumping into Trish and April. Both here, freeloading on your food."

"They just dropped in on spec."

"Is Trish still a barmaid at that old biker's pub?"

"Well, not exactly a barmaid, more than that."

"So she says. And what about April, still living in that awful place?"

"She had to move somewhere cheap to fit Kate in."

"Deadbeats!" says Helen. "Surely you move in different circles now. Whatever do you see in them?"

"They've been good friends to me. And they're fun." Sam now knows that Helen is on the attack, but she cannot see what she has done to cause it.

"Fun!"

"I do like having fun, you know. When I get the chance."

"You've always had fun. You've done exactly what you wanted all your life." Sam is stricken with guilt, maybe Helen is right, maybe she has always got her own frivolous way. But somehow the description does not sit comfortably. It is not how she thinks of herself. She is the one that always makes the compromises, that pacifies, that organises and ends in the back seat of the car. That never has time for her work.

"You've always wanted to get on with your 'art'," continues Helen and makes the classic two-handed gesture to show that art is in speech marks. "I wasn't any good at it. Michael was though." She is silent and continues feeding Salome. Sam misses Michael again, Michael who has always been so loving: it is easy to love Michael whereas Helen has always been prickly. But Michael left.

"You both have different talents." Helen shakes her head and pushes backwards as Sam came towards her, standing up and putting Salome over her shoulder to burp her. Salome begins crying, the prelude to her screams. "Maybe she wants changing?" Sam suggests gently, Helen sniffs her bottom and then frowns at Sam and looks towards the changing bag she's brought in.

"The least you could do is change her then. I do it all the time." Sam picks up Salome and carries her crying from the room and into the downstairs shower room. The resulting fight is messy, long and tiring. Salome is doing really large wet poos now that need a bag full of wipes. Sam wants to put her under the shower wholesale but knows this will be regarded as over egging the pudding.

She needs rubber gloves she thinks, grabbing Salome's hands away from her shit-filled nappy. By the time she has cleaned both of them and returns to the kitchen Helen is nowhere to be seen. Just a note on the table,

'Back later, H x'

Six

Monday afternoon

April runs as quickly as she can back to the town hall, which is not very fast at all, but a crouched stretching lope, easily overtaken by pensioners with zimmer frames making for the bus. She pants up the stairs and tries her usual ploy of taking off her coat in the toilet and hanging it behind the door, then appearing at her desk quietly, as if she has been to the loo. Sneaking to her seat, smiling at her colleagues, she opens the bag of pick and mix she has bought from Woollies on the way back, and immediately opens letters with a flourish and inputs, ostentatiously following the checklist. She thinks she's got away with it, but two minutes later, Becki appears beside her desk.

"Ah April, can I just have a word?" April follows silently as Becki leads the way to a small office that is on one side of the department, passing the curious stares and sympathetic expressions of other staff on the way: one of them winks at her, another grimaces. April sits down nervously as Becki opens a large file on her desk in silence and clears her throat.

"April, you assured me on Friday that everything was alright 'down there'." April waits with her head on one side as Becki looks at her expectantly until she realises that Becki is referring to her lie about going to the doctor. She nods hurriedly and swallows, terrified in case she is asked for the name of her GP. "So, there's nothing physically wrong with you?" Again, April nods. Instantly Becki alters tack and becomes a large earthmover, bearing down on April with intent.

"So, April, I just need to know why you were so late back from lunch? It is now 50 minutes after you should've returned. Your lunchbreak started at 12:10 and you returned at 2:00 You should've been back at 1:10. This is not a formal disciplinary meeting or warning, at the moment, but you must give me a clear explanation for your behaviour. Do you have an explanation?"

"I went to the bank."

"And?"

"There was a queue."

"And?"

"I spoke to the manager."

"And?"

"It took longer than expected?"

"I can see this, April. I really can see this. What I can't see is why you think this is a good explanation? Everyone goes to the bank in their lunch hour. Everyone fits it into their working day, except you." April knows this is not strictly true. She has covered for a few people who are often late back from lunchbreaks and the smokers spend ages out of the office. She has wondered about taking up smoking again, but the cost is phenomenal now and the walk to the official smoking zone is miles.

"I'm sorry, it won't happen again," says April, almost tearfully. If she loses this job, she will never be able to help Kate, let alone pay her own bills.

"No, it certainly won't," says Becki, "in fact it can't. This is your last chance. I don't want to have to speak to you again about it. Do we understand each other?"

"Yes, we do," says April. "I'm really sorry."

"So you should be, I don't want to speak to you again."

"You won't have to."

"Next time will be disciplinary, and we all know where that leads, don't we?"

"Yes, I understand. Totally. You won't need to speak to me again."

"Just one more little thing," says Becki. "Your dress…"

"My dress?" says April, she isn't wearing a dress, she is wearing a green and red kilt, a blue blouse with a pink cardigan, a pair of white trainers and blue Norah Batty tights. She buys everything at charity shops, loves colours and 'real' fabrics, hates black and anything formal, will only ever wear comfortable shoes. Most of her clothes are tight, she has expanded to bulge them but cannot bear the thought of throwing them away.

"You do represent the Council when you are on the desk and we want to create an impression of an efficient and effective service. Do you have anything, shall I say, less gaudy? We have given you a jacket to wear, which would help, but I never see you in it."

"I've grown out of it," says April, casting her mind over her wardrobe items and knowing that most of them are brightly coloured.

"I'll issue you a new one immediately, what size are you now?"

"18. I'll see what I can find to wear underneath it."

"Also, your bag?" April never goes anywhere without her large red leather handbag crammed with tissues, a newspaper, safety pins, paracetamol, pens, an umbrella, a torch, a bill that needs paying and anything else that she's wanted at one time and now forgotten. It causes her to tilt to one side and makes a strange rattling noise when she picks it up and puts it down. "Could you put it safely out of sight? Somewhere no-one will fall over it? Julian almost sprained his ankle the other day."

"Of course," April wonders what else will be asked of her: whatever it is she'll say yes.

"Thank you. I hope this is the last time we need to have this little talk, eh?"

"Of course. Thank you," says April and meekly retires to her desk, flattened and digs into the remains of the pick n mix. She leaves a message on Trish's mobile before settling down and trying to concentrate on her work.

At the end of her working day April goes home with relief. Parking outside her block of flats she looks nervously round for any sign of the gamblers' car but sees no plush strange cars in the parking lot, just the usual beaten up old ones that her car merges in with. She looks up at her block of flats, only four storeys, an offshoot from the council towers next door. It is filled with people who need to keep their heads down, mainly foreigners who grimace placatingly, squeezing into the stairway of the main building in silent groups. The industrial estate opposite advertises its bleak interior with factual billboards and plot numbers.

Coming back here always depresses her.

Once inside she switches on the water heater to ensure that there is hot water for a bath and goes into Kate's small single room once more. There is no sign that she has been there, it already feels empty and neglected. The old photo of her mother and grandfather posing is gathering dust, flat on a bookshelf. Up on the wall there is a space where the picture of Kate in her graduation robes hung. It is no longer there. April loved that picture, it showed Kate looking proud and beautiful, smiling out to a new future, the first escapee from generations of poverty. It is a visual vindication of all April's efforts to maintain balance and joy and optimism in a harsh world. She searches for it and finally finds it at the top of the wardrobe and hangs it back in its place, wondering why Kate has taken it down. She dusts the glass tenderly, feeling afraid and tearful. She circles restlessly and rubs her hands then leaves, closing the door firmly.

She takes off her bra without removing her top by pulling the straps down through the sleeves, scratches with relief, puts on her slippers and unpacks the food she's brought, everything past its sell-by date. The remnants of her cake-making still lie around, but she leaves the washing up for the moment; she is sucked of energy. Every single thing she's tried today has gone badly. She draws the curtains and sits down on the sofa with a cup of tea, the local paper and some remaining cake scraps. Her brain just seems to be sluggishly going around in the same circles and getting nowhere; she's so tired, so worried about Kate and the money. She puts her feet up on the sofa and switches on the TV to watch the early evening rubbish that she calls 'chewing gum for the mind'.

She wakes up with a start with the phone ringing. She is momentarily disorientated and realises how little sleep she has had over the last few nights. She rubs her forehead and tries to focus but the answerphone is already speaking as she clambers slowly off the sofa. The minute she hears her mother's voice saying her name, she grabs the phone off its cradle.

"Mum! Mum! Are you OK?" and her heart beats heavily in her chest. There is only one payphone in the care home, and it is too complex for her mother to handle unaided, so April knows at once that it must be an emergency.

"Oh April. You're there!" Her mother sounds anxious and almost tearful.

April, in her panic, is barely conscious that her front doorbell is ringing. "Mum, are you OK?" and April speaks louder, both to get some answer from her mother and also over the insistent ring of her doorbell. Her mother mumbles a few slurred words. "I can't hear you, mum, there's someone at the door!"

There is a cry of panic at the other end of the phone. "Dun answer t' door! Dun answer t' door!" April sits down suddenly with the receiver to her ear, feeling weak, her mother's Yorkshire accent always surfaces more strongly in times of stress.

"I won't, mum, don't worry! Is it the gamblers? Have they been to see you? Are you OK?" She cannot think why the men should have terrified her mother or how they would have even found out about her, but she hopes her mother is safe.

"No, no, not t' gamblers!" her mother sounds irritated by the suggestion, "worse, much worse." The doorbell rings again whilst April sits down on the floor in shock, hiding behind the sofa, wondering who can be worse than the gamblers. She ignores the bell. She has seen enough horror films to know that you don't go down dark corridors when there is a killer loose.

"But what's it about?" She feels strangely calm. The only reply is heavy erratic breathing and April knows that her mother is sobbing. "Keep calm. Don't worry," she coaxes. "I'm OK. I'm here. I'm fine. Are you OK, mum?"

"I'm awright. There's nowt wrong wi me but t' same." Her mother sounds as if she is recovering now. There is the background murmur of a voice and April realises with relief that her mother is not alone. That of course explains how she has managed to make the phone call at all.

"Who's with you?" asks April.

"A friend."

"Thank goodness. But please tell me what's happened." There is the background murmur again and her mother speaks again.

"You'll be OK. Just don't open that door. It's nowt really. I'll tell you when I see you." The phone goes dead. April sits staring at the phone and wondering what she should do next. She phones her mother's home and it is finally answered after a long wait. April asks to speak to her mother but the woman at the other end says that most of the residents are getting ready for bed, or are in bed already, and asks if it is really necessary. April decides that she doesn't want to upset and tire her mother further by bringing her all the way downstairs to the phone in the office, so she tells the woman that she will visit tomorrow.

It is now clear that the person who needs help is not her mother, but April herself. She peeps out from behind the sofa, gets up and crawls to the door and puts the chain on it, conscious that she is an older woman on her own in a ground floor flat with no one near that will give immediate physical help. After the gamblers' ultimatum, she certainly cannot call the police (not that she would've done that anyway). The brick walls suddenly feel like cardboard and every window seems delicate and as if it can be shattered with a small blow.

There is nothing really between her and the dark, cold outside world where the stranger is waiting. She wonders if she should phone Trish or Stuart, but knows that Trish is working tonight at the pub, and anyway what is the threat? Is anyone outside? She creeps towards the window and tries to peer round the closed blinds and can see little at first in the darkness, but then a police car drives slowly along the road and its headlights shine on the wet empty parking space. Feeling reassured, she starts making some supper. April loves making complex dishes with enthusiastic ease, and soon she is engrossed in making ravioli stuffed with butternut squash and ricotta. Kate loved this recipe, and April eats with nostalgia, remembering when they sat at this very table together.

She becomes calmer and so does not notice the flash of car headlights through the blinds until the doorbell rings and frightens her back to the present. When she nervously peers over the kitchen windowsill, there is a police car in the car park with an officer sitting in it. She cannot see her front door but guesses that another police officer is there. Her mouth goes dry at the thought that they may have found Kate in some terrible accident and she runs to the front door. Opening it slightly with the burglar chain still attached she sees a policeman.

"Mrs Roberts?" He stands straight in his uniform with his walkie talkie buzzing on his shoulder and his identity card held out in front of him.

"Yes?" she replies, suddenly dreading that he is going to give her some awful news. She takes off the chain and opens the door. "Is it about Kate? Is she alright?" and she steps forward anxiously to see, if by chance, Kate is standing somewhere to one side.

"Can I come in?" he asks. "It's not about Kate, whoever she is," and grins. The smile, though not welcoming, does not seem to herald disaster and she lets him in. As he steps firmly in through the door, she gets a good look at him. He is maybe in his early forties with a square face with something about it that reminds her of her grandfather's harsh morality. His uniform is immaculate, clean and pressed, looking as if he has barely started work today, and his boots are polished to a high shine.

"Come in," she says and offers him a cup of tea, which he refuses. April shows him to the worn sofa where he sits, takes off his hat revealing very short thick hair and then looks around the room and most keenly at some of her photographs that she keeps on a side table next to the sofa. There is nothing to hide in them (not like some others that are thankfully stashed away), being only of her mother's 70th birthday party before her first stroke, Kate sitting outside a tent in the New Forest and Sam, Trish and herself laughing when they had a celebratory meal out for Trish's 50th birthday several years ago. She sits down opposite the police sergeant and waits anxiously for him to speak.

"This will only take a second. Just a precautionary visit. I did call earlier, but there was no reply," he says.

"Ah," says April, feeling immediately relieved, "the thing is my mother phoned and told me not to answer the door, so I didn't." She sees his look of surprise and knows that it is all coming out wrongly. "Well you never answer the door in horror movies, do you? Not if someone tells you not to? Not unless you want to get beheaded or your eyes gouged out or turned into a flesh-eating zombie." His expression tells her that he is starting to think that she is bonkers. How can she be such a coherent liar and so bad at telling the truth? Then he sits up straighter on her sofa and speaks clearly.

"My name is Henderson. Sergeant Henderson."

April sits still, wondering why the name is familiar to her.

"I can see that my name means nothing to you." He continues calmly. "Despite the fact that my father gave you £5,000 of his hard-earned savings! Did you even look at the cheque before you cashed it?"

April's mouth falls wide open and her hands grip each other so that the nails leave marks in her palms. He looks at her with shrewd eyes and then around the room with disdain. He stays seated and even settles back into the sofa, uncrosses his arms, rests his hands on his knees and spreads his fingers. Every movement he makes is controlled and deliberate and he speaks straight across the room to her.

"Now, Mrs Roberts. Let me tell you about my father. He bought me up single-handedly after my mother died and is a respected father and grandfather. He is a kind man who has worked hard all his life in a bank and put aside savings scrupulously. He came from a poor background and his mother was ill for most of her life, but he always looked after her, even when his own wife died. He started off as just another bank clerk and then slowly worked his way up to a bank manager and then a regional manager through hard, continuous work. He never had a day off ill. He brought me up and cared for his mother with devotion. He never missed a parents' evening or a Christmas concert.

He is a wonderful, caring man. Unfortunately, he now has severe arthritis and Parkinsons and me and my family were unable to provide him with the round the clock care he needed. So, after consulting for a long time with nurses and doctors, he was taken from our house and put into the nursing home wing of the care home your mother is in. They have taken extremely good care of him. He is capable with all his faculties about him but in a lot of discomfort most of the time and finds it hard to move in a controlled way at all." He pauses and stares at her. She is unable to say anything, she is not being physically threatened, but she is being made to feel ashamed.

"Do you want to say anything?" he asks. April slowly shakes her head; she does not know where to begin. She can't give the money back. He stands up, leans forward slightly and makes his statements clearly and precisely with controlled vehemence.

"I do not know how you made him give you the money. My father said he gave it to you as a gift voluntarily, so I can't do anything officially. He did not want me to come to see you at all, he said something about an old debt to your mother but he's never even mentioned her or you before at all, so I know that you have exploited him in his weakened position in some way. And I will find out how, believe me.

How you could take money from an old defenceless man is beyond me.

He would never give so much money to a stranger and you are a total stranger to him. Your actions are despicable! I do not know what you are spending it on, maybe drink, maybe drugs. But I just want you to know that from now on me and my colleagues will be keeping a keen eye on you.

If you so much as park on a double line for a minute or drop a sweet paper, I'll get you. We'll be watching you, Mrs Roberts. We'll be watching every time you go out, wherever you go, we'll be there! We'll be watching you even if you don't see us." He steps towards her and April cowers back. "And we'll find something. You'll slip up somewhere, sometime and when you do, we'll be there." He picks up his hat and moves towards the door, then turns and points a finger at her.

"Oh, and don't go anywhere near my father. Don't speak to my father again. Don't go into his room. Don't even look at him from the doorway. And make sure your mother doesn't go near him either!" For the first time she can hear his voice losing control. Then April hears the front door open and close and a little while later the sound of a car starting up and moving away.

She sits on the sofa for a long time and moves shakily to the window and sees that the police car has gone. By God she needs a drink! At the very back of a deep cupboard she finds a dust-covered quarter bottle of cooking brandy.

Pouring herself a hefty amount and taking a swig, she wonders what to do. She cannot give the money back till Friday, no matter what happens, as she has put it into a building society. But having it now does not make her feel victorious, but guilty. There are terrible consequences to whatever action she takes but by swigging the brandy she is successful in numbing the fear and letting tonight's events fall into a remote corner at the back of her mind. It starts to feel as if the whole episode has happened to someone else.

She will visit her mother tomorrow who might have a perfectly good explanation for why April should have the money, and why Mr Henderson has given it to her. With her mother, anything is possible. There's a chance (that increases as the brandy decreases in the bottle) of a real debt that has never been repaid. There is no use thinking about it now, she can do nothing anyway, everything can be left on hold until Friday.

She knows what she'll do; she'll bake a cake, and when she sees her mother tomorrow, she will give it to a nurse to take to Mr Henderson. She'll send a note to tell him that she intends to pay the money back. It will not be a gift, but a loan.

Seven

Tuesday morning

Trish wakes up to the sound of her mobile ringing. She picks it up, stretching over Stuart who is snoring copiously beside her, his long grey hair snarled on the pillow. She sees whose call she has missed, swears, and gets out of bed. She makes a call, hears it default to voicemail and leaves a message.

"April, April, what's going on? Are you OK? Give me a call back."

She goes downstairs, lets the dog out and fills his food and water bowl, noting that she will have to do a shop today, which means asking Stuart for some financial contribution. She does not envisage this as a problem; he offered early on in the relationship to contribute to costs and has kept his side of the bargain, all a bit of a novelty for Trish. She digs for a mug, finds one beneath the pile of crockery in the sink and washes it. She knows that anyone looking round her house would see a mess but what she sees are signs of life, signs of living. She believes that an ordered life is a stunted and warped life, chaos is where the energy is. The kettle is working again. Her mobile rings as she is making herself some tea.

"April, what did you want?"

"It's Sam's check-up today," comes April's quietened voice. "I only just looked at my calendar and realised. You know I promised I'd go with her, but things at work are really, really tricky at the moment. And I need to go to the pawnbroker's this lunch hour as you suggested, to try to get some money. But I'll chance it all for Sam, you know, if you can't go?" Her voice echoes and there is the sound of a flush; she must be in the loos at work.

"Bloody Hugh, he should be going," says Trish, trying to find a place to sit in the front room that isn't coated in motor bike parts.

"Too right. I don't think they're getting on well at the moment."

"Understandably if he won't give her any money, considering how she's helped him make it! All those days in that damp Brixton basement! Don't get me going! But she rolls over for him of course, always has. And as for bloody Helen! I can get to the hospital of course, pleased to, you just need to tell me where and when."

"You'll have to just turn up. You know what she's like. I can't get in touch with her." Trish sighs; Sam, through a sense of artistic allegiance, has made technology her enemy. Won't use computers, can't set her own central heating and doesn't watch TV. Helen once bought her a mobile, but she lost it immediately; the minute she's away from the house there is no hope of contacting her. Trish dashes round the room looking in all the usual places for a biro and paper to write on, without success, eventually settling for a large felt tip pen and a discarded free newspaper. She makes some brief notes on this and is just letting the dog back in, when the house phone rings. She picks it up expecting April again, but instead hears her father's voice.

"Who's that?" he asks. Trish is confused, she can't remember the last time her father phoned her.

"Papa it's Patricia, why are you phoning me?"

"I pressed this button…" Trish thinks it must be the last number recall button, which explains how he's made the call. Her mother has phoned Trish repeatedly, asking her to apologise, saying she ruined the anniversary party for them all. Trish has made sure no-one answered and deleted every one of the answerphone messages without listening.

"Patricia, Patricia, your mother has disappeared. She's gone. I woke up this morning and realised she hadn't come to bed last night. I've looked round the whole house and she's nowhere to be seen. Patricia, is she with you? Are you there?" Trish is astounded. Surely her father isn't asking for her help? He sounds old and worried and, despite herself, she responds to his plea with kindness.

"Pater I'm here."

"Oh thank God. Is she with you? She said she might go down to your place. Is she there?" Trish is appalled at the thought.

"Of course not. She only visited me once after Ricky was born." She kept her gloves on the whole time, Trish remembers.

"Oh blast it. I don't know what to do. I'm so worried. Do you think she's OK? Do you know where she is?" Trish goes through all the likely people that her mother may have gone to visit, knowing that her knowledge of her mother's circle of friends is limited. Both her brothers are away or not replying, her father says. It's the cleaner's day off. He will phone her friend Marjorie, if he can find the number. He is really at his wits end, but he'll try everyone again and have another look round the house and grounds. If he can't find her, he'll phone Trish back. Reluctantly Trish gives him her mobile number, hoping that he will not pass it to her mother. Running upstairs to get ready she sees that Stuart is awake and getting dressed, wandering round the room wearing only socks and a T shirt, searching out his clothes which lie muddled on the floor amongst hers.

"I need some money for shopping," she says, "and the dog needs a walk."

"Hiya Stuart sweetie," replies Stuart sarcastically, "good morning, how are you?" Trish kisses him on the lips, telling him that her father seems to have lost her mother, he holds her tightly for a moment and chuckles.

"Ah, that I can understand. Do you think he's murdered her?"

She heads for the bathroom as Stuart strolls downstairs, whistling for the dog on the way.

*

Sam leaves the house almost the minute she hears the door close behind Hugh, and goes to the bus stop, walking through the damp morning air, noting the bushes with their radiant red berries. She likes seeing the colours of autumn gripping the woods behind her house and hearing the high-pitched chatter of starlings. The countryside is where she feels most at home and the wilder the better: muddy slopes, jagged clifftops, wheeling buzzards and the wild Cornish seas. Despite Hugh preferring the groomed parks and gardens of National Trust properties she still misses the outings they used to make together to the countryside when they strolled the grounds and chatted in the tearoom. That stopped when she was diagnosed and has not been reinstated. Nothing has been the same since.

At the hospital she makes her way through the labyrinth of ramshackle buildings to find the canteen run by volunteers. She wonders if April has remembered the appointment but knowing that her friend has other priorities at the moment steels herself to be on her own. She has not felt it appropriate to ask for April's attendance at such a routine activity when her mind must be full of the danger she's facing. Sam just wouldn't be top priority and is reluctant to put more pressure on April by making unreasonable demands.

Sitting there, she begins to worry about what the consultant is going to say to her. It has been six months since her last visit and she took a blood test and a mammogram two weeks ago. The cancer and treatment have made her feel ill for so long, it's hard for her to know whether she's back to normal or not. She never forgets she's ill, but maybe this is as good as it gets, a sort of 80% return of energy. More worrying for her, is a persistent pining, an uncredited mourning, which is creeping into everything she does. She looks at the lives of those around her and wants more of what they have; meals out, concerts, walks in the country, fun; all very mundane to others. Hugh is so busy making money he has forgotten why he wanted it in the first place. She sighs and sips her tea. She wonders if she still loves him, then shakes her head, that is a question she cannot ask herself.

She stands up and walks towards the outpatients' department.

She is still early but decides to sit in the waiting area, read some of the magazines and see if April turns up. She has trouble finding a seat as it is crowded with people of all ages and walks of life, many of whom have brought all their family along. Mothers and daughters sit together whilst grandchildren play quietly. Older fathers swap quiet jokes with their sons. Sam imagines Helen or Salome here and the ensuing chaos. Why doesn't she have kind, thoughtful, supportive families like everyone else has? One little girl stands next to her grandmother and looks at her adoringly and holds her hand, why does Salome never do that to Sam?

Sam gives her name to the receptionist and picks up a magazine. One of the advertisements is for a cruise on a small sailing ship around the Caribbean; it looks wonderful. It is ages since she's swum in the sea and she knows that this one would be warm. Trish has been there and says the water is like silk. She hears her name and looks up to see Trish in person standing in front of her. Tall and curly blonde, wearing her usual jeans and leather jacket, but smiling at her welcomingly and opening her arms for a hug so that Sam stands up, embraces her and gives a small sob of relief. Trish sits down next to her and Sam pats her hand.

"I was just thinking of you," says Sam.

"Only good things I hope?"

"You've been to the West Indies. You once said the water there is warm and smooth as silk. I've always remembered that."

"At last! You want to travel a bit. Well Hugh's got the money and you have the time. That should be easy."

"If he can spare both," says Sam. Trish looks at her questioningly and gives her hand a squeeze.

"April can't make it," says Trish, "some trouble at work that means she can't take any time off."

"I bet it's that new manager," says Sam, "she sounds a bit jobsworth."

"But she said she would definitely be here if I couldn't make it." She pauses. "What's brought on this desire for the Caribbean?"

"I don't know, just thinking. I'd like to see a bit more of the world. Go somewhere where I can swim in the warm. I'd like to sketch a different wildlife with different colours. Wear few clothes. Feel hot sand under my feet. Maybe it's the time of year," she shrugs.

"This is such a change for you, you've always seemed so happy to be here, such a home lover. And your house is lovely, mine is such a mess." But Trish smiles as she says this, she does not envy Sam her home.

"I'm so glad you came," says Sam. They sit for a moment in silence then Trish smiles again.

"I know what I meant to tell you and April. One of Stuart's friends can get Stuart two tickets for Glastonbury, so I'm going back to Glastonbury in June. Whooppee, hey?" Her voice rises as she gets excited and one of the nurses looks up and frowns at her.

"Oh Trish, I'm so pleased for you. You'll love it."

"April was there," says Trish. "Remember?"

"You were with Roger and her boyfriend was his best friend at that time."

"Yes, Roger, my first awful choice."

"My brother Roger," Sam sighs, "What did you expect? You met him in a pub!"

"Moved straight in with him. I thought I knew everything. Soon found out!"

"You were only 16," says Sam "and he was dark and dangerous, all my friends fancied him. But ... but ...." Her voice tails off as she tries to mentally absolve her hopeless alcoholic brother who still asks wistfully after Trish whenever he calls to cadge money off Sam.

"I can't believe we thought April was so cool and sophisticated, she seemed so much older and wiser then."

"She'd been around a bit. Anyway, she is the eldest one of us, you're the baby," and Sam pats Trish's knee.

"At that age I was, I spent a lot of time with your brother getting drunk and being stoned," continues Trish, remembering her mother coming to fetch her home from Roger's rented flat and them both looking down on her from the windows above an off-licence, stifling their laughter, and pretending they were out, her mother must have heard them giggling.

"You could stop when you wanted to. Roger's never learnt that. Mind you, April's choice wasn't much better," says Sam, remembering Ernie late one summer night at Glastonbury, leaning in to stroke her breast and her swatting his hand away, hoping April didn't see.

"Terrible man," says Trish. "Still, he brought April to meet us, so I'll forgive him. What a Glastonbury that was!"

"It was so sunny that year, we never wore any clothes, we were stoned all the time. We laughed so much. We jelled immediately." She recalls the warmth of Trish and April tumbled across her on a sunny afternoon on a grassy slope whilst someone was playing a penny whistle. "We slept out; we had no tents. I can't remember being cold or uncomfortable," Sam remembers, giggling, watching the stars and seeing the early light of dawn as Bowie sang.

"Bowie played," added Trish.

"Just what I was thinking."

"Fairport Convention were there too. Didn't the Grateful Dead play? It was brilliant!" Sam's face was alight with good memories.

"No they weren't there at that one. When did we last go? All of us?"

"It was 1979. Helen was conceived that year, that's how I remember."

They had made a batch of 'biscuits' and sold them. "So long ago! It feels so near!"

"Samantha Wright." Sam's name is called. They both stop smiling and get up and make their way to the nurse who is holding Sam's file in her hand. The nurse is turning the file over in her hand and smiles at Sam welcomingly, greets her by first name and is introduced to Trish.

"Dr McGiveney will see you now," she says and leads them round the corridor and into a small room with an older doctor sitting at a desk in a lurching chair. He heaves himself out of it as they come in and holds his hand out.

"Samantha!" he says and shakes her hand and then smiles at Trish.

"My friend Trish," says Sam.

Dr McGiveney takes Trish's hand and looks at her keenly but then

86

sits down in the wobbly chair and opens Sam's file and looks on his computer that is placed on top of a desk piled high with notes and papers. The nurse stands beside him protectively. He turns towards Sam again and rocks on the chair. He laughs and so does Trish.

"Whoops!" he exclaims and goes on to fully concentrate on Samantha, asking her how she is, whether she has felt any itching, swelling, puckering, bumps or lumps. He goes through her test results, explaining what they mean: good, going in the right direction. He listens keenly to all her answers, asks her about her appetite and how she's doing with the exercises. Sam responds positively and opens up under his questioning, her eyes brightening at his professional matter-of-fact reassurances. He asks if he can examine her fully, so the nurse draws the curtains that are around the couch and Sam goes into the resultant cubicle.

"Don't you work at The Old Duke?" the doctor asks Trish.

"Well yes, don't tell me you've got a bike?" Trish feels herself blushing.

This is always happening to her, middle-aged men who've just bought a bike and want to talk about wheels with a biker bitch. But this is Sam's time, Trish does not want to get diverted. Trish can hear Sam changing behind the curtain and realises that she has not asked Sam whether she is welcome at the examination or not.

"Of course. A Honda Goldwing." Trish smiles; a good safe comfortable bike, a sensible choice for an older man who wants to tour in style. "But you've got that lovely Harley Fatboy," and he smiles at her appreciatively and Trish can't stop herself from straightening up a little and smiling back. She feels young and dangerous again.

"I came on it today actually."

"Hrrmph!" and the nurse is making her presence and disapproval felt. "If you don't need me in the cubicle, doctor," she continues.

"The patient has indicated that her friend," the last two words are strangely stressed, "can be at the examination."

"Of course," the doctor continues "I know you have loads on." The nurse picks up a phone on a desk nearby and starts speaking in a low voice with a disgruntled backward look at Trish.

"You can come in," says Sam's voice from behind the curtain. She is not worried about being seen naked. After the scars from Sam's op semi-healed they all three sat in Trish's garage, smoked a joint, downed some beer, took their tops off and compared breasts whilst giggling and prancing to music from the radio. Trish's youngest son, Ricky, opened the garage door innocently, gasped in horror and rushed away. They laughed so much they had to sprint for the loo and Trish, being ousted, squatted behind the garage.

The examination continues well, the blood test and mammogram results being OK, Doctor McGiveney sounds hopeful and suggests another six-month follow up just as a precaution. He asks again about reconstructive surgery, but Sam refuses. He stands up from his chair, shakes their hands, takes a moment longer clasping Trish's and escorts them to the door where the nurse appears with a stern face. He smiles again at Trish while the nurse turns sharply away and points towards the reception desk advising them to make sure they have a follow up appointment booked. Sam notices Trish stepping away with a bit more than her usual sway and looks back to where the doctor is gazing after Trish.

"For God's sake, Trish," she whispers. As they approach the reception desk, Trish's mobile rings and she answers it immediately and walks to one side. The nurse complains loudly and points to the notices showing that no mobiles should be used but Trish is engrossed in the phone call and can clearly be heard to say, "Oh No!" then "Oh no!" then "OK OK I'll come up if there's absolutely no-one else." Then "Alright, OK" then "Yes yes". Sam at the reception desk is booking another appointment whilst all the staff and some of the patients look at Trish with disfavour until finally Trish ends the call and then comes towards Sam apologetically.

"I'm so sorry, Sam, it's my father, I'll explain everything over coffee." The nurse glares at Trish.

"Ah, nurse Perivale," says Trish in her most carrying voice, leaning forward and reading the nametag. "So sorry, a bit of an emergency at my end I'm afraid."

"If everyone used their mobiles in here who wanted to …"

"I have said I'm sorry," says Trish. Then looks more closely at her nametag. "Perivale. The worst fuck I ever had." The nurse stares at Trish disapprovingly for a moment then raises her eyebrows.

"Same here," replies the nurse, "that's why I divorced him."

*

April makes her way out of the office over lunchtime, hunching her shoulders as she pulls up her hood to stop the autumn drizzle from reaching her hair. She notices a long black car out of the corner of her eye. It drives slowly beside her, at her walking pace so she looks up and sees that the person inside it is the tall man with the crooked nose who threatened her on Saturday morning. April calls him in her mind The Enforcer. The younger man is driving the limousine that has blacked out rear windows, and the Enforcer is sitting alongside him nearest to April, so close he could touch her. He stares hard at her, making sure she sees him, nodding and pointing at her as he passes. April steps to one side with shock and stands still for a moment, watchful, until they go. The car accelerates and is lost in the high street traffic. She trembles. They have made their point: she is unprotected. She shakes her head, pulls her hood further forward and almost runs down the road to the pawnbroker's.

The pawnbroker's is in a small side street right at the furthest end of the High Street. From the outside it could be mistaken for old-fashioned jewellers specializing in watches but the window does not allow any passers-by to see into the store itself. April opens the door gingerly and hears a bell ring to announce her presence. She sees a room with a bare floor and a counter, behind which is an open door to an office. A couple of display cabinets round the wall contain electrical equipment and odd items, including a rather moth-eaten stuffed fox. As she looks more closely, she sees that the fox is wearing a most incongruous grin. A man standing at the desk coughs at her, so she straightens up and faces a thin elderly man with a long pale face, unkempt grey hair and a rumpled suit. She asks him if he can look at some bits of jewellery.

"Is this to sell or to pawn," he asks.

"What's the difference?"

"Well I can make you an offer for both and let you decide. Are the items yours?"

"Oh yes," she says, although strictly speaking the brooch belongs to her mother, a present from one of her admirers when she was a Tiller Girl, causing a rumpus in the house in Leeds. April's grandfather said it was 'the wages of sin' and her mother had to give it back, she refused of course and handed it to April, 'to keep safe'. But her grandmother took it away immediately and hid it in the tea caddy before her grandfather found out. April only re-discovered it when she cleared out her grandparents' house after their death. She roots in her bag and fishes out the plastic bag containing all the jewellery she found this morning, including the brooch. She lays it all out and is tempted to snatch it back when she sees its memory-catching familiarity. The drop earrings Kate gave her when she got the London job as a thank you for being 'the best mother in the world'. The ring from Ben to say sorry when he wouldn't leave his wife, a truly beautiful ring from a wonderful man, but it has to go, she has hung onto it too long anyway.

Other stuff: birthday and Christmas presents, a cross of her grandmother's, cuff links, a button hook, a signet ring, more earrings, just looking at each one makes her feel nostalgic and tearful.

"Have you been here before?" he asks her and as she shakes her head he reaches behind him to pull out a form. He gestures to the chair and gives her a pen "Read that. Fill it in and sign it." He scoops up her valuables and disappears into the back room with them. She hears voices. April looks at the paper she's been given which is headed 'Loan Agreement'. There is a lot of it. She skips the small writing and goes straight to the back pages where she has to give details of herself. She is busy filling these in, which is a job she absolutely hates, when the doorbell pings. She crouches forward to hide her face in case it is anyone who might recognise her. The man in the office behind the counter comes out to see who has entered, but then springs to attention and nods at the person.

"Hello Sergeant, any problems?"

"No, not at all," says a familiar voice and April looks over her shoulder and sees Sergeant Henderson glancing over at her. "Just checking if you've seen our latest list?"

"Yes, of course, nobody has offered me any of those. I would've told you if they had."

"Well, we keep a close eye on law breakers," and he sweeps round to look directly at April who is bright red, having started one of her hot flushes. She knows this makes her look nervous and guilty and tries to smile, which only makes the sergeant frown more deeply. "We all need to keep on our toes and make sure decent people are protected."

"We've never been in trouble with the police. You know that. Not like some I could mention." The owner is clearly on the defensive.

"Of course, of course. I may call in later. Just to ask you a few questions about a particular person who's very much on my mind at the moment." He stays half turned and then looks directly and warningly at April as he leaves. She is so distracted she fills in the form wrongly and has to ask the man for another. He also seems disturbed and goes into the back room again where she can hear him complaining to someone unseen.

"…fed up of this …tantamount to harassment … we've never …" After a moment he returns with April's jewellery and goes through each piece, asking her about it, handing a couple back to her with a little shake of his head. He has obviously been spooked by the Sergeant's visit. He gives an estimate and it all seems ridiculously little: £450. April wonders how burglars make a living. He then carefully goes through the difference between a loan and selling them and the variation in price. April tries to hurry him, but only makes him flustered and repeat himself. She is late already. She hopes Becki has gone to a meeting. As she lopes back with the money burning a hole in her handbag, she sees the police car passing her again and the Sergeant tips his cap at her. She tries to smile cheerily in response but he glares back at her.

April creeps back into work feeling defeated. She is not going to come up with the money this way. She is too dispirited to go through her usual pretence of having gone to the loo, but just goes to her chair and plumps down. Taking off her coat and pulling out some mints from the pocket, she looks up and sees Becki's eye upon her and knows that her lateness has been noted. She wonders if there is a reasonable excuse she can give. She nods and simpers at her, hoping that looking innocent might make Becki wonder if she's got her timings right. Becki picks up the receiver and makes a phone call and April, relieved, turns on her computer and puts in the password. She has barely finished when Becki comes over to her.

"April can you follow me please?" April heaves herself out of her chair and follows, trudging along behind her, feeling like a prisoner going to death row. She passes the usual line of gazing younger faces who now look concerned for her. One person holds up her crossed fingers, another puts their hands in a prayer position. April grimaces back and tries to straighten her top over her stomach.

Becki has obviously had some trouble finding an empty interview room at short notice, so finally they sit down opposite each other in an overheated, airless attic room at the top of the old town hall. The furniture belongs to the old building, wooden chairs, a badly scratched small desk missing a drawer and a desk lamp without a bulb. Nothing has been said as they come here. Now Becki motions to the empty chair furthest from the door and opens the file she has brought with her.

"April, I'm forced to take the disciplinary proceedings to the next level. This is now a formal warning that will go onto your file and may result in dismissal." She pauses and looks at April questioningly. April regards her without saying anything. "Do you understand?" April nods. "Would you like anyone else here with you? A union rep? A work colleague?" April does not want any person to hear the obvious truth; she is late again, it is a fair cop, what acceptable excuse can she give?

"You left for your lunchbreak at 12:45 and were not back in your seat until 2:15. Do you dispute this?" April shakes her head. If only there were some way to escape all this. Her whole life is lurching from bad to worse in every direction. "I have spoken to you only yesterday about the importance of timekeeping, you were late then and I reiterated the council's lunchbreak policy and sent you a copy of that which you have read." April nods. She just wants all this to end. "Yet despite this you were late again today. Breaking that policy most deliberately."

April feels one of her hot flushes coming on and, hoping that this one will go away quickly, she flaps the front of her blouse so that the cool air can hit her chin. It does not help, sweat breaks out on her cheeks. Becki speaks without looking up, "Both before and after lunch. You left early without permission and you came back late. Over half an hour late in fact. Do you dispute this?" There is a silence. April shakes the front of her jumper madly and wipes the back of her neck with her bare hand knowing that her face has gone past flushed and is now approaching traffic light red.

"Er, yes, I mean, no...." she manages to stutter out, inwardly cursing her inability to control her body. Becki looks up questioningly. April stops all her movements. "Er yes, I was late back. Well a bit late back. There is a reason." Becki, looking unsympathetic, writes a few words in the file, and continues.

"You do know how serious this is, don't you? I have explained to you previously the importance of timekeeping. You have broken council policy! And, it appears, quite deliberately." Becki pauses for a moment and, still looking down, she taps her pen on the papers in front of her. "I can think of no reason why you should take an extra-long lunch hour. You will have to explain further. Though I have to warn you to think carefully before you speak."

But April hardly hears anything Becki says. The whole of April's body has gone out of normal temperature boundaries into nuclear meltdown and now soars to a heat that would've made the inside of a volcano feel cool. Large drops of sweat trickle down her nose and fall into her lap, the blouse clings under her arms, even her socks feel damp. April brushes the wet from her forehead and waggles her other hand feebly. The room is full of stale humid air, which is stifling her. The noise of her quickened heartbeat blocks her ears. She can bear it no longer and, without thinking, she stands up and flings the window behind her open and leans out into the cold air, pushing her vermilion cheeks frantically into the wind. The windowsill cuts into her ribs as she bends forwards and gulps, trying to lower her temperature by the only means possible. Behind her, there is a surge of activity and Becki's voice cries out,

"NO! No! STOP!"

The next thing she knows is that two hands take hold of her shoulders and she is wrestled away from the window. She looks up in some surprise as Becki pushes her firmly into a chair and stands squarely in front her.

"Get away from there! Stop! No need for that!" says Becki, who must've moved at speed and now is guarding the window. Surely it isn't Council policy to prevent the windows from being opened, thinks April.

"I'm sorry," she mumbles. "I was at my wits end." Becki turns and closes the window with fumbling hands. April cannot think what the matter is with her and offers to help. "Let me," she says, standing up. But Becki sharply tells her to sit down and then smooths her blouse, brings her chair and places it next to April. She stretches a hand towards her but diverts it to pat the arm of April's chair.

"I didn't want to distress you unnecessarily. I might've been a little firm. But really there's no cause for you to think about, well, ways out."

"Ways out?" says April, wondering if there is a fire exit over the rooftops, she wouldn't put it past the Council in such an old building. Becki nods and raises her eyebrows.

"You know…" she whispers, "ending it?"

April regards her with astonishment and gives a gasp. Becki immediately turns and presents her with a tissue. "Yes, do feel free to cry. Let's just have a chat about it, shall we?" April ducks her head, accepts the tissue and covers her bemusement with it. She realises suddenly how the rumours about Becki and the previous 'personnel problem' and her nickname of the 'Black Widow' might explain her reactions. Some member of staff in Becki's last job must've tried to commit suicide. April hides behind her tissue, clutches it more tightly and thinks how she might turn things to her own advantage.

"I'm just so stressed!"

"You're not hiding any bad news from the doctor when you visited on Friday?" asks Becki. For a moment April is tempted and opens her mouth, but quickly realises Becki would be sure to ask for a doctor's report and she hasn't seen her GP in years, so reluctantly shakes her head.

"Is it about your mother?" asks Becki. "Your notes said you had some time off earlier this year when she had her stroke? Is she bad again?"

"Yes," says April, pleased for being given a viable lead.

"Has she had another stroke? Is she ill again? Where is she? In hospital?" asks Becki. But April realises that any such statement by her could be easily verified and tries to think of a more general situation.

"I'm so worried about her," April stalls for time and answers another one of the string of Becki's questions. "She's in a home."

"So you think they aren't treating her properly?" replies Becki, linking the two previous statements together.

"I've noticed a few things," says April, wondering where this conversation is going.

"Has she got bruises?"

"No," replies April quickly, thinking that to accuse the staff at the home of physical abuse would be cruel, "but she seems very frightened."

"Is she frightened of a particular member of staff? Has anyone been threatening her?" Becki clearly wants to get to the bottom of it all. April, on the other hand, who is at the end of her inventiveness, casts around for a way out and then resorts to loud sobs in order to distract Becki. But Becki still gazes at her expectantly, only stopping for a moment to reach for more tissues, so April stands up and looks at the window. This does the trick. Becki becomes flustered and asks April to sit down again.

"I don't know what I'm doing," says April, putting her head in her hands. The most truthful statement of this meeting. "I mean, I don't know what to do." But this last admission seems to activate Becki, who asks her a question, takes silence as assent, and then leans over and picks up the phone. April, meanwhile, with one ear open, is pretend mopping her eyes. She hears Becki ask for an appointment for 'April Roberts to see a counsellor as soon as possible,' and is relieved. April straightens and gazes vacantly at Becki.

"I think you should feel better once you've seen a counsellor," states Becki and April smiles at her gratefully and rises as if to go. "Oh but," continues Becki, "under the terms of our protection of vulnerable adults' policy, that I know you're familiar with, I have to take a few details of your mother's residential care home."

"Oh no," says April, sitting down suddenly. "I really don't want to cause any trouble."

"I'm sure the social services will be discreet," says Becki firmly. There then follows a painful ten minutes as April reluctantly gives the name and address of her mother's home, hoping to escape after that. She sees Becki opening her mouth to ask more questions and has no alternative but to break into pretend sobs as a distraction. At last she escapes from the room, leaving Becki making phone calls to other departments. Outside the door, she pauses to let her trembling stop, gives a sigh of relief and then scuttles to the rest room where she has been told she can 'recover herself' before returning to her desk with her head down.

Eight

Tuesday afternoon

Trish arrives at her parents' house at about 3:30 and parks Betty on the driveway. She takes off her helmet and then walks heavily towards the door. The ride here was lovely. None of the usual homicidal maniacs were loose on the road nor was she bothered by any men with very small willies speeding close to her, determined to prove that they had big dicks. So she travelled unhampered and it has done her good. She is not looking forward to seeing her parents again so soon after Sunday, but for the first time in her whole life she hopes that her mother will be in her home and her usual self. She rings the doorbell and her father answers it; he is wearing carpet slippers, a sign that he has not even been out in the garden today. When he sees her, he smiles in his usual charming though absent way.

"Ah Patricia! How good to see you. Come in, come in." He starts towards the drawing room but then catches himself. "Tea? Coffee? Or something a little stronger?" he asks her as she takes off her gloves and leather jacket and waits in the large hallway looking and feeling a little lost. She says that she wants coffee and so they go to the kitchen. The Aga is on and throwing out a good heat and her father immediately sits in one of the chairs round the large oak table, not even bothering to make the coffee, which is alright by Trish, who likes standing and moving around after a ride. They talk as she prepares coffee and finds biscuits.

"So you haven't heard from her?" asks Trish though she knows the answer.

"No and I don't know what to do next. Nobody seems to know where she is," he is looking round the kitchen expectantly as if his wife might suddenly appear, stepping out of a cupboard.

"Didn't anyone say anything at all?"

"No, nothing, nobody has any idea," he sits there looking mystified, "she said she was just coming to bed and then when I woke up she wasn't there!" Trish grits her teeth and forebears from mentioning that he has already told her that at least three times.

Trish has been thinking about what to do on the ride up and has come to the conclusion that the first thing is to search the whole house and grounds really well, and then if her mother still hasn't been found, she will phone up the local hospitals to see if anyone has been admitted. She sips her coffee, looking round the kitchen for any signs and starts to make a rollup, but at her father's protest agrees to light it when she is outside in the garden. This is unnervingly reminiscent of her teenage years. It is getting on; she'd better start the search before it's dark.

"I'm going to look round the garden," she says, striding out to walk across the large garden, only stopping briefly to light the cigarette. There's a huge number of places where an elderly woman could have fallen and then lain unnoticed. She examines behind a row of fir trees, the edges of the rose garden, in the summer house, around both garden sheds (which are locked) and in the greenhouse.

She calls out continually, listening carefully for any noise in reply. She paces round the edge of all their land and sees nothing out of the ordinary until she notices that the gate to the common is unlocked. This is unusual, both her mother and father make a point of making sure this is padlocked, as they once disturbed an intruder who entered from this direction. Trish opens the door and sees by the muddy marks that someone has gone out this way recently. She curses. The common is overgrown and huge and if her mother has fallen or been taken ill there she might not be found for days. She decides to phone the police immediately. If she wastes any more time, she could be endangering her mother, who may be slumped on the common suffering from hypothermia. She hurries back inside to tell her father the bad news.

The police come in a remarkably short space of time, one male, one female who arrive together, question them both and individually look round the house and gardens making copious notes. They phone up the local hospitals to see if anyone with her mother's name or answering her description has been admitted and have no luck. It is now dark and getting cold and Trish worries, imagining her mother lying somewhere alone, cold, frightened and in pain as a second night approaches. The dog handlers come, and their dogs are given the scent of her slippers and then race madly round the house, garage and gardens without discovering her. One of the dogs is taken to the gate to the common and leads the handler around this piece of scrubland for a good hour but returns without success. Other officers arrive and trek round the common with torches.

The kitchen is the natural hub of the whole operation and so Trish makes sure that her father is comfortably settled in the quiet of the drawing room, away from the noise and confusion. He has made several comments which have not been at all helpful and will keep asking questions about when she will come back. The police and dog handlers make themselves at home and drink enormous amounts of tea and eat any biscuit put in front of them with no shame or restraint. They devour three packets of her mother's favourite Duchy biscuits like hungry seals swallow whole fish. Despite herself, Trish finds herself developing a feeling of gratitude towards them. Her previous experience with police, both here and in the US, has made her dislike them with an almost pathological hatred. But now she sees them as both professional and human. They are careful of both her father and herself, showing concern and keeping them informed with unfailing good humour. When she nips out for occasional rollups, she invariably bumps into one or other of them having a sneaky fag by the back door and they are always keen to talk about her Harley and tend to be knowledgeable about motorbikes in general. It is now approaching 9 o'clock, it is cold and has started to rain. She is now deeply concerned. She pictures her mother weak, helpless and alone in the cold and dark. The police start talking about search parties and helicopters. They are also planning to put out a description on local radio and TV stations and are choosing which picture of her mother would be clearest for this purpose.

Trish spends her time between making tea for the police and dog handlers, making sure her father is OK, smoking rollups and answering the phone that keeps ringing; it is always neighbours asking whether her mother has been found yet. She goes to the phone when she hears it ringing yet again and, as usual says the number.

"Patricia?" Her mother's irritated and shocked voice comes over the line. "What on earth are you doing there? Is your father OK?"

"Mother? Where are you? Are you OK?" There is a hush suddenly in the kitchen behind her and she knows that one of the policewomen has unobtrusively followed her and has told everyone to be quiet.

"OK? OK? Of course I'm OK. Or as well as you would be if you'd just had your gall bladder removed. Whatever are you doing there and where's your father?"

"He's here, he's OK. But he is terribly worried about you when you disappeared. He didn't know where you'd gone or what had happened."

"For God's sake I hope you didn't do anything foolish like calling the police?"

"Well actually they're here now! They searched the house and garden and even the common!"

"Oh no! How could you! I bet they've trailed their muddy boots over all the carpets!" Trish glances around and sees that this last remark is true. There are an enormous variety of foot and dog prints throughout the whole house, smeared across every floor covering.

"Where are you?" asks Trish in desperation, the conversation is reaching Alice in Wonderland proportions of weirdness. She needs to sit down and have a good long beer.

"In The Haven. I told you! I've just has my gall bladder out. I was phoning to say everything's OK and could he come and collect me tomorrow at about 1!"

"What's the Haven?"

"It's a private hospital of course, in Haversham!"

"Well how was I supposed to know that!"

"Well your bloody father should've! He dropped me off here yesterday afternoon!" There is a silence as Trish digests this. "Don't leave him on his own. You'd better stay the night and come and see me tomorrow, early, before I get out," says her mother. "Believe it or not I should be resting and away from stress and excitement today. I only phoned to make sure your father collects me. I have had an operation today; I need to rest. God knows I get little enough time to myself."

"Alright, alright mother," Trish knows the signs of approaching martyrdom, "I'll stay and make sure he knows he has to be there tomorrow. How will I find the address?" There is a momentary silence on the line.

"I think," says her mother's very restrained voice, "I think you'll find that your father has it in his trouser pocket."

Trish turns around to find an array of police faces looking at her and goes back into the kitchen where the police are already packing up and getting ready to leave. She apologises profusely, signs some paperwork and waves them on their way then returns to where her father is sitting in the drawing room.

"I've just spoken to mother. She's in The Haven having her gallbladder removed. She's fine." Her father looks unsurprised and only nods at her.

"Is she? Ah yes. Jolly good." Trish isn't clear that he's fully understood. "She's fine."

"Of course. I remember now. I made a bit of a fuss, eh? Well, I think I'll have a glass of whisky, then go to bed." He makes his way to the drinks' cabinet. "Will you join me?"

"Yes please," says Trish, watching as he pours two large glasses.

"Down the hatch!" says her father, tipping it into his open throat with a shaky hand. "I must say, Patricia, thanks a million for coming to my rescue. It's been great of you!" He sloshes in another tot. Trish examines him more closely, noticing his general untidy thin pallor, a hesitation in his actions and wandering pale eyes. He is just tired; it's been a long day and he's had a shock and a lot of stress.

"Could you just look in your pocket?" she asks. Then watches as he draws out a series of papers, some with blu-tak others with

Sellotape still attached; they have obviously been stuck around the house and he has picked them up and pocketed them. Each one says the day, the date and The Haven For Gallbladder and gives the address and phone number.

"Well I never!" he says whilst Trish picks up each one and gulps her whisky.

Later as she stands under the front porch, blowing the smoke from a rollup into the rain and sipping her third large whisky, she thinks about the day. She's come all this way for nothing and been worried for no reason. She's been left out of a family information loop and made to look an idiot, all because no-one tells her anything. She slams down the stub of her cigarette, grinds it into the stone flooring and returns to the hall to phone Anthony, her nearest brother in age. Her father said he was away. The answerphone kicks in at his house and an upper crust female voice asks the caller to please leave a message. It is now about 10:00 p.m., early for Trish but no doubt late for Anthony and his wife.

"Anthony! Anthony! Are you there? Anthony? I'm at The Cottage with father! Anthony! Why did no-one tell me about him? I'm so fucking pissed off, I came all the fucking way up here and ..." There is a click and a tired older male voice answers suddenly,

"Patricia! Must you swear on my answerphone? It's late, whatever is so urgent!"

"How could you NOT tell me about father! You must've known that he's absolutely losing his memory." Anthony protests and tries to interrupt but Trish keeps going. "Why didn't you tell me? How was I to know he wasn't telling the bloody truth? I came up to see him when he said he couldn't find mother. I looked and looked all over the place and phoned all her friends and got really worried. Finally, I called out the police. They came, then they called the dog handlers, everyone searched the common…" She stops. Anthony is laughing. He is chuckling with the deep familiar sound that Trish hasn't heard in decades.

"Dog handlers!" he says weakly and Trish suddenly laughs as well.

"Yes, the dogs followed her scent around the common." There is a loud bray from her brother that sets Trish guffawing again. She remembers that he was the one that first gave her some dope. They sat up a tree in the garden smoking, him showing her how to inhale and then they watched their mother walking around, sniffing the air and examining the compost heaps whilst trying to locate the smell of burning grass. They had almost fallen out of the tree for laughing. Trish must've been 14 or so, and he about 17.

"Well of course they would go around the common, she goes for a walk there every day. The same one she used to take when the dog was alive." Trish, hoarse with laughing, has to sit down to mop her eyes as she remembers all the things that will make her totally house-proud mother annoyed.

"We had to break the door open on one of the garden sheds because I couldn't find the key. They tipped out the laundry basket. They went up into the loft and unrolled that old rug that used to be in your room and now covers that stuffed stoat of grandfather's. I think they thought my father may have done her in. There are muddy footprints and paw marks all over the house. They've eaten every biscuit there is; my mother's favourite Duchy biscuits. There's no milk left from all the tea and coffee they drank. And … and…." she stops and tries to form words though she is becoming increasingly unclear, "they were just going to call out the helicopters and set an alert on the local radio and TV. The only photo I could find that might be suitable is one when she won fourth prize in the village jam-making competition. It is a close up of her and she is holding up a jar of blackcurrant jelly." She sits back in the chair and simply howls with laughter whilst Anthony joins in at the other end of the phone.

"Where was she this time?" he asks finally, still half-laughing.

"What do you mean, 'this time'? You mean he's done this before?"

"Of course he has! At least four times! Surely you knew?"

"How the fuck would I know! Nobody told me. You mean the police have been called out before?" says Trish suddenly remembering why she has wanted to speak to him in the first place.

"No," he laughs, "nobody's called the police out before! You're the only one to do that! She always comes home from the shops or a friend's or the WI in time. After the first time we tended to ignore it."

"Why did nobody tell me?"

"I thought mother has or someone would…" he tails off. "Where was she by the way?"

"In hospital having her gall bladder taken out!"

"Oh, she finally decided to have the operation, did she? She never told me she'd booked in. She must've told Geoffrey, she seems to tell him most things and he's getting a little forgetful himself."

"Why didn't she tell me? I didn't know she was ill at all."

"Dear Patricia," he uses his superior older brother voice, "you've made it quite clear that you think she's bonkers. You've never seen eye to eye with her since you were 12 and decided you wouldn't go to ballet lessons again. You've stayed away from us all as much as you possibly could. You rarely phone her; you've made it clear that you don't like her phoning you. You've never invited her to stay. Why would she tell you anything?" There is a moment's silence and then Trish finds her voice.

"I've been busy," she says feebly.

"We've all been busy. But you've been busy for over 30 years!"

*

April calls into her mother's care home on the way back from work; a mid-week visit she usually avoids unless absolutely vital. But she needs to see her mother and has brought a cake to give to Mr Henderson. However, as the car splutters to a stop in front of the nursing home she looks on the back seat and realises that she has not put the cake into the car: she was concentrating on the jewellery she wanted to pawn. However, as she is here, she might as well go in, see how her mother is and get a bit more information about the police sergeant's father.

Mrs Weekes greets her at the door and immediately summons her into the office. April's whole life is turning into reprimands, with every official body intent on correcting her in some way. It is what she has come to expect of authority, she has had to fight officialdom for her rights throughout her many years of existence. She slouches into the small room overpowered with filing cabinets and drops into the chair opposite Mrs Weekes.

"Just a word in your ear, Mrs Roberts," says Mrs Weekes. "You must've heard there was a bit of an incident here yesterday."

"Sergeant or whatever-his-rank-is Henderson called on me."

"He accused your mother of theft."

"I know."

"But I spoke very carefully to Philip and Philip says it is no such thing. He says it is a gift. Rather a large gift if you don't mind my saying."

"It's a loan," says April firmly. "I was calling to tell him that." Mrs Weekes looks instantly flustered.

"Please don't go near him. I've promised his son that neither you nor your mother will go ANYWHERE near him. Philip is physically ill but is not mentally impaired and is still capable of making his own decisions, but he is vulnerable.

He's an absolute sweetie and he and your mother hit it off immediately, but we've had to put a stop to that. We can't have him being preyed on ..."

"He's not been preyed on, I told you it is a loan."

"Well he says it is done willingly, so there's nothing else I can do," says Mrs Weekes, standing up and looking at April with disapproval. "Just don't go near him and I've told your mother to stay away. If either of you are seen in or near his room, I'm afraid your mother will have to be found other accommodation."

April winces, she has spent ages finding this place for her mother and getting the council to pay for it, other council funded homes are much worse.

"We will stay away; we won't go near him. I promise you." She asks to see her mother.

"She's in her room. She has a urinary infection; which you know she gets rather frequently, and she has been prescribed antibiotics. I would not stay long. She's sleeping a lot. If she is awake, please make sure she drinks some water." April leaves the office and goes to see her mother who is asleep on her bed and seems quiet, so she scribbles a note and goes away without disturbing her.

On the way out she looks at her watch, though she doesn't know why, the date is always wrong, and the time is variable, but it forces her to think. It is Tuesday. She's nowhere near getting the money she needs. There's still no sign of Kate. Will she have to take up Martina's offer?

*

Sam has made an effort with the evening meal, she has bought steak, which she knows is Hugh's favourite, and she has laid the table with a vase of flowers and candles ready to be lit and has opened a bottle of red wine and let it breathe. She is dressed in something that she knows Hugh likes, not her usual long flowing autumn-coloured linen dresses, but a pair of tailored trousers and a more figure-hugging green top. This is the fairly traditional stuff that Hugh usually appreciates. It is late, after 8, when she hears him come in and calls out,

"Hello dearest. I've got something nice for dinner!" Hugh looks round the door of the dining room and sees the table.

"Oh no," he says, "I have quite a bit of work I need to do tonight. I didn't know you were planning this." His comment is a demonstration of how low down she is on his list of priorities. She feels like crying, but her mind settles, readjusts, and she knows she will not.

"Come on, Hugh, you can take an hour off at least. You've been working late at home every night this week." Hugh looks at her and consciously makes an effort but there is irritation in his tone.

"Really dear…" he says and stops.

"You don't want to be bothered," Sam hears herself saying.

"No dear, of course not, not tonight. I thought you knew how busy I am." Sam turns away and, brushing past Hugh, leaves the room.

"Oh Sam, dear," she hears him say, "don't get upset." He follows her out, his whole attitude one of a man at the limit of endurance. She walks upstairs and he follows her into the bedroom. "It's been a hard week for me."

"And not for me?" says Sam who is sitting on the bed and carefully removing her earrings.

"Well of course, dear, but it's not quite the same, is it?" But there is a forced tolerance in his voice. Ice creeps into Sam's heart.

"And why is that?"

"Well you don't have millions hanging in the balance, do you? Or other people's employment relying on you. Do you?"

"No, I don't, that's true. So not a matter of life and death then?"

and she gazes at him quizzically with her eyes wide and innocent. Hugh is taking off his suit jacket and hanging it up carefully, looking away and so is not forewarned.

"Well if you put it like that…" and he smiles at her.

"So how did my visit to the oncologist go then?" Hugh freezes. Surely it could not have been this week already? She has told him, and he's forgotten. He consciously changes tone.

"Oh, was that today? I'm so sorry. I presume it is all OK?"

"Don't bother about it. It's not important. Not as important as YOUR work. With so much money to be made."

"You know I didn't mean that."

"What did you mean exactly then?"

"Look I've had an exceptionally busy week…"

"You've had an exceptionally busy month. No, year. No, YEARS. And I just don't figure in it at all. I'm so unimportant that even my cancer doesn't register in your life." Hugh approaches her appealingly but she sidesteps him, "and you're still not bothered. Not really bothered. Just irritated that I'm making this scene and stopping you getting on with something REALLY important."

"That's not true!" he says but his eyes shift sideways.

"I don't want to talk about it," says Sam. "You just get on with your work as ever."

"Oh, Sam, come on. We'll have that meal. Tell me about the oncologist visit. I'm sorry. I'm just so stressed and tired." Sam stalks out of the room and goes up the stairs to her attic studio. She can feel the white heat of anger cooling, changing. She no longer cares what Hugh thinks. A cold and solid indifference is settling in her abdomen. Hugh climbs the stairs slowly and opens the door. He looks out of place and ill at ease.

"Can I come in? Will you talk to me?" Suddenly Sam is tired: tired of putting on a good front, of coping, but more tired of quarrelling. She bursts into tears. Hugh puts his arms around her, and she turns and sobs into his shoulder. He strokes her hair and his body tenses as his worry builds.

"You know I love you," he says soothingly, "Come downstairs and have a glass of wine and tell me about the oncologist. Please." He continues, "Everything's OK there?" She nods and he relaxes. "Come on now," he says and pulls her up. "Let's have that meal, but first we'll have a glass of wine eh?"

Later, after the meal and discussion, they sit in silence. She knows that Hugh's mind has once again turned towards his work and feels mean about stopping him from going to his desk. He has told her of the problems surrounding him. The language problems which confuse his getting across what he wants, his second in command going off after a road accident, the unreasonable demands of the employers and the trouble with the employees.

She has not told him about Trish's problems or about April's continuing problems. She knows he would regard these as minor, just more of her crazy friends' trivialities, not his big man's serious stuff. She does not want to expose her friends' lives to his judgements.

He does not ask her what she is doing over the week whilst he will be working. He assumes that she will just continue in the same way. She suggests that he gets on with his work and she gets on with hers. She goes upstairs and, feeling uninspired, looks around her workroom and tries to get on with enamelling. But the fact that Hugh has made a comment about the costs he bears of her jewellery-making disturbs her, she wonders how financially reliant on him she really is.

Nine

Wednesday morning

Trish wakes up to the birds singing and her head aching and in immediate dismay. She is in the room where she spent most holidays and some weekends, her parents called it her room. One summer holiday she painted it black, but the minute she left her mother redecorated and now its fresh ordered cleanliness brings back all the claustrophobia of her childhood and adolescence. She throws back the bedclothes and jumps out of bed feeling a surge of panic. Why didn't she go home yesterday and defy her mother as she would've normally done? She knows the answer as she scrabbles in her bag for an aspirin to try to get rid of the too-much-whisky needles behind her eyes. Dressing quickly in yesterday's jeans and T-shirt she finds her father in the kitchen staring at the kettle steaming on the Aga: he is wearing slippers, old trousers and an unbuttoned pyjama top.

"Where's the tea?" he asks her, showing no surprise at seeing her. For a moment he looks at her blankly. "Patricia?" he says. She nods, reaches round him and gets down the tea and makes some for them both. "Of course," he continues, "I made a bit of a mess of things yesterday eh?"

"I have to go," says Trish. She really cannot bear being in this house anymore and the thought of having to spend more time here, waiting on her father, makes her feel physically sick. She puts down her teacup firmly and heads for her jacket. The phone rings, her father picks it up and wordlessly, passes it to Trish. Her mother's voice is clear,

"I want to speak to you, Patricia."

"Oh mother no!" says Trish, who feels she has endured enough during the last 24 hours and was hoping she could leave early and not see her mother after all.

"I've been thinking, that maybe we could try to reach some sort of agreement, some way of being together without always rubbing each other up the wrong way. I was speaking to one of the nurses last night and …"

"For God's sake, mother, I can just imagine what you've been saying about me!"

"Hold your horses. She was pointing out that you came to your father's aid, you called the police to look for me, so you must care about us after all. So, I thought that …" Her voice tails off. "I promise not to shout at you or get angry. If you come to the hospital, we could have a little chat before you go back to your house, couldn't we?" Trish recognises that she is being offered a peace token and by her mother of all people. She waits for a moment, feeling the anger surge within her, remembering all the accusations her mother has thrown at her and wondering if she has the strength to forget.

"All right," she says reluctantly, "but I must be quick, I have to work this lunchtime. I'll come around now."

"I'm so glad, Patricia, I'll look forward to seeing you. Can you put your father on the line again?" Trish wanders round the kitchen finding bread, making toast, whilst her mother directs her father to a cupboard where some pills are kept in a pod containing all the days of the week. She watches as he takes out three under Wednesday and swallows them. The doorbell rings and the cleaner appears, a young dark nervy woman who speaks little English but goes straight to the cleaning cupboard and starts gathering her materials with a sharp sideways glance at Trish and her father. Trish recognises all the signs of an underpaid employee who has been thoroughly harried by her mother. She picks up her keys and kisses her father fleetingly on the cheek and leaves. She waits for a moment outside, smoking, and notices her wheel marks from Sunday still on the otherwise pristine lawn, then grinds her butt end into the gravel driveway and rides to the hospital.

It is a small modern building, with a discreet entrance, and a reception that includes a waiting area with leather sofas and free tea and coffee. Trish gives her own and her mother's name to both of the well-groomed women behind the wide desk and helps herself to a large black coffee. She has barely sat down when she is greeted by a woman wearing a blue uniform who smiles at her and holds out her hand.

"You must be Patricia," she says, "your mother is expecting you. My name is Hetty, I'm the nurse assigned to your mother whilst she is here." She escorts Trish around a corner and into a lift. As the lift ascends, Trish inspects her, she is small, thin and looks of Philippine extraction and is speaking perfect English.

"Are you the nurse my mother has been talking to?"

"Your mother is doing really well after the operation; she should be able to leave today after she's seen the consultant again and spoken to the dietitian."

"Not exactly the answer to my question…" says Trish.

"Your mother has had a surgical procedure and is recovering and spending time here to relax. She needs it."

"So she has been talking to you!"

"I'm just a nurse here. My only concern is for the welfare of my patient." The lift doors open, and the nurse walks a few brisk steps and leads her into a private room leaving Trish thwarted of a quarrel.

Her mother is sitting up in an adjustable hospital bed flicking through a magazine in a spacious bright room with a wide picture window over a padded seat, a large bedside table, a screen that is connected to a whole entertainment and communication system, and a door that leads to an en suite bathroom.

"Do you want anything?" asks Hetty of them both.

"A cup of Earl Grey please, dear," says her mother, putting down her magazine and holding out her face to Trish. Trish clasps her coffee cup firmly and leans forward to kiss her mother's cheek.

"Hiya mater," says Trish and plumps herself down on the foot of her mother's bed, rumpling the pristine sheets and blankets. "I suppose a fag would set off the alarms in here?" It isn't really a question and her mother knows this but has obviously set herself to be tolerant so only raises her eyebrows.

"Ah Trish. So?" says her mother, seemingly unable to start the conversation.

"Well papa is OK. The house is a mess, I tidied a bit, but the cleaner is in, so it should be sorted by the time you're home. How are you?"

"The op went well. I could go home now, just a few more checks, but I felt I needed a bit of time to myself. I've asked Marjorie to call in and see that Archie is OK until I get home." She is wearing her own white cotton nightdress and her face is made up perfectly, she pulls the blanket towards her to straighten it a little.

"You didn't tell me he is getting so forgetful." Trish dangles a Doc Martin'ed foot off the bed, she's never comfortable with too much softness around her.

"To be quite frank you never seemed that interested in how we were. I thought that phoning you up to tell you he'd been diagnosed with dementia and I am spending most of my time looking after him would be seen as just another ploy by me to get you to visit." Her mother's tightened lips show that she is maintaining calmness at some personal cost.

"That's a bit unfair."

"Well the only times you've come has been to ask for money." Trish knows this last statement is true, so stays silent. "It's been very difficult, you know. He's been forgetful for some time, but last year it got much worse. He couldn't remember the simplest things; I can't tell you how often he lost his keys and put things in strange places. I once found a full milk jug in the wardrobe. I took him to various doctors, and he had all the tests and they said he has vascular dementia. There's no cure, just these pills that can slow it down a bit, I honestly haven't seen any improvement. The only thing is, thank God, that he isn't unhappy, just more withdrawn." Trish wonders how often her mother has repeated the same story and whether this is genuine stalwart angst or if the apparent calm fortitude is another form of affectation. So many of her father's family are charming, affable people who ruthlessly underpay their employees, send their children away at the earliest opportunity, yet profess love and concern. It is an attitude her mother strives to emulate. It's always been hard to know who is behind the posturing.

"I didn't know."

"When the boys phoned, I told them, they're so good at keeping in touch."

"I'm sure they're devoted sons."

"At least they phone to see how we are."

"You could call me."

"It might've escaped your notice but in the last couple of days I have left about five messages on your answerphone. So far I haven't had a single reply." Since the messages that her mother left were filled with vitriol, demanding an apology for Trish's behaviour at the diamond wedding celebration, Trish has never contemplated replying.

"Well, I'm here now."

Her mother pauses and struggles for a moment. "I just wondered how you were?"

"Why?"

"Well we didn't really get a chance to talk at the party, so ...."

"Mama, I'm fine. Living as I want. I've been fine for decades."

"So just let me know," her mother's voice hardens, "why you came to the party if you were just going to disrupt it? Was that your intention all along? Or did you just come to cadge money as usual and then decide to make me a laughing stock?"

"You treated me like shit," says Trish.

"When I complained about your rude and disgraceful behaviour? When you showed me up in front of everyone?"

Trish puts down her coffee cup and stands up, reminded once again why she has never felt she belongs in this family. The lies, the pretences, the jostling for social position. When she was 14, she remembers cornering her father in the summerhouse and seriously asking if she were adopted. No such luck, she's stuck with this gene pool. She is no longer outraged, just resigned, reminded again of the distance between them. She walks towards the door but stops as she hears her mother's voice, almost pleading.

"Trish don't go. I didn't mean... Everything I say comes out wrong. I'm sorry. I am cross. But …." Trish has never heard her mother apologise before and sees that she is visibly trying to control herself and is, surprisingly, paused. "You have my temper, always had. My temper. My impulsiveness. Maybe we're more alike than you want to know. Please sit down. Let's start again." Trish slowly lowers herself onto the leather chair beside the bed, noticing that beneath the careful make-up her mother looks older and is speaking quietly now, almost as if to herself. "I don't know what I've done. I never know what I've done. You seem so angry with me all the time. I don't want to fight with you. I want us to make peace." Trish cocks her head. "Please take me seriously. Just tell me what I've done. What have I ever done to you to make you so angry? You started when you were thirteen and you're now, what? 53? So, 40 years. What did I do to make you 40 years' worth furious? You are my only daughter for God's sake. The family had such hopes for you."

"Ah there we are." The sentiment Trish has lived under but now openly expressed at last, "I've let you down. I've not been what you wanted me to be. I haven't married a wealthy man, I haven't bought a nice house, I haven't got a decent job. All you see when you look at me is a missed opportunity for you to boast to papa's family. Do you really know what I'm like? How I live now? What's important to me?"

"The only thing I know is you're wasted. You were one of the brightest girls in your school. You used to be in the first team for athletics, near the top of your class, you were so intelligent, elegant and beautiful. All your school reports said you would do well at university." This is a shock to Trish, she never got that impression from the school where she spent most of her time sitting in an empty classroom, the clock ticking, as she wrote lines, whilst the other girls played lacrosse outside.

"Not what I recall, mama."

"Then it all changed." Trish remembers this, looking out of the attic room at home, filled with discarded band equipment left when the last brother went to University. Blowing cigarette smoke out of the window and seeing the lights of the cars in the distance, all going places and knowing that a world was out there filled with different sorts of people, living on the edge, being free. She determined to taste it.

"I never wanted the life you led. You know that. I had to get away."

"You never passed any exams, did you? Never got any qualifications at all. You were so busy running, you never looked back. That's my gripe. That's what makes me cross." She bangs her hands together in frustration. "You've been so busy rebelling against us all that you've never turned to see what else you left behind. You loved music." Trish learnt the cello for a few terms, was teased mercilessly for having such an ungainly instrument and never made it into the school orchestra. Her mother, oblivious, continues, "I always thought you'd go to university, maybe become a professor."

"Or marry one."

"Forget marriage. Quite frankly I wish I had."

"At last! Some honesty."

"Don't patronise me. I grew up when if you got married you stayed married. If you had children, you tried to make a better life for them. End of story." She shuffles the pillows behind her back to sit more upright.

"Ah the good old Catholic upbringing."

"At least I've stuck it out, whilst you, madam, have been swerving and slumming it for 40 years." At this critical moment there is a knock on the door and the nurse comes smilingly into an atmosphere thick with reproach. She brings the Earl Grey tea and a fresh coffee for Trish. Apart from her questions about the beverages and biscuits the silence lies unbroken until she leaves. Trish swigs her coffee and stands up.

"Well, mama, it has been jolly pleasant, but I really have to rush." This is true, she has to be at the pub to open up as Vince is taking the day off.

"I do try, Patricia, I have tried to understand, I'm not your enemy, really I'm not. You are my only daughter. I just wanted so much for you."

"But it isn't what I wanted."

"That's what I'm going on about. How do you know? How do you know it's not what you wanted? If I said eat caviar, you'd eat chips on purpose, even if you loved caviar!"

"Ah caviar! Much overrated!" and Trish leans forward to both their surprise and kisses her mother's hair and smooths a wrinkle from her forehead: the first time she's touched her affectionately for decades. Her mother briefly pats her hand, watching as Trish leaves the room. On the way to the lift Trish starts rolling a cigarette and lights it as she strolls towards her bike. Loosening her hair from her neck she straddles the leather seat. It feels like coming home.

*

Becki stares at April who is late, of course, and frowns. April is totally exhausted after yet another night of no-sleep, waking at every sound, hearing cars pull up outside, going to look, seeing police cars and the black limousine. Resting in Kate's room, amongst her sheets, crying, missing her, wondering where she is, how she is. Being angry for leaving her on her own to face the mess. Each day passing makes her worry more, not less. Last night she drank the brandy Sam gave her, hoping it would make her sleep, but it made her feel sick.

She woke this morning with a headache, still frightened, fretting, worried, thinking.

Arriving at work feels like a haven away from it all. She hopes that here she may have a chance to quieten her mind, but Becki comes over to her desk and speaks to her softly, in the tone of a hospital nurse speaking to a small and unruly child that needs pacifying. She lays a jacket on April's desk and asks her to cover the public enquiry desk today. It is the most difficult part of the job, because there is an endless supply of members of the public coming in with parking-related issues, most of whom are angry, some confused and some downright devious. Becki asks in a lowered voice whether Health and Wellbeing has been in contact. April, who has forgotten Becki's request for a counsellor, recalls this now and wants to slump forward over the desk, she is so past caring. Becki says she will phone a counsellor who will be in touch. April's head aches, she takes another paracetamol, opens the jacket and grapples it on. As she goes down to the public area, pulling the stiff nylon material down, someone wolf-whistles.

She sets herself at one of the enquiry desks and logs on to the computer and sitting back straightens her shoulders. She has barely finished putting in the third password when her phone rings. There is a moment's quiet on the other end and then just as she is wondering whether it is a miscall, a young male voice speaks calmly.

"Hello, I'm from the Council's health and wellbeing department. I believe that you want to speak with a counsellor?" April, who most emphatically does not want to speak to anyone, let alone a counsellor, finds herself saying that she might. "Well, your manager thinks that you need to see someone urgently, do you think that she's right?" April makes a non-committal sound that might have been a 'ya' or a 'na' as the man continues, "because it just so happens that I have an appointment this afternoon free?" April makes a sudden reversal as she realises that with a bit of luck she can get the afternoon off work.

"Ah yes yes," she says eagerly, "I do need to talk to someone really quickly!"

"I'll book you in for this afternoon then at 2 o'clock," he says, "this will be for a 45-minute exploratory session. I'll explain further when you come along.

Essentially, it's to see if we can help in any way or if another service is required. My name is Thirsten and it'll be at room 342 opposite the training suite." April, who is overjoyed at the appointment time, accepts the offer immediately, assures him that she knows where to find him and puts the phone down, feeling like jumping up and punching the air. Yet another small victory against fate.

The morning progresses; there is a steady stream of visitors, either paying parking fines, getting resident's permits or making enquiries and April deals with the requests with the usual boredom creeping in. She calls out the number of the next person in the queue and opens the home screen on the database.

"I'd like a car permit," a familiar voice says, and April lifts her head to meet the gaze of the gamblers standing opposite her. Neither of them smile at her, but push together and block her view. The Enforcer has spoken and is looking at her coldly.

"Can I have your name and I'll see if you're registered on our database," she manages to blurt out.

"No, Mrs Roberts, I won't give you my name. Just 'ere to check. We've seen a few strange things round where you live. We 'ope you've not said anything to the police?" April forces out a laugh which sounds shrill to her and makes her neighbour look at her strangely. Nobody laughs in this place.

"Oh no, why would I do that?"

"We've been keeping an eye on you and we've seen a police car.

What's going on?"

"That's not strange," she lies, "there's always something going on in my block."

"Hmmph. We'll keep dropping in, but any sign of anything funny going down and you know what'll 'appen. I 'ope for your sake that you've kept your mouth shut."

"I've not told anyone, honestly," stutters April. Of course, she's not told anybody except Sam, Trish, Stuart, her mother and Martina.

"We know where you live, where you work, where your mum is ..." He pauses whilst April pales at the thought that she has been followed so persistently. They have found out so much about her. She is not safe anywhere.

"That won't be necessary, I'll have the cash by Saturday," she tries to sound supremely confident and smiles.

"We'll be there, Mrs Roberts, believe me, we'll be there and if the money ain't, the action will be fairly immediate if you know what I mean."

"I know what you mean," she replies and watches as they saunter off in a solid slow-moving block, turning for a moment to stare at her. She tries to concentrate but has another shock when she looks up again to see Sergeant Henderson in front of her booth, dressed in his full police uniform, hat tucked under his arm.

"Can I help you?" she asks, hoping that the gamblers have not seen him.

"Just letting you know I'm here," says Sergeant Henderson. "Whenever you want to return that money, I'll be waiting..." He smiles, puts on his hat and then turns once more to look at her and finishes his sentence, "and watching."

He strolls out of the door without looking round. April automatically asks for the next person and manages not to cry.

Ten

Wednesday afternoon

It is almost two by the time April gets back to her desk giving her just enough time to dump her coat and make her way over to Thirsten's department on the top floor of the modern extension to the old council building. The corridor outside gives views to the High Street and April knocks at the door number she's been given, looking around wondering what on earth she is going to say to Thirsten. As she waits her head begins to twinge again, so she finds another two paracetamol and has just taken them out of the pack when she identifies a police car circling the block and stopping for a moment. The police sergeant gets out and looks up at the building and starts walking towards it. He glances up. April, shocked, backs away from the window and walks towards the office door. It opens and a tall man in his thirties smiles at her.

"April Roberts?" She nods, and barely touching his outstretched hand, dashes into the room behind him. Thirsten is clearly taken by surprise and turns to look at her as she stands in the middle of the room glancing at a group of chairs, a small sofa and a desk round a coffee table. "I'm Thirsten Gallagher, your counsellor, please take a seat," and he gestures invitingly towards the group of chairs. But April loiters for a moment, feeling too agitated to sit down. Thirsten has a square face with hazel eyes and the sort of unthreatening demeanour that means young foreigners would ask him for directions.

"You look nervous?" he sounds genuinely concerned.

"I'm being followed," she blurts out and looks out of the window behind the desk whose dark-tinted glass gives a view onto the reception area. The inspector has made his way inside the building and is talking to Doug. She shies away from the window and retreats towards the door.

"Who's following you?"

April throws her arms out hopelessly and throws herself down on the small sofa that is furthest away from the window.

"The police…" she says.

"Why do you think that?" says Thirsten, pulling up a chair and sitting down opposite her.

"He called on me the other night and said he would be watching me, him and his mates the other police officers. And now he is." Thirsten picks up a pen and notebook and scribbles quickly.

"Well April, there's only you and me in this room. Are you comfortable there?"

"OK I suppose, at least he can't get in here."

"That's very true. You're safe here with me," he seems puzzled by her. "There's a few things I should run through before we start. You do realise that this is just an assessment meeting? Your manager has asked me to talk to you to see what help we can offer you. I will be writing down my recommendations after our meeting and they will go straight to her. Are you OK about this?" He looks intently at her, waiting for her assent.

"That bloody manager, really seems to have it in for me, watches me every moment, never lets up. There are plenty of others late back. Why does she always pick on me?"

"I'll be reporting back to her, nevertheless. Is that OK?"

"Fine," says April and gets up to peer out of the window again. The sergeant is still there. Doug is laughing. What on earth are they talking about? She realises she is still holding the tablets and puts them into her mouth quickly and swallows.

"What's that?" asks Thirsten with some alarm.

"Paracetomol, I've got a hangover."

"Have you been drinking?"

"How else would I get a hangover?"

Thirsten regards her with concern and gestures towards the sofa again. "Would you like to sit down again?" April does so, hesitantly.

"You must think I'm mad," she laughs. Thirsten keeps a non-committal expression, "I was in a bit of a state this morning. I've hardly been sleeping. I've been so stressed."

"Well maybe you can tell me a bit more about it?" he smiles and waggles his pen invitingly over his paper. April shrugs.

"I've been to quite a few counsellors in my time," she says.

"Oh really?"

"Well it's not really surprising with my upbringing. No father, farmed out to strict chapel-going grandparents, mother flitting around taking small parts in stage and screen, picking me up for a while then dropping me again, marrying weirdos ...."

"It sounds like you've had a lot to cope with," he writes busily, his pen rushing across the paper.

"I suppose so, but no more than some others."

"You mentioned your mother?"

"She's in a home now. But she's the cause of it all really. The police sergeant is after her as well. He's got it in for both of us. Well actually it's all my fault. I thought I was doing it all for the best but now I seem to have called down the wrath of God onto my head. My grandfather always warned me 'As You Sow, so Shall You Reap'. I hear him so clearly sometimes; he's telling me I've brought it all on myself and chuckling. I can hear him now. Well he's right, isn't he? I'm really reaping it at the moment."

"This all seems a bit of confusing."

"You can say that again. Actually, it's not mine or my mother's. It's Kate's fault."

"Who's Kate?"

"She's my daughter. She's nowhere to be found. She's run away I think."

"This sounds extremely serious! How old is Kate?"

"Oh she's a grown woman now. If only I could find her. I'm exhausted. I can't remember the last time I had a good night's sleep. I lie in bed and worry about Kate and then the police keep driving past. Sometimes they park outside for a while. Sometimes I think I see them but they're not there, it's just a different black car."

"Maybe they're just doing their duty."

"That's what he said, the sergeant. He said he'd get me, and I've been so careful, though he keeps popping up suddenly. He was here this morning. He's here now. Then there's this offer. My grandfather would say it comes from the devil; it seems I must do it. But it's wrong, I don't care how it's justified. I've never done anything criminal before. Well maybe during the miner's strike, but that was only running at a policeman. He was going for my grandmother. But this, this, is much, much worse. Should I even consider it? I seem to be worried all the time. Now I'm frightened I'll have to do something really bad."

"How long has this been going on?"

"Well it kicked off on Saturday. But it all started before that. These men called on me…. But I can't tell you about that or there'll be real trouble, they said I mustn't tell anyone about them. And this other thing, don't write it down. Oh God, maybe just mentioning it will make it worse. Don't write it down, don't let anyone know." She jumps up and looks out of the window. "Are these walls soundproof?"

"Do you think someone's listening?"

"I don't know. They could be, couldn't they?"

"I've told you, you're safe here."

"But I have to leave at some time. I can't stay here forever, then I don't know what will happen."

"What do you think will happen?"

"Well he might arrest me for a start." She points towards the window. Thirsten gets up and looks out towards the reception area and sees only Doug talking to someone on his phone.

"See," says April.

"I do indeed," he says and scrawls some more notes for her file.

20 minutes later April leaves the counselling suite a bit bemused. Thirsten has told her NOT to go back to work on any account. He will talk to Becki. She has to go home immediately and rest. He has been firm in saying that she needs time off. He is going to recommend that she has a fortnight off and he will organise for someone to come and visit her. April agrees with enthusiasm but leaves the room only after he has assured her that no-one is lurking down the corridor and she has looked both ways before leaving. Clutching her bag, she makes it to the reception desk and hisses at Doug, "What did he want?"

"Who?"

"The police officer?"

"Oh, him. I don't know he spent some time here just talking about theft, safety, any problems I might have. Anyone suspicious I'd seen. Quite frankly, April, I thought he was just bored and occupying the time. Left his card with me in case anything came up that worried me."

"He didn't mention me?"

"Now why would he do that? Don't tell me you've been robbing banks again?"

"Ha ha! Sorry Doug. I'm just a bit on edge." She takes the stairs to her office in order to say goodbye to her colleagues and collect her coat. She has almost got into the main office when she meets Becki coming towards her in a hurry.

"Whatever are you doing, now?" asks Becki, continuing before April can say anything. "It's three o-clock! You left for lunch at 1 p.m. Two hours you've been gone. This is too much!"

"I've been …."

"I don't care where you've been. You left your coat on your desk. Was that meant to fool me? I've been looking for you all over the building."

"Not all the building ..."

"Don't give me that. I've had enough of you..." April finds her voice at last and speaks calmly and clearly in the same patronizing tones that Becki has used on her.

"Becki, Becki. I went to the counselling suite." She sees Becki give a start of shock and continues soothingly, "Now, I quite understand you're a woman in a man's world, but really, do you need to be this brutal? We all know you write those reports for Toby who never credits you, you collate those statistics that nobody ever uses and you harry your staff. All pretty thankless stuff. Why not copy how the men do it? Delegate everything. Be careless. Work shorter hours.

Talk about football. Relax. I'm off home." Becki stands, opening and shutting her mouth whilst April pats her arm and tells her to speak to Thirsten in Health and Wellbeing. April collects her coat, waves to her colleagues and leaves the building.

*

Sam is sitting in Hugh's BMW being driven towards the pub and listening to Hugh's diatribe against all other road users. "Why didn't she signal if she's going left? What does she think her indicators are for? God and she's slowed down now almost to stopping. You're only going round a corner! What's that cyclist doing now? At last, he's getting onto the cycle path, at least he's got his lights on, so many of them don't bother. They'll only have themselves to blame if they're in an accident! Oh no, a biker is right behind me just waiting for his chance to overtake on this narrow road, his headlamp is really bright. Why anyone would ride a bike I don't understand, they're so dangerous."

"Trish rides and is OK," says Sam mildly.

"My point precisely. Remember when she came off because that white van swerved to the right in front of her?"

"She only broke a leg." Sam deliberately downplays Trish's accident. She went to see her in hospital and was shocked by the leg hoist, neck brace and Trish's pallid lethargy. But Trish bounced back again, as ever.

"Spent three months in plaster!"

"You broke your arm in that rock pool and spent three months in plaster."

"Not my choice, you know I stepped on a sea urchin." Sam is tempted to say that Trish didn't choose to be cut-up by a van driver either.

"Well it's freedom to Trish and Stuart and others," says Sam, staunchly defending her friends' choice of transport.

"Hmph! Not freedom if you're maimed is it? Dangerous for no reason."

"I like that it's different."

"Commonplace now. The hospitals are filled with older men who want to re-live their youth and have bought motorbikes and then get into accidents." Statistically he is right, but his assumption of superiority because he's staid enough not to ride a bike makes Sam queasy.

"Stuart has been riding since he was 18."

"Good for him. And how many accidents has he had? You only have to look at some of Trish's friends to see the damage done." This is unfortunately true. The last BBQ they attended at Trish's was filled with old bikers swapping accident and near-miss stories and limping their way to the beer table.

"Well at least they are living their dream," Sam says defensively.

"Some dream that is!"

"What does it matter if it involves an element of risk!"

"Might as well bungee jump or go to Las Vegas."

"But they are out there, living!" She is getting agitated and she doesn't know why.

"Foolishness! Do you really think that's a good way to spend your time?"

But Sam, knowing she can't dent his smugness, is cornered into silence. They stop for a moment outside the pub in the car park where Hugh turns to Sam and says, dutifully, how nice she looks. He asks her why she has seen so much of the girls this week and she is forced into a lie, saying blithely that it's just the way it goes; but she wonders why he hasn't made the obvious connection between this and April's need for money. Then she thinks that he has forgotten

April's situation, of course, to him it is unimportant. Hugh looks round the car park and comments on the modern bikes that must cost a fortune, then points to a row of cars and says that at least there are some normal people there. Sam keeps her objections to herself on registering his use of the word 'normal' and opens the car door. But he has not finished.

"There's an old beaten up Saab! Goodness that's old. I used to have one of those, remember?"

"I remember," says Sam sadly, reminded of them sitting in it eating fish and chips beside a Cornish harbour one rainy night, and laughing as they threw chips to the quarrelling gulls. He tells her to be careful and, jokingly, not to get too drunk as she kisses his cheek with irritation. He says he'll pick her up at 10 and watches her making her way across the tarmac.

Once out of the car, Sam steps lightly towards the pub.

The pub where Trish works was once an inn, so it is large, retains some suggestion of faded grandeur and is set back off the road with a car park at the front and a beer garden at the back. It has an upstairs room that is used as a popular venue for local bands. It is managed by a biker, has a clientele of old bikers and is popular with others, including and increasingly, young bikers, for its authenticity, good beer and music. Trish is more than just another member of staff; she is used and valued by Vince the manager as a reliable assistant and adviser, she specialises in event management. He is limping along behind the bar at the moment, wiping glasses and grumbling whilst Trish is sitting talking to a couple of other bikers of mixed ages who all seem eager to engage her in conversation. She is rolling a cigarette and laughing with gusto and obviously totally at ease and enjoying herself. The minute she sees Sam, she stands up and waves and moves over to let Sam share her stool. She introduces them, orders her a drink and continues the conversation.

"Biff here is talking about his 'magic road' and I was trying to get out of him what he meant," laughs Trish, "but the others seemed to know what he is talking about."

"You know! You know what I'm talking about!" protests Biff. " You were going on about Route 50 the other day, saying that the Missouri stretch is wonderful. Don't tell me you don't know. I only mentioned the Lake District in the early morning, full of twisties yet great sight lines, though it's only an English road and that doesn't compare with any of your beloved American routes!"

"Over here it's all so small and so soon over," says Trish, mock mournfully.

"Hey, Stu! She's talking about your sex life again!" calls Biff as he sees Stuart approaching. There is a general shout of laughter and Stuart greets everyone with a smile and a slap of hands and squeezes Trish's waist.

"Not boasting again! All of you must be so fed up of being put to shame! She just can't keep up with me."

But Trish only smiles in reply, and soon the talk has flowed around her and she and Sam have moved into a rather gloomy deserted back bar with a billiard table and darts board. Trish sits down and inspects her friend.

"You look tired. Are you OK?" Sam nods, pushing back the sleeves of her coat. "Bloody granddaughter again I suppose?" Sam is about to say more when April appears, making her way slowly towards them carrying a tray of glasses, crisps and a bottle of red wine, which, she informs them Biff has bought. She sets the tray down and takes off her jacket. There is a moment's silence and she looks at them both with some trepidation. She is wearing a shapeless blue, purple and white patterned dress, cut low at the front but then hanging round her with the voluminous capacity of curtains in a church hall. They all know that her taste is execrable, but how she has chosen this particularly unflattering monstrosity is beyond Trish and Sam. Trish opens her mouth, but Sam speaks first.

"That certainly looks cheerful!" says Sam, Trish shuts her mouth and April smiles and sits down in her chair, opens a packet of crisps and they all raise their glasses to each other.

"To us! To Taylor's Three," says April. "To Thirty-five grand!" and they all take hefty swigs of their drinks. Sam almost chokes on hers and has to be slapped on the back by April.

Trish asks them both how things are going but before they can respond, carries on immediately, "I have to tell you about father." And she keeps them chuckling as she recounts the story of the mother who isn't lost and the police search at her parents' house. April, feeling more confident than she has for a decade, then tells them about getting a sick note for a fortnight and shocking Becki. They ask her exactly what she said and April embroiders a bit, makes out that she was really brutally rude to Becki and both of the others congratulate her wholeheartedly.

"Having a free day gives you more time to get the money together," says Sam. "But then what will you do after all of this?" It is a question Sam has asked April often without getting a satisfactory reply and, once more, April shrugs.

"I got £450 today for pawning the family jewels."

"So you sold Ben's ring?" says Sam with a mournful face.

"You know I loved it, but there was other stuff of my mother's."

"I never knew you had family jewels?"

"I haven't anymore."

Trish congratulates her for making a real effort to raise money and for confronting Becki. There is a pause as Sam asks if there is any hope of getting the money and is greeted by blank stares and mini head shakes. She puts her glass down and asks why April seems so calm about getting the money as the deadline is creeping closer. Trish raps the table and looks at April pointedly, telling her to let Sam know. April turns to Sam and tells her about Martina's offer.

"I didn't tell you before Sam. I discussed it with Trish who said hold off, maybe something will come up, but it's Wednesday now. I've got to face it. There's no way I can make that amount of money legally. None. So, it has to be done. But I forbid you from doing the thing, absolutely. I know that it absolutely isn't your thing. But if you don't even want to hear about it, you can go in the next bar and chat to Stu. We'll love you always, anyway Sam. We won't think the worse of you whatever you decide." Sam is obviously shocked and asks how safe it is. April says that Martina has said it is a doddle, but Sam needn't get involved. She and Trish will do it. They've got it in hand. "Just, we had to tell you, let you know, so you can leave at this point before Martina arrives."

"We did think about not telling you, quite frankly," admits Trish.

"I'd never have forgiven you! Why was I the one who was left out?" asks Sam.

"You're so respectable now," replies April, refraining from mentioning that she is still officially ill.

"So are you. With your job on the council."

"But I never wanted to be."

"What difference does that make?" replies Sam, "I hope this isn't because you still think I can't cope with it physically?" She notices April's sideways glance at Trish and continues, "because the doctor said I was fine. You were there, Trish."

"Darlin's, can you remember watching our squat being raided by the fuzz?" says in Trish.

"Of course, but what's that got to do with anything?" says April.

"Well, we've all changed since then, haven't we? Got a bit duller? Less risk-taking? More careful?" Trish's tone is regretful.

"Isn't that a good thing?" asks Sam automatically, then remembers her irritation at Hugh earlier in the evening. Hugh, whose idea of a good time is a night in with a box set and a glass of wine; who likes 'decent' people. "When did we get to be so 'normal'?" she adds with a sigh. "What happened to us?"

"Well ultimately it's up to you, Sam. But only do what you're comfortable with darlin'," says Trish. Sam doesn't hesitate and says she'll stay, she's sure she can help out somehow then raises her glass in a toast and they all join her.

"To Taylor's Three," says Sam.

Trish and April discuss what they'll need: dark clothes, torches, gloves, and how they'll get there. They'll go separately, Trish on her bike and April in her car. They'll park in different directions two or three streets away. They hear the door creaking and Martina comes in quietly and quickly, wearing her usual funky sports outfit, but now with a black jacket. She has obviously run here.

"Hiya April," she says, "shall we go to another table?" she puts her hands in her pockets and nods her head sideways. April asks her to look more closely and she surely recognises Trish and Sam, her old friends, who will be advisers and helpers. Martina then notices both of them. "Of course I remember you. You called yourselves The Something Three." She exclaims. "We like, went on that brilliant camping trip! The first time I abseiled! The weather was, like, great at first then it rained for two days. We got so wet and muddy that when I, like, got home, my mother threw all my clothes away. It was cool! So good to meet you again. You're the artist one. I had a crush on you. You sketched me and Kate once. I think I've still got it."

Martina sits down, leans forward and goes through the plan again. "The table is booked early for 6:30 so that her son can be there as well. It's one of those places that have 'little meals for little people'." Her voices goes mockingly squeaky as she says this. "SHE's always late. They're going by car so she can put the precious brat in the car seat. I'll let you know when they leave. Oh!" She digs into her jacket pocket and gets out a mobile, "I bought another pay-as-you-go mobile. My father will ask to see my mobile. I know he will. He'll immediately think I might have something to do with it. So, I'm keeping this one separate. I'll send you a text, April, so you know this number." She does so. "Only use this from now on. I'll text you when we leave the house and afterwards when he pays the bill. I'll leave the gate and the back door open, then you just go upstairs, nab the stuff and leave. Easy?"

"Which room are they in? And where are they kept?" asks Trish.

"In her dressing room, that used to be MY bedroom." She takes out a piece of paper and they see it has a rough map of the layout of a house on it. She traces a path on this with one finger as she speaks. "You go up the stairs from the basement where I am, then into the hall and ground floor. Up another flight. Like, big stairs now, very grand. Opposite the front door. Then turn first right on the first floor, takes you into their bedroom. The en-suite is on this side and the dressing room is on the other. You used to be able to get into it from the hall when it was my bedroom. Not now. First thing she did was turn me out then close up that door and build a connecting door from the bedroom. It's enormous. It's where she tarts herself up and keeps her clothes: rows and rows of them. All names, all labels. Masses of them. He used to grumble at the bill if my mother bought a cardigan from Marks and Sparks. Anyway. In front of the mirror there's a place where she puts on her make-up. There are two boxes filled with jewellery, the oldest box is what my mother left. She's mixed her stuff up with mine and my mother's now, so best take it all. I'll sort it out later."

"How much of it is there?" asks Trish again.

"Oh, not that much," her hands mime a small pile.

"So, the whole thing should take about 10 minutes at the most?" asks April.

"Easy. In and out as I said. Only…" she pauses and looks at them, "you'll have to take some other stuff. Go into some other rooms. Turn things over a bit. Make it look like you were searching. Otherwise it's clearly an inside job. See what I mean? If there were two of you…. then one could get the stuff. The other could mess up the rest of the house a bit."

Trish and April look at each other quizzically, "You know I was going to come anyway, darlin'. But it looks like you'll need me there. I can jumble things round a bit whilst you get the stash." Trish says.

"Are you on?" asks Martina. Trish looks at April keenly.

"Are you certain, darlin'? We can hide you for a while, you know. Just leave it."

"They know where my mum is," says April, "I have to pay up."

"Think for a while," says Sam, "don't do anything quickly, dearest. Maybe there are other ways? I'll have about two grand I've sneaked out of the cashpoint daily."

"Thanks Sam. But that won't touch the sides. I've tried everything I can think of. Unless either of you have more ideas?" They both shake their heads as Martina gets up and walks round the billiard room. Finally, April calls her back and tells her that she'll do it.

'Wicked! I don't want you to contact me in any way from now on," says Martina, "I'll text you on the new phone. Once it's done, I'll meet you with the cash at your home, April, on Friday. Then we can sort through stuff."

"Best not make it my place," says April, thinking of the police sergeant, "we'll meet at Trish's," and gives the address.

"Just check you've got my text," says Martina and April looks at her phone and nods.

"I won't see you tomorrow. See you Friday. Here goes. I'm well pleased. Thanks so much, April. Best of luck." And she jumps up, pushes open the door that clearly says 'no exit except in case of fire', and runs out, leaving it open to the cold air so they see her jogging effortlessly across the car park and round a corner. April watches her with a frown and as Sam gets up to fetch more drinks Trish leans forward and speaks softly, "You do know she's up to something?"

"Of course. Sneaking back her mother's, no grandmother's, jewellery," replies April, looking at her phone. Trish opens her mouth and then shuts it again.

Eleven

Thursday afternoon

At her mother's care home April barely gets through the front door before Mrs Weekes meets her quite forcibly, blocking her way. April proffers the cake tin apologetically.

"I know I can't see Mr Henderson, but do you think you could give him this?"

"You know I can't give him anything from either you or your mother," says Mrs Weekes sternly. "I made that quite clear to you last time you called. Take it away. Of course, you may go to see your mother if you want, you are her daughter and naturally concerned and she is still a bit under the weather. But do not go anywhere else, just immediately up to her room and back. And whilst you're there please make sure she drinks some water." She waves her hand and watches closely as April walks upstairs, carefully holding the chocolate cake in its tin.

April opens the door of her mother's bedroom and sees that they have pulled a table across her mother's bed and placed on it a jug of water and a glass. Her mother is propped up on pillows looking pale but awake. She looks up as April enters, but her eyes are blurred and her unmade-up face droops more noticeably, and April knows she must be really unwell as she hasn't put her teeth in. April puts the cake down and bends to kiss her.

"How are you?" she asks cheerfully but her mother's hand shoots out and grabs hold of her wrist.

"Ah April, I'm to blame," her voice is more slurred and reverts to her broader Yorkshire accent which it often does these days, especially when she's tired. Her mouth seems formless and her cheeks flap as she speaks, she squeezes and shakes April's wrist, trying to draw her attention.

"No mum. It's not your fault." April replies automatically, remembering her long list of grievances and how hard she has tried not to feel resentful: the forgotten birthdays, the sudden abandonments, the expected admiration. Most of all, the refusal to apologise, to admit how badly she'd not just treated April but her own parents, all of whom kept picking up the pieces she broke. She holds her mother's hand, feeling the papery skin wrinkle over the bones, stroking the palm, calming the fingers, and senses a relaxation. Her mother lies back more easily in the bed.

"Aye, t'is … if only I'd told ya…."

"Never mind, mum. Just drink some water now." April holds the glass as her mother sips from the good side of her mouth, but a weak hand rises up again and taps it away.

"I wish I'd told you. An' he don't know. I wish we'd both been more canny."

"I don't know what you're going on about," says April, feeling her mother's head. She doesn't seem to be running a temperature, but she is flushed. "Just rest now." She makes her mother take some more water and watches her as she lies back, breathing more evenly, her face easing onto the pillow, asleep.

Picking up the cake, she gets up to go and is walking away when she hears her mother's voice speaking softly and returns and leans over to hear. Her mother appears to be speaking in her sleep.

"We did nowt right, neither of us. Ah'm sorry, so sorry."

Mystified, April leaves, almost bumping into Mrs Weekes who is waiting at the bottom of the stairs, clearly on alert and eager to see April completely off the premises.

"How is she now? A bit better?" Mrs Weekes walks her to the front door.

"It's hard to tell," April tells her, "at least she was awake for a while, but she was rambling."

"Ah yes, that happens, but once the antibiotics start working, they get back to normal quickly. You'll be amazed at her improvement in a day or two."

"She's had quite a few of these, hasn't she? But this one looks worse. Why does she get so many?" April stands by the opened front door and turns to face Mrs Weekes.

"Some people are more prone that's all. Especially women. And she has some physical problems left over from that nasty childbirth. They weren't so advanced then, were they, medically?" She shuts the front door behind her firmly.

On the way home April wonders why no-one has mentioned that her own birth was difficult, in fact she remembers her mother saying that it was a breeze, wondering why modern mothers made such a fuss; a very bad preparation for Kate's birth. But the car is stuttering again and so she concentrates on getting it to go up the hill towards her flat.

Once inside she opens the cake tin and looks in, tempted to try a slice but then glimpses the door to Kate's room. She opens it tentatively, knowing all is the same inside and wondering why she is doing this. She breathes in and gazes slowly round, seeing if she can sense Kate's presence. She lies down for a moment on Kate's bed and sniffs the sheets, missing Kate so much, imagining her well and happy, sending this image out across the land towards Kate, telling her she loves her. She talks to her in her mind, hearing her voice replying, telling her not to worry. She gets up and opens the wardrobe yet again, touches her clothes, opens her drawers and lets her fingers run over the T-shirts, pressing them down in places, recalling how and when Kate wore each of them. Finally, she closes the drawer and leaves the room, wiping her eyes with the back of her hand. She needs cake. And to prepare.

April parks a few streets away, remembering Trish's instructions, takes off her coat, locks the car, puts the keys above one of the tyres and walks a block down a side street which is not busy. Trish and she meet silently, as arranged, at the top of the alley behind the long row of Victorian terraces where Martina's house is situated. The dark pathway connects the remote end of the high street with a parallel street that is purely residential. On one side are the gardens of the terraced houses behind a variety of walls, gates and doors whilst the other is the concrete back of a block of mews buildings. It is narrow and grubby, only used by locals taking their dogs for a walk or as a shortcut. The entrance at the top is dark, away from the light of the lampposts and hard to distinguish, only a bollard shows that there is an opening here. For the first few yards its high walls on either side are covered in graffiti, then the darkness descends. It is a damp cold night, April is clutching her mobile phone, waiting for the text from Martina.

Trish, dressed in black jeans, T-shirt and leather jacket, smiles tightly at April then takes another look at April's outfit and sniggers.

"Whatever are you wearing?"

"Damart undies, Kate gave them to me a few Christmases ago, two layers, and a black scarf as a sort of short skirt whilst I'm out here, they're the only thing I could find that was black," she pulls down the vest top and tucks it into the long-johns, revealing for a moment her spare tyre in all its dimpled glory,

"Nobody'll see me." Trish shakes her head and asks whether April has got a torch, a head covering and gloves. April nods, waves her hands and gestures at her forehead where she has pulled on a headband with a torch attached, she pulls down a balaclava so that the headband pings off and falls to the ground. They see the lights of a car coming along the road and move further into the alleyway as April scrabbles for her torch. Trish's eyes get used to the gloom and she gazes round warily: the only light is the glow from April's phone which is clutched in her hand and seems to be mesmerising her. "I can't believe I'm doing this," she whispers.

"We can back out," says Trish, "just go home. If you want." April considers this for a moment then shakes her head.

"I can't see any other way, it's Thursday. We've all tried. This is the only offer for big money I've got. They will be after me and Kate. Martina says it'll be a doddle. It should be easy. The stuff is hers anyway. Let's do it. Get it over with." She looks down anxiously as the phone pings and there's Martina's text. "They're leaving now," April whispers and they both push further into the alley where its walls are patched with ivy and the tarmac humps and lumps under their feet.

They wait in silence, standing next to each other, their breath steaming and April's heart beating faster. It seems like ages before Trish looks at her watch and says they might as well get on with it.

"Lead on," she whispers, "don't switch on your torch, it'll draw attention to us, but pull your gloves tight." As they make their way along the alley, groping at the walls as they go, the bare branches of the trees in some of the gardens rattle in the wind as April nervously leads the way. There are about 20 gates of differing shapes and sizes on one side of the alley, tall metal gates, short wooden gates, swing gates, house doors with bells, April passes each one and gets almost to the bottom of the alley when she stops.

"I can't remember what the gate looks like from this side, I think it was further up, I think we've passed it." She whispers and Trish curses and turns sharply to retrace their steps. They go slowly. April examines each gate and what she can see of the garden and house behind it carefully, trying to remember the type of gate and wall but with no success. None of them look familiar. They almost reach the top when it is clear she has missed the house once again.

"For fuck's sake!" says Trish.

"I'll try a few gates as we go from this way. It was nearer the top," says April and tries a gate that opens immediately.

"You go in," says Trish "and let me know if it's the right place," April disappears and then reappears quickly shaking her head. The next couple of gates don't open and then one does, April goes in and is gone for a little while. Trish waits in silence but loses patience and pokes her head slowly round the gate and calls quietly for April. There is a courtyard with tables and chairs and then a row of plants in terracotta pots and behind these a small area where there is a blur of activity, hard to distinguish in the dark. On getting closer Trish sees it is April petting a very overfriendly cork-coloured hairy mongrel who is jumping around her, whimpering and wagging its tail. "For God's sake," says Trish, and the dog turns and gives a little bark and a light goes on in a back room, revealing a tall woman looking outwards. Both of them desperately whisper soothing words at the mongrel and back towards the gate, petting and stroking and trying to calm it. But the nearer they get to the gate the more agitated it becomes and starts chasing round the garden and yapping, its pale tail waving madly. It obviously thinks it's going walkies. Trish picks up a stick from the garden and throws it between the pots saying "Fetch!" and the dog barks in excitement and runs as a woman comes up the steps and calls the dog's name.

They head for the gate, slamming it behind them, and run madly up the alley as the woman shouts, asking who's there. Trish makes it easily to the top and around the corner, but April is slower and ends up pressed against a wall amongst some overhanging ivy, pulling in her stomach and trying not to pant loudly. The back gate opens and a shrill voice calls out again asking who's there. The woman does not come into the alleyway but just pokes her head out and says firmly she knows they're there. She waits for a moment as April's breath hovers in the air but finally slams the gate shut. Stepping out from the ivy April plods to the top of the alley where Trish is rolling a cigarette.

"You'll have to go round the front and count how many houses down it is," she says. "We must get in and out quickly, let's not waste any more time." April nods, pulls off her head torch, balaclava and gloves and walks round to the front of the row of houses, trying to look respectable. She ventures down the opposite side of the road and counts seven houses down and returns to where Trish is sitting on the bollard and smoking. They once again make their way along the narrow pathway, counting the back gates carefully as they go, then April stops.

"Somebody is coming along here!"

"Act casual, and keep moving," says Trish and they both walk towards the stranger, making inane conversation as they go.

"Such cold weather for the time of year," says Trish.

"Nasty," continues April, "so different from Saint Tropez!"

"Breezy too. A windy night." Trish is stopped as the stranger says both of their names and glancing at her they recognise Sam. April's first instinct is to hug her, but Trish speaks very firmly, backing away from her,

"What are you doing here, darlin'? No, don't tell us. You must go home. At once!"

"I'm not going, I've made up my mind, I'm staying. I'm joining in."

"No Sam. This is not for you," says April, more gently than Trish. "We love you too much and you can't be doing this sort of stuff."

"You're not coming and that's that! Come on, April, let's get going for God's sake we've wasted enough time as it is!"

"I'm staying whether you want me to or not. I'm going to be lookout! See!" and she rummages beneath her coat and scarf and pulls on a tape until a yellow plastic children's whistle pops out, which she blows. It makes a sharp high sound and all the dogs in the neighbourhood bark in their various tones, producing a surprising variety of sounds from high pitch whimpers and squeaks to low long deep bassoons, causing Trish and April to put their hands over their ears. Sam is a little surprised.

"Goodness there's a lot of dogs round this area! But at least you'll hear."

"For God's sake, Sam darlin'. No! Martina is going to text us. We don't need anyone blowing any fucking whistles."

"I'm staying," says Sam doggedly as April and Trish walk away from her with her trailing behind them and standing a little away as they open the gate.

"Go home, Sam," says Trish as first April then herself enter the back garden. Once assured that it is the right place, Trish speaks

148

clearly and quietly saying they must be back here at 7:15, but April, tugging on her balaclava, looks at her watch and curses quietly as it doesn't light up; she had no idea until now, it was her mother's and she thought it was the best timekeeper. The only other one she possesses loses a minute an hour, that's why she took this one, she might as well have bought the other one. She witters on nervously until Trish tells her to shut up, just lead the way for God's sake. April crosses the paving where there is a stone table and chairs next to a small pond with an abstract sculpture in the middle, past a small formal knot garden, round a hedge hiding the dustbins, and finally down the steep narrow steps that go down into the basement. At this moment she adjusts her head torch and presses a switch. Nothing happens so she presses it again until it produces a bright flashing light. She swears and presses every button it has and finally turns to Trish whispering that it worked fine at home she doesn't know why now it would only flash. Trish swears again, tells her to switch it off and goes in front of April, carrying her small torch. Trish breathes deep as they push open the back door and are in the damp basement.

The corridor extends darkly in front of them. The carpet sticks to their feet as they tiptoe, pausing at each step for a moment, listening and looking, waiting for their eyes to adjust, their ears to hear any breath, any movement. All is quiet, so April gestures to the right and they both go up the back stairs. They stop behind a heavy door before reaching the hallway and listen again. Trish finally pushes the door open and peers around the corner. Her torch beam shows a spacious hall with black and white tiles, a solid oak front door flanked by a coat and umbrella stand, several other doors leading away and stairs curving up to the next floor landing. There is a lamppost directly outside and it gives an orange glow to the hall. Trish turns off her torch and they wait.

April is shaking with nerves; every noise she hears from the street makes her jump and turn. She is in the grip of one of her hot flushes and uses the ends of the scarf round her waist to mop at her face. Finally, Trish tells her that she must go up to the next floor and Trish will mess up the rooms down here and meet her upstairs. They creep into the hallway and April makes her way upstairs, gasping at every creaking floorboard, watching every step, her gloved hands holding the banister. She hears Trish moving stealthily through one of the rooms below and the sound of drawers opening, once a clang as if Trish has thrown a metal object to the ground. She reaches the top of the first flight of stairs and walks a little way along the hallway before turning into the bedroom. It is huge, about the size of April's flat, high walls, a chandelier, thickly carpeted and with shutters fitted behind draped curtains, an enormous double bed and an array of drawers and cupboards. April opens one and looks inside then turns suddenly and freezes, she has seen a movement in the room. On one wall, a dark blob of a person with greying hair stares back at her. April's heart does a backflip, and as she jumps along with the other person, she realises that it is a mirror and that large lump in the reflection, is herself.

She rests for a minute on the bed, getting her breath, and goes to another doorway opposite the foot of the bed. This is a black marbled bathroom with a stroll-around shower behind a glass screen, all looking really high tech with total surround spray jets and a large waterfall. April remembers that she hasn't had a pee and her nervousness has made matters worse. She eyes the large bulbous loo and stops for a moment to relieve herself. As she gets up, she sees her reflection in another mirror above the basins and hears a scraping sound she can't place. She flees and immediately sees the door on the opposite side of the bedroom. Going through this she is in the darkness of the dressing room with its closed shutters. This must be the room, so April turns on her flashing head torch and takes a deep breath.

Two sides of the room are covered by units for clothes, rows of jackets hang above rows of trousers, lines of tops range over lines of skirts, a long clump of dresses, shoes on slanting racks reaching from floor to ceiling. So much, so many. April turns in wonder, seeing it all in strobe lighting, it's like an up-market department store. She jumps again at the sight of herself in the large mirror behind her but looks to one side. There is a tall chair in front of a table arranged for make-up with another mirror surrounded by lights, the sort of thing April has seen in backstage dressing rooms. She peers more closely; this must be what Martina described. The make-up table. Perfume bottles and makeup are in a backlit cabinet to one side. On the other side is an open unit displaying jewellery: earrings, beads, watches, chains and pendants but directly below the mirror are two boxes.

April's breath catches. She knows that she has found the target. Both boxes are made of wood, one with brass fittings and the other with delicate marquetry. She makes the guess that the marquetry one is the older one and tries to open it. It will not open. She looks round for a key with it tucked under one arm. She wonders if it is the right box after all, puts it down for a moment and opens the other one. This is filled with the glitter of stones, necklaces, some rings. Realising she has nowhere to stash everything, April unpicks the scarf from around her waist and fashions a rough sling, roughly putting everything from the box that will open into it. She selects randomly some of the array of earrings, brooches, and necklaces that glisten and dangle on the bars beside the mirror. On the dressing table there is just one ring apparently carelessly thrown down. It draws her eye; it is very like the one that Ben gave her that she pawned and she can't resist taking a glove off and slipping it onto the top of one finger where it sticks whilst she turns it round to the light. A noise outside makes her realise she is wasting time and picking up the marquetry box she tucks it under one arm, adding a couple more rings onto her finger. Back in the bedroom she suffers another shock at seeing Trish. Recovering herself with a gasp she whispers,

"I can't open this box."

"For fuck's sake come on," says Trish. "Just hurry up." She pauses as April flashes her finger at her, showing how cleverly she has stashed the rings "where's your fucking glove?" April runs back into the dressing room and grabs her glove from the table and, not being able to pull it over her ring-decked fingers, takes off everything and wedges them into her cleavage, making chinking noises as she pushes them down. Meanwhile, Trish rushes in behind her asking what she's touched and grabbing a jumper from a rail rubs the dressing table and the door handle. April rubs the jewellery display on one side with a pair of tiny silk pants, feeling doomed and tearful. God knows what she touched.

"Let's go!" says Trish. "Let's just get out of here." They run down the stairs and April bumps into Trish who has stopped to listen in the hallway. Trish knocks over the umbrella stand which crashes down and its contents roll and slide across the floor. Trish curses April quietly as they make it down the basement stairs, treading carefully now. Trish takes the lead with one hand holding April back. They turn the corner, go along the corridor and open the back door.

There is a cacophony of dogs. Someone is blowing a whistle.

"Bloody Sam," whispers Trish, "you would've heard from Martina if they were coming back!" April smirks, feels for her mobile. Grabs Trish's arm.

"I left my mobile in there!" They freeze for a moment, for once neither of them swear, "if anyone finds it we're done for, Martina's texts are on it." April almost weeps, she has always known this would end badly.

"I'm going back to get it, you get out," says April, thrusting the box, scarf and most of the jewellery in her bosom at Trish who runs to the back gate and finds Sam blowing her whistle. The minute she sees Trish she stops and bounds forward.

"At last you're here. Thank God, thank God. They're back, they're back," says Sam in a frantic whisper. "I went round to the front, I saw Martina getting out of a car. Thank God you're here, where's April?" Trish grabs Sam and pushes the box, scarf and spare bits of jewellery at her, many of which drop to the ground.

"April went back," whispers Trish, "the stupid fucker left her mobile. It has Martina's contact and everything on it. Fuck. FUCK." Sam turns pale and Trish freezes for a moment then turns, saying, "Bloody hell there's stuff all over the place." She bends and picks up a bracelet in the garden and then moves a bit further on to pick up a glistening earring, she calls quietly over her shoulder, "Stay around, I need to pick up these pieces. I'm collecting the bits she dropped." Sam protests faintly whilst picking up stray pieces that have fallen outside the gate as Trish disappears into the back again. She hears shouts coming from the house. Lights are going on, illuminating the garden, an angry male voice is coming up the basement steps. Trish flings herself down behind a box hedge just in time and sees a stout man in a suit stomp past, going to the back gate.

"Shut up Martina! Shut up! Just for once shut the hell up. The gate IS bloody open. You didn't bloody lock it! Nor the back bloody door!" He produces a key and locks the gate, puts the key in his pocket and slams down the steps still shouting at her, telling her how useless she is. He's going to call the police. It's all her bloody fault. She can't be trusted to do anything. This is all her fault. This is the end.

Trish lies behind a box hedge, flinching as a piece of stone digs into her back, and waits. She knows she's trapped. The gate into the alleyway is six feet high, set into the brick wall, with only a foot gap at the top of it and a few inches at the bottom. He locked it. She is stuck here now. She sits up slowly and moves to the edge of the garden and creeps to the back gate and whispers for Sam. She waits hopefully and eventually Sam answers. They debate what to do in whispers whilst Trish passes under the gate the spare bits she's found and urges Sam to get away and go home with all the stuff.

"If we're caught, we may be able to tell a semi-believable story as long as we don't have anything on us," she finishes in a desperate whisper. "I'll find a way out of here; the walls aren't that high. You must get the jewels and evidence hidden. Go home." Sam reluctantly agrees and disappears.

Trish stands up by the back gate and suddenly grins. The feeling of danger enlivens her, she remembers sneaking out of hotel rooms, squeezing through the bars of a fence to get to the squat, lying under a hedge as police walked past. This challenge is a familiar one, she looks back on those times fondly, times when she felt alive with the danger, risk and adventure. She peers around, noticing that the wall leading to the next garden is shorter by a few feet. She looks around to find anything to stand on and tries lifting one of the chairs in the seating area, but it is carved out of stone and immoveable; her back protests as she heaves. She searches for alternatives that are portable but substantial enough to bear her weight, but it is useless. The lights are on in the house, yet no-one appears to be looking this way, but they will only have to glance out of any window to catch sight of her. With a flash of creativity, she remembers the capacious wheeled dustbins and races down, grabs them and drags them one by one, to

154

the side wall. They are surprisingly heavy and make her pant and her arms ache, she has to get each one in separate journeys. She realises that she has done little to no real physical activity for years. Out of breath she manages to clamber up, using one on its side as a precarious step. Perched uncomfortably on the top of the bin with her knee protesting, she shifts, pushes a leg out, noticing with surprise that it is shaking. She falls onto the wall just getting astride it. It is significantly wider than her Harley. Her hamstrings tighten at the sideways stretch and a sharp piece of stone bores into her crotch as she stops for a moment and looks down to the other side. Below her is a thicket of bamboo. She shifts and restrains herself from swearing aloud with discomfort. She cannot locate the ground beneath, it must be some way down, her courage deserts her as she remembers the pain when she fell off her bike, her shock, how time slowed when she knew the fall was coming. She definitely does not want to get hurt again; it might be better to try another way.

The noise of a police siren gets louder and stops close by. The police. She hasn't thought about them. They will find her for sure: they may have dogs. She flattens herself out along the top of wall wondering whether she can get down safely. Another police siren sounds and stops. She has no alternative but to get into the next-door garden in whatever way she can. She holds her breath and tries to roll and slide down the wall but loses her grip and falls backward, grabbing hold of some canes, cracking and breaking them as the ground meets her. She lands on her back and all the air leaves her body. She is drowning and draws in air with a screech that sets all the dogs barking again, she cannot breathe, she gasps and gulps, biting the air. The dogs continue barking and someone is coming down the garden she's just left. Someone is walking back to where the dustbins are and waiting. A face pops over the wall above her.

It is Martina.

"Trish!" she whispers. Then looks at her again, "Got the stuff?" Trish splutters yes and can see Martina smiling in response. "Cool! We all had to come home early. Sorry. The bitch felt sick. They've called the police. I'll take the bins away."

"Wait," stammers Trish, as Martina starts to go, "April. Still in there. Went back for her mobile. She dropped it somewhere."

"Fuck, fuck, fuck," says Martina and disappears and Trish can hear her quietly pulling both bins together back to their original places away from this wall, before running to the basement.

Trish rests for a while, getting her breath and feeling her heart slowing. She shifts, feels the damp earth and the cold seep into her, making her shiver. Above her, the wind rattles the bamboo. She sits up slowly, every bone aches, her jeans are torn in parts under her buttocks and knees. She has cuts on her neck and cheeks, her bum hurts, one ankle really burns and her ribs stab with each breath. She limps to the back gate keeping under the wall; the door has a Yale lock that opens easily from this side. She edges through, keeping guard, and sneaks up the alleyway and crosses the road. There is no sign of Sam. She considers riding to Sam's but needs to recover herself. She walks towards her bike slowly, avoiding looking down the road where she knows the police car will be parked. She turns a corner and sees her bike ahead when someone grabs her.

Twelve

Thursday evening

April enters the house again and goes up the back stairs without thinking anything except she must get to the dressing room. Most likely she put her mobile down there when she took her gloves off. As she pushes the door open to go into the hallway and runs forward, she hears a key turn in the front door lock and the oak door moves inwards. She immediately steps sideways into what she sees is a study. Voices sound out, the father has seen the umbrellas scattered over the floor and is asking Martina if she did that. She replies in a loud sullen voice asking how she could have done that since she's never allowed upstairs anymore, it was most probably the brat.

The father is moving round and opening and closing doors. April ducks down behind the large desk just in time as the study door is pushed further open and then left fully ajar. He opens the drawing room where Trish has flung a lot of stuff around and she hears a series of curses and then he is swearing at Martina, saying she must've left the back gate open. Two sets of footsteps go along the hall outside the study door and away down the basement stairs, accompanied by quarrelling voices.

April creeps to the study door and looks round cautiously, she can hear someone throwing up noisily in the loo next door. She takes a chance and legs it up the main stairs and into the bedroom with the sound of a loo flushing downstairs making her feet move faster than she knew she could. Breathing heavily, she looks around the room.

Standing in the doorway of the dressing room is a small boy. They look at each other silently for a moment until April picks up the sound of someone coming upstairs. She puts her finger to her lips and, keeping her eyes on him, treads slowly and smoothly round the bed and ducks, then lies down. The bed stretches to the floor, if anyone comes round to the window side she will be seen immediately. Someone sits on the bed.

"So sorry, sweetheart," says a young female voice, "were you looking forward to your milkshake? Mummy's not well. So sorry. Are you trying to say something? Clever boy! Ooops!" The bed rocks slightly, quick light steps go into the en-suite bathroom where they echo and are supplanted by the sound of retching.

April stands up and almost falls over the boy who has obviously come around the bed to stare at her. She keeps her finger on her mouth, tiptoes briskly round him and goes into the dressing room, closing the door firmly behind her. She switches on her torch and searches quickly for her mobile, keeping an eye open for where she should hide in case anyone comes in. She looks carefully round the dressing table area, on the floor, on the tabletop, in the drawers. Nothing. She hears the loo flushing and switches off her torch. No sign of her mobile and now she is in pitch blackness.

Her glimpse of the room has been enough, there is absolutely nowhere to hide. Every available inch of space is taken up with racks and lines, hangers, open shelves, drawers, every part of the room is visible to the back of all the units. She moves carefully towards the window and stands for a moment behind the door wondering how the hell she is going to get out. It is useless. She is sure to be discovered. She is trapped in here. She begins to plot what she is going to say to them when she's discovered. A moment of madness? A strange menopausal urge? The problem is: how to protect Trish and Sam?

She catches the sound of murmuring and movement in the bedroom, but nothing else happens. She waits breathlessly, leaning against the wall, any moment now someone is sure to come in. As her eyes adjust to the darkness, the light from the bedroom seeps round the edges of the closed door and shows her the outline of a chair. The rooms are quiet, and she wonders if the woman has fallen asleep. A police siren comes closer and stops outside the house. She knows then she is going to be found and arrested for sure. He must've called the police. But no-one seems to have discovered the theft of the jewellery yet. No-one has been in here. It's rather odd.

The front doorbell rings. The light patterns round the door vary as if someone is moving around. The door opens and the light is switched on in the dressing room, making April blink. She cannot see who is standing there as the door hides them, but hears a woman's gasp as she rushes over to the dressing table and begins throwing things around and screaming out.

"Harry! Harry!" she goes out of the room and calls downstairs, "Harry! They've taken my jewellery from here too! Harry! Harry! Come here at once! Harry!" She leaves the bedroom and April can hear her calling down the stairs and a replying call from Harry. April runs out of the dressing room, looks out of the bedroom door and seeing the back of the blonde woman turns quickly, scampers back, and swerves into the bathroom, barely getting there before a male voice comes hurrying into the bedroom. The female has returned to the dressing room and is still crying out about her beautiful rings, her lovely necklaces, all gone. April looks round the bathroom for somewhere to hide. It is black slate and marble with a large transparent shower partition and in the adjacent corner an enormous stand-alone white oval-shaped bath. But on one side there is a laundry basket. She goes towards this and thinks she can just get herself behind it if she kneels and then wriggles backwards. She is halfway there when the door opens slightly, and she is staring at Martina.

Martina jumps in, shutting the door behind her. There are more voices and conversations outside. Martina bends over the bath and asks April if she has found the mobile. April shakes her head and backs behind the bath in response to Martina's gesture, feeling her back aching. Martina starts to run the bath which has a high wide waterfall spout, the pipe of which burns hotly against April's ankles as she squeezes between it and the bath. Martina runs to one side of the bathroom and fetches a pile of towels that she dumps loosely over the laundry basket, obscuring April more, she gestures to April to lie down fully. The door to the bathroom opens and a police officer looks in, Martina is sitting on the edge of the bath, apparently testing the temperature of the water, waving a towel around aimlessly.

"Nothing missing in here?" he asks.

Martina shakes her head, "What would they take in a bathroom?"

The police officer strides over, opens the cabinets above the double basins and looks at Martina.

"Nothing in here?" he asks, and Martina shakes her head saying 'only Viagra' with a wink that sends the officer away. She continues sitting, the steam is rising, misting the mirrors and making the room warm and moist, April feels sweat dripping into her eyes, the balaclava is making her head itch.

"Whatever are you doing?" Martina's father, Harry, has come into the room. "For God's sake, you know you're not allowed to use this bathroom. Emily is feeling sick again. She's so upset. I'm furious with you. This is all your fault."

"I'm upset as well!" says Martina, "it seems my jewellery has gone too. Can I make a report to the police?" She stands up. A police officer comes into the room and asks if Mr Chowdhury could just help clear up a few matters. Martina says that she wants to report some stolen jewellery herself and leads him out of the room, Harry following spluttering that it isn't her jewellery. The water stays on and the steam rises. April, crushed, tries to loosen one arm to wipe her face, stretch her leg. She feels hot and uncomfortable, with the bath pressed against her, a solid mass, the pipe delivering water sears her. She tries to remove her feet from the hot pipe but ends up jamming them further in. Her head is outside the bath and hopefully hidden by the overfull laundry basket, but the position makes her back twinge further and her ankles ache and she has to lie on her arms. A spare bit of jewellery in her bosom is making a hole in her breast. All she can do is curve round, hoping she is less noticeable in the falling steam, and freeze whenever someone comes in. She can see diagonally across the bathroom floor which means that the loo is fully in her sight and through the opened door she glimpses a corner of the bed and an expanse of cream carpet. Martina's stepmother runs in and bends over the loo, retches, smooths back her hair, retches again, gulps and wipes her forehead. She goes over to the basins, and now April can only see her lower half but hears her brush her teeth and rinse her mouth. She must then notice the water running into the bath and strides over to turn off the taps and sits for a moment on the side of the bath, whilst April, doomed, waits to be noticed.

She turns on the water again, opens the door and April can hear her talking to someone outside and soon she is back in the bathroom bringing the small boy with her.

"Make sure we're not disturbed will you, babe?" she calls out. "Your little Emily wants her mummy time." Harry comes in and gives her a kiss, picks up his son and flies him round the bathroom with both of them making aeroplane sound, puts him down and tickles him, accompanied by squeals and squirms. Finally, Emily says he is overexciting his son and he stops.

"Daddy, daddy, I saw a lady! Black!"

"Yes, the waitress was very kind, she gave you some chips to take away, didn't she?"

"Hush!" says the boy, putting his finger to his mouth.

"You funny little thing!" says his father, ruffling his hair, "after the bath I'll give you a drink and put you to bed." He turns to Emily. "This is all Martina's fault, I'm so angry with her." He strides up and down the bathroom. April, catching glimpses of him, notices that he is significantly older and fatter than when she last saw him. He must be into his sixties and Emily looks in her twenties. April's theory is that for every 10 years of age difference between an old man and a young woman you calculate five million. 40 years or so difference here. He must be worth 20 million. Loaded! And if Martina's stories are true it seems that Emily is intent on getting as much of it as she can.

What she overhears next means that April stops feeling guilty about the robbery.

"Oh, babe. I really feel for you. You've been so kind to her, letting her stay on here despite her being so old now. Almost 30, is it? And this is how she repays you!"

"She's only 25 …"

"Not getting a proper wage though, is she, yet? But I don't want to upset you more, babe. All your valuables and mine, taken. All because she left the gate open!"

"Don't mention that to the police. It'll ruin the insurance claim. Martina's so forgetful. I don't know what gets into her. Sometimes she just doesn't think."

"She doesn't know how lucky she is, having you for a father, spoiling her. But this is the last straw, this is how she repays your generosity and kindness! Surely you can see now how little she really considers you? You must tell her to leave."

"She is my only daughter."

"You're going to have a new daughter!" During this process, Emily has been undressing herself, and now starts peeling the clothes off her son who looks sleepy and is sucking his thumb. "Just feel the water will you, babe, and we can let him splash in there for a while." But Maximilian, dressed only in his nappies, goes into the other room and returns with his blanket and then sits on the floor, holding the blanket up to his ear.

"Oh babe, I can't stop being cross. My jewellery has been stolen as well, you know."

"My poor sweetie. Your beautiful jewellery!"

"I'm so upset. You gave me those gorge earrings. They've gone. That beautiful bracelet. There's so much I've lost. You know I love my gems and stones. I'm so annoyed. They must've walked through our bedroom. It makes me feel strange. Then the other stuff in the safe! So much you've lost too. I loved that necklace. You were going to give it to me."

"Don't worry, I'll get you them again, and better. The insurance will cough up."

"Oh babe. Really?"

"You bet. I'm completely covered, as long as we keep telling them the back gate was locked. You just relax and think of what you would like when the money comes through. I'll get it for you. Whatever it is."

"You're so sweet to me. You spoil me. I WOULD love that Cartier diamond watch we saw in London."

"Of course, whatever you want. I couldn't spoil you enough. Don't worry about the police reports. You can add to the details later. I have most of it anyway. It's been a bad day for you. Take as long as you like, relax. I'll tell them to leave you alone. You and my little man!"

"And soon to be daughter!"

"Oh yes, sweetie. You have a long soak. I wish I could join you. I'll bring you whatever you need."

"Daddy, daddy, hush!" Both the adults laugh.

"You're so wonderful to me. Happy birthday, babe. I should be treating you!"

"I'm so lucky to have found you whatever the day is."

"Give me another kiss, handsome!" There is a silence whilst April watches two pairs of legs intertwining, and the boy plays with something on the floor near the loo. "My lovely cuddly wuddly bear."

"My pretty little squirrel-irrel. Does ooh want her daddy-waddy?"

"Squiggly loves her gorgeous daddy-waddy." More movement and leg mingling.

"Feel that! Can't wait till they've gone."

"I'll be ready. You know I'm going to give daddy bear his special present later." Some moaning sounds and April fears they may be going to get down onto the marble floor. A male voice is calling from the other room, so the lovers finally break apart and Harry leaves the bathroom, blowing a kiss before he closes the door. "Daddy bear loves sexy squiggle!"

For the next four hours, April is treated to a front row seat at the world's most intimate and boring show. Emily and the brat (Maximilian) have a long bath together and play with some ducks, with Harry tending them. Meanwhile, April hears the tramping sound of police officers going in and out of the dressing room. Emily disappears into the bedroom with Maximilian. The TV is switched on and April hears the unmistakable start of Thomas the Tank Engine.

The police seem still to be clumping round next door, but no one comes in here. At one point the door is slightly open and April spies an official dusting the outside door handle and speaking quietly over his shoulder to Emily, who is replying in disgruntled tones.

After a while Hugh returns, closes the door, walks in a circle, letting out a couple of flobbily farts, then has a very slow large difficult shit and a shower. He wanders round a bit in the nude, scratches a lot, inspects and washes his testicles and penis, shaves and brushes his teeth.

Nothing happens for a while. April is wondering whether they are awake next door and if she can look at her watch when the door opens and Maximilian is there, obviously half asleep, sucking his thumb and dragging his blanket. Harry appears behind him, obviously irritated, and asking what he wants in there. Maximilian says something about looking for his mofo, then darts behind the door and picks up a small black rectangle from behind the loo and holds it to his ear. April, who at this point is almost in a stupor of boredom and discomfort, sees immediately that he's holding a mobile in his hand and freezes with shock. This is what he must've been playing with earlier, how stupid of her not to have seen. Harry asks him what he's doing in there and does he want a pee. She cannot breathe, there is nothing she can do, she can only watch hopelessly. They are all going to prison. Maximilian presses the mobile to his ear but then pokes at it, looks at it, presses a few more buttons, says hello hello, presses it to his ear again. He turns towards the door, grabbing his blanket over it and returning to the comfort of his thumb and yawning. Harry, talking to Emily, closes the door. There is silence.

April, in a fever of anxiety, wonders what the hell is happening, but takes the chance to stretch out and move the ring embedded between her breasts to one side again, feeling sure they must've found the mobile. She shifts but then has to freeze with her feet half up the wall as the door opens and Harry comes in without switching on the light and opens the medicine cabinet, picks something from a cellophane wrapper, and takes a sip of water before almost running back into the bedroom. After a while she hears some activity next door and soon identifies it. There are groans and yeses and the steam clears in the bathroom, surely they would not be having sex if they had found the mobile? They would be calling the police. But they can find it anytime, it only needs Maximilian to show it to them, or leave it somewhere. She waits and the door opens finally, and Harry appears and has a lengthy pee and wipes his penis. Emily has a pee, rinses her mouth, brushes her teeth and takes some time in front of the mirror. There is a conversation next door which April can't catch. Then silence. April squirms, one leg and an arm are dead, maybe they are better that way. The door is closed. The light goes off in the bedroom.

It has been a terrifying night for April. Hidden, but in sight, sure she would be seen. Hearing the love talk was sickening but luckily that doesn't last long. Seeing genitalia at such close quarters keeps her awake but not in a nice way. Unluckily, the only part of the room that she can see clearly is the loo. At one point during Harry's large, smelly and pained bowel movement she thinks of declaring herself with the idea that her sudden appearance might actually speed up the process. She stays as still as a rock, which takes a toll on her back, adjusts her position when the room is empty, scratches underneath the balaclava, moves the ring around in her breasts, turns her face to the floor and closes her eyes. On one occasion she faces away from the bath and squashes into the wall, a really bad choice. The need for a pee grows slowly but insistently.

In the silence she is left with her rambling thoughts. This house is so luxurious, the bedroom is huge with crisp white bed linen and thick cream carpets, the bathroom is as big as her kitchen and living area. Why does anyone need a dressing room? Everything is modern, elegant, robust. Not like where she lives. Or wants to live, she realises. All she wishes for now (apart from getting away unseen) is for Kate to be OK. She doesn't care where she lives as long as her daughter is safe. It doesn't matter what Kate's done. She just has to be OK. Anything else April can fix. She will sort it out. For the first time in years she feels her determination rising. If she can steal some jewels, get time off work, brave the gangsters then she can definitely make things OK with Kate. She only has to show the courage that brought her here to this house to steal. She used to be braver many years ago and in the past few days she has reminded herself of how it feels to take that step into the void, to risk the consequences. She can do it. After all, Kate can only get angry. Scared people are angry.

April waits and thinks through her escape. She looks at her watch. It's too dark to see the time. She decides to try to creep out. She wonders which room is the boy's, she might have to find him. She shuffles forwards and manages to free herself. Cautiously she stretches each limb, letting the blood return, adjusts all her clothes and thinks about having a pee here but decides to wait and grips those muscles tightly. She tries crawling on all fours to the door but finding the pain in her back gets worse she stands up for a moment and stretches and curves her back and legs. Hearing no sound from the bedroom she opens the door slightly and listens and waits. She touches the handle and slowly pulls until she can peer round, her ears open for the slightest sound of alarm. It is completely dark so she can only hear rhythmic snuffles and the light woof of an outbreath. She gets onto her knees again and leans forward onto her elbows and shifts slowly across the bedroom, placing each arm and leg carefully, one at a time. Near the door she moves with swift smoothness and stands up without looking backwards, opens the door and is through it as quickly as she can manage. She releases the handle slowly and exhales.

Maximilian is standing there, gripping his comfort blanket and gazing bleary-eyed. He points at her sleepily. She puts her finger to her lips and they both say the word 'hush' as she creeps towards him. He looks confused, drops his comfort blanket and something black falls with it. He bends slowly, still looking at her, to pick them both up. But April, with a speed she never knew she possessed, darts forwards and snatches the mobile. He howls. She runs as his screams fill the house. She is down the stairs and across the hallway when she hears a door opening above and a male voice asking whatever the matter is.

"My mofo!" screams Maximilian from the top landing. "My mofo!" He is taken, crying shrilly, into the bedroom. April opens the door to the basement and sneaks down the steps. She rushes into the front room and finds Martina toking on a large joint and stretched out on top of one of the sofas.

"Get it?" asks Martina and April nods. "Anyone see you?" April shakes her head. "I'll lock the door at the top of these stairs," says Martina and she is up and moving away, handing April the joint as she passes. April takes a large inhale and hands it back to Martina when she reappears. "Loo?" she gasps and follows Martina's pointing finger to a cramped damp bathroom where she enjoys a luxurious long pee.

Returning to the front room, Martina, halfway through the joint now, smiles at her.

"Thought you might make it. Best place to be, the bathroom. Black bathroom and you in black, like merged a bit. Once SHE was in it, like, the police kept away. Where was your phone?"

"I dropped it in the loo then Maximilian had it. Just got it at the end. Bloody lucky!"

"Sick! Fuck. Saved!"

"Lets us all off the hook," says April.

"I kept them busy, pointed them in places away from the bathroom, acted robbed. I've been banned from going upstairs. I've been, like, looking everywhere for your mobile: windows, shelves, cupboards, drawers, all the rooms in the house, this garden, next door garden, alleyway. Said I was, like, looking for dropped jewellery. I actually found a couple of pieces, like, but pocketed them. Like, kept bumping into police. Kept on being told to 'lock up'. They've been to see the neighbours, like, quite a few people saw someone 'behaving suspiciously'. There have been other thefts down here. We're starting up a neighbourhood watch. I'm gonna be the main contact." They both grin, April giggles despite herself.

"We only did this for the money," says April, unsettled by Martina's cool reactions, but presuming she's over-stoned, "remember that. Only because I'm desperate. Be at Trish's house at noon with the cash. Now I need to get out of this place. You go ahead of me." Martina goes down the garden with her and unlocks the back gate and walks with her up the alleyway, 'just in case'. April, feeling every inch of her age, plods to her car. She reaches it and leans down to get the keys from the front wheel where she left them.

Suddenly she is engulfed from behind by two arms and inhales Sam's familiar scent. She turns.

"Thank God! Thank God!" and Sam grabs her and won't let go. "You're OK. Were you arrested? Did you find the mobile?" April just clings on, staggering slightly under Sam's pressure, wordlessly delighted to see her and realising how terrified and alone she has been. Then Trish is asking if she's OK and whether she's found the mobile.

"Yes," says April. "But only by accident. I spent all the time stuck in the bathroom, hidden behind their fucking huge waterfall bath."

Both Sam and Trish groan and grip her. They lean in to hear as she tells the story. "The things I've seen! Give me the Texas Chainsaw Massacre any day! I'm suffering from post-traumatic stress or whatever soldiers get. That bathroom is the worst place in the whole world, shiny black with spotlights. Why do you want spotlights in a bathroom? It means that every hair and pimple on his bum was highlighted! I've seen more close-ups of cocks and testicles since Deep Throat. Have you ever watched someone having a shit under a downlight?" She shuddered. "It's seared into my brain!"

"We've been waiting by your car," says Sam. "The stuff is under it. We couldn't leave you there on your own, dearest. We took it in turns and wandered round sometimes just to see what was happening, but no sign of you." She hugs her again.

"It would've been easy if I hadn't dropped the bloody mobile. I'm so useless," says April. "I owe you both bigtime!"

"You bet!"

"You weren't discovered and you got the mobile. That's the main thing."

"It was so brave of you," says Sam, "you could've been spotted anytime. And the mobile! You got the mobile!"

"The gods were on our side."

"Makes a change!" says April, though something she heard in there is making her nervous.

"Let's hope they stay there," says Sam.

Thirteen

Thursday night

April and Sam arrive at the Old Duke in April's car, with Trish behind idling along on Betty. They park up in their respective spaces and meet at the pub doorway, linking arms with April in the middle, and enter in a triumphant group. There is a band playing upstairs, so they easily find a table in the downstairs bar, although it's noisy with the sound of the rock beat making the ceiling vibrate. They chatter cheerfully whilst warming up, but then pause, huddle round and lean towards each other, elbows on the small table.

"Do you think we really got away with it?" whispers Sam. "I can't believe that when we get home there won't be a police car there."

"There's no reason why you should be involved at all," says April, "you have to stay out of this, you've done nothing. Just remember, you came out for a drink with us, that's all, say you were at Trish's place first. In case the sergeant has been watching my flat."

"I'm not leaving you in the lurch!" protests Sam, taking hold of Trish and April's hands.

"Actually darlin'," drawls Trish, "that would be the safest thing to do for all of us."

"The least people the better," agrees April, "I'll just say it was me. They need never know there was anyone else or that I was stuck behind the sodding bath…." Now both Trish and Sam join in and start arguing and justifying why it was better that they were the one, how each was the most sensible choice.

"You need to keep your job, April, Vince will keep me on here no matter what."

"I'm the one that can give them details, neither of you know where the jewellery was."

"They won't connect me to Martina, at all," says Sam, "so she'll be safe as well and can still pay the money. I insist I'm in this with you. I won't be left out."

"It's Kate's debt, I'm her mother. I must take this on my own and face the consequences. I don't want either of you to be in more trouble than you are already."

"I have form," boasts Trish, referring to the time she was arrested for growing dope, charged and let off with a suspended sentence.

"I haven't," says Sam in a patient tone of voice, "so they are more likely to view me leniently."

"Hugh would divorce you," chips in April.

"That might actually be a benefit," snaps Trish. They all sit back, glaring at each other.

"He could have custody of squealing Salome," and April makes a whining noise which Trish joins in. Sam looks momentarily disconcerted, but then as the noise gets louder, she covers her ears and starts smiling. Trish leans forward again and speaks,

"Sam, darlin', you can't even tell your own daughter to stop dumping Salome on you. How on earth would you stand up to the police?" April intervenes immediately,

"That's different, it's much harder to tell your nearest and dearest the truth. Much, much, harder."

"And how would you know that?" asks Trish.

"Stop, stop," begs Sam as April sits back suddenly. "Look, everyone, we've had a really terrible evening and now we're just taking it out on each other. We can't do this. We must stick together. Trish... Trish ..." she begs.

"OK. OK. I know I've overstepped the mark a bit. I'm sorry. You know how I get. I just really don't want to see either of you in jail."

"I'm sorry too," and April grabs their hands again, "it's my fault for involving you. You're my dearest closest friends and I'd never forgive myself if anything happened to either of you."

"Pax?" asks Sam as they all squeeze hands, "we most probably won't need to even think about it. I'm sorry I brought it up. Gosh I need a drink." Nobody has any money on them but Trish spots Biff, one of Stuart's friends, who comes over as she beckons. She talks to him in a low voice and he nods his long beard, at one time looking sideways towards where Sam and April are sitting and smiling, he whispers in Trish's ear who looks surprised and then he pats the side of his nose.

"He's loaded," says Trish as he leaves and makes his way to the bar, "and before you say anything, I've said I'll pay him later." She pauses for a second as the other two wait and gaze at her expectantly. "Well he said he was only too happy to buy us all drinks, especially one particular member of the party that he says is looking amazing tonight." April and Sam look knowingly at each other, shake their heads and grimace.

"No shame," says April fondly, "you have no shame."

"Well actually, it was you," continues Trish, "he likes to see a woman who's not averse to displaying her curves." April looks shocked and tugs at her double damart underwear and scarf, sees Sam's face and laughs. She stands up and turns around.

"Well I have to say," says Trish, "that the outfit is a definite improvement on some of the ones I've seen you in, darlin'."

"Actually," Sam adds, "I can see what he means. It's so long since I've seen you in something that shows your figure." April does a further twirl, pats her midriff bulge and stretches the scarf over her buttocks, tightening the knot on one side. There is a moment of silence.

"On the other hand ...." Trish begins but pauses as Biff appears, hugging the drinks that he dumps unceremoniously in front of them.

"One pint of best, two glasses and a bottle of red, I remembered from yesterday. Are you going to become a regular?" and he winks at April and strokes his bald head. Sam and Trish are suddenly busy getting the drinks in order whilst April blushes and looks at the table. Trish gives her a nudge.

"Thanks Biff," she manages to stutter out. Biff smiles at her and turns away and goes back to his place at the bar. Covertly (she thinks) April watches him, noting his jeans, loose T-shirt, firm rotund stomach and earring. He turns and smiles back at her, a warm smile, a friendly face, not in any way handsome, a bit strange with a combination of long greying beard and bald head. She picks up her glass of wine to find Sam and Trish both looking at her questioningly with raised eyebrows.

"OK. OK," she protests, "not my type. But a nice face." Sam turns slightly to look at Biff and smiles back at April.

"And the rest?" she asks.

"Come on now, Sam, I am still in shock. I've seen so much pudenda I didn't want to see tonight. I think I'll wear a blindfold from now on."

"What was his tackle like?" Trish laughs whilst April groans.

"Please don't ask me to describe it!" Trish and Sam press in closer and fire questions at her.

"Circumcised?"

"Droopy bollocks?"

"Length?"

To each question April shudders and takes another swig of her wine, not saying anything, then chuckles, leans forward and starts describing. After a little while they all raise their glasses to toast each other before going upstairs to join the dancing.

Fourteen

Friday morning

April and Sam arrive at Trish's on a large council estate. The apparent disarray outside mirrors the inside; there is a system in it all, but it is hard to find for those who are not living amongst it. The whole house is not a refuge but a place to start from, to sleep in and then get away, a variation on a nomad's tent but in brick.

"Hello April and Sam, sweethearts," calls Stuart "didn't expect to see you back so early." He chuckles, and his usually fierce face relaxes into warmth.

"A night never to be forgotten. I think we'll celebrate it every year," says April.

"Trish is inside," he says, "expecting you." April pats the dog as they pass a huge gothic mirror in the hall with its mass of scrawled and stick-it note messages. In the front room Trish sits, swearing madly at the computer and repeatedly poking the return key to the dead bell sound of something wrong. She is perched in a white garden chair that is obviously too low for the keyboard that lies on an ornate Georgian desk whose tooled leather top is covered in marks.

The whole room and house seems to have been furnished at random; in this room an obviously cheap sofa from a garden centre stands alongside a couple of Lloyd loom chairs, a brass standard lamp and a bookcase made of planks and bricks. Most surfaces are covered with biker mags and spare parts.

"At last!" Trish says, getting up and they form a trio hug. "Recovered from last night?"

"The heist? Or after?"

"The heist of course, I expect you both to be able to manage an after- party."

"I slept well," says April, "just a bit of a shock again this morning, woken by Martina's bloody phone call. Just phoned you, got dressed and came here. Still not really awake."

"That might explain your choice of clothes," says Trish, referring to the puce trouser suit April is wearing.

"Bloody cheek, you old tart," retorts April "getting your mother's habits?" There is a wry smile from Trish whilst Sam tells them both to cool it and goes into the kitchen.

"So? What did Martina say?" asks Trish as Sam returns and begins collecting crockery and taking it to the kitchen as they speak. This is no reflection on Trish's appalling housekeeping, but a need Sam has to put order into chaos and to repair a bit of the damage they made last night when they returned here. She takes one overflowing ashtray into the kitchen.

"Said she had to see us IMMEDIATELY and would we meet at your place, like, as soon as poss, like. I asked if we'd been, like, found out and she said no, like, more complicated than that."

"OK, OK. I get the gist. I'll have my ears 'liked' by her soon enough. I hope she's quick. I have to go to work."

"Had a bath yet, April?" calls Sam from the kitchen with a chuckle.

"Don't start! I'm never going near any bathroom ever again, especially if it's black. I could barely go into the loo this morning, luckily mine is so old it's still avocado-coloured."

"Where's the tea, Sam?" yells Trish, "you're taking your time."

"Bloody cheek! I must be doing about two months' worth of washing up, here, just to get to the mugs. Anyway, I thought washing up was men's work."

"Marigolds Maketh Man," shouts April, her usual after-dinner remark.

"Don't fucking bother with the stuff," bellows Trish, "there will only be more, there always is! Just do four mugs!"

"Do you look at your sink ever? First I have to find the mugs in all this."

"Must be novel for you, with your flash dishwasher, to actually dip your hands into a washing up bowl."

"Well I like that! This mess has clearly not seen your hands for months."

They are cheerfully insulting each other, when Martina runs lightly up the path and into the house and pops her head round the front room door.

"Hi all. Where's Sam?" Sam calls out from the kitchen, saying she's a slave to tea and she'll make one for Martina. April clears a few chairs so they all have a place to sit. Trish makes a roll-up while Martina walks round the room.

"I can't get the money," says Martina bluntly, a remark that drops like an elephant onto a brass band.

"I thought so," says Trish. April merely stares. Sam is silent in the kitchen.

Martina shakes her head.

"I, like, tried, this morning, but they want my mother to come along AND they, like, want 24 hours notice so they can get the cash in. I gave them that."

"So we're fucked," says April.

"Well I do, like, have this idea."

"Stop fucking saying 'like'," splurts out April, flinging herself down on the old garden chair that skews sideways as she lands. "Not another bloody idea!"

"Look, I really mean to pay up. This is a wicked idea. It'll work absolutely."

"Shut up, Martina, shut up!" Trish is shouting and slamming round the room, throwing a magazine, an ashtray, a bike part to the floor, swearing. April, slumped in her chair, half-heartedly joins in the abuse. Martina stands still, looking shocked, she opens her mouth, but Sam comes in from the kitchen, having heard everything, and pulls her softly back.

"Let me," she says quietly to her. "You've done enough damage. Bloody annoying, if you don't mind me saying." Sam walks into the middle of the maelstrom and stands calmly whilst Trish storms and April despairs.

"Bloody annoying," she says. "Really irritating." Trish lets out a barrage of swear words, but April looks up and Sam sees that she is near to tears.

"What'll I do now?" she asks Sam, "what's going to happen? I've no chance of making it." Trish is silent for a second.

"Hush," says Sam, handing April a tissue and patting her shoulder.

April suddenly snorts, "If you only knew how often I heard that word yesterday!"

"Sam darlin', 'really irritating' doesn't begin to describe being absolutely conned!"

"I stole!" says April. "I'm now officially a criminal. My grandfather would turn in his grave! And all for nothing."

"Clever girls," says Sam. "I'm really proud of you both. Daring women. Doing what needs to be done."

"It wasn't really stealing," says Martina's voice from the doorway, "just getting what's mine and my mother's."

"So why didn't you do it, then, if it was that simple?" asks April as Martina walks round the room.

"He said he didn't have some bits of jewellery, said he'd not seen them. He, like, wanted big tits to have them. But he, like, has now declared to the police that he has them AND said that they belong to my mother. That's all down on the police report. So, he can't say, like, he doesn't know where they are anymore. I don't want to cheat you. I really do want to give you the money."

"So that's what it was for!" says Trish, sitting down on one of the battered Lloyd Loom chair. "For your mother."

"Are you going to give them to the police?" says April, flabbergasted. "Please answer without saying fucking like!"

"Of course I'll turn them in. I'm not a bad guy. A friend is handing them in as we speak."

"How can he?" says April half-laughing "when we still have them," but Trish interrupts and glares at Martina accusingly.

"So, there's another bit to all this?" she asks and seeing Martina rest back in her chair say, "I knew it."

Martina takes her place in the middle of the room and explains, turning to speak to all of them.

"You have to understand. Mum has these jewels, a really wicked set: a necklace with a matching bracelet and ring. They belonged to her grandmother. They always go to the eldest daughter. They're special. Called Navratna, that means nine jewels set in a particular order and each one has to be perfect. They're not just beautiful. My mum believes they bring blessings. But they are ..." she stops and widens her hands, " just ... Wow!" She pauses and looks round at the three women. "Wow!" she says again. April shrugs. Martina continues, speaking faster.

'They're mine really, eventually. But definitely my mother's. But she just upped and left and said I could have them. But then ... then ... He showed them to bouncy boobs. She started wearing the necklace. I saw it. I told him my mum wanted them back and that they were mine. Then he told me he didn't have them. I just couldn't believe it! I knew where they were. So, I asked you to do a robbery. I know it's a strange way of doing things but it's just righting a wrong really. Getting back what belongs to me and my mother. Mum says I can have part of the value of them. I'll be able to put a deposit on a house, get away from them upstairs. Or maybe just stay in the basement annoying them."

"A deposit?" exclaims Trish.

"How much are they worth?" asks Sam.

"So, you haven't seen the local paper this morning?"

"What!"

"What do you mean?"

"What have you done?"

"Together, like, with the rest, they're worth about half a million pounds. They've reported it in the Downland Herald."

Quiet drops over the room. There is the most stunned silence, this one has depth, open mouths, slack jaws, staring eyes, no breath.

"The value means detectives are being sent to investigate. That's why they have to be handed in. I don't want all that money; mum will be coming back at some time and she'll need it."

"Fuck me, why weren't they in a safe?"

"They were..."

"No they bloody weren't," says Trish, "when I was messing up the place I went into the drawing room and the safe door was open behind that picture and it was completely empty. I remember thinking how strange."

"Actually, like, they were in the safe. I opened the safe and cleared it out before we left for the restaurant. He doesn't know I have the code. He hasn't, like, changed it for years. What you have here is worth nothing, maybe a couple of grand or so in total."

"For God's sake," exclaims April, "what have you done? I can't believe you've landed us in such a mess! You've set us up."

"Don't worry. My friend's reporting he's found them," says Martina, "Will be happening any time now. They'll call off the unit once the stuff is, like, returned."

"God, you're tricky," says Trish.

"Always was," says April. "I remember now, in the bathroom she said something about other stuff in the safe… it didn't make sense at the time."

"I thought the open safe must be normal for your dad," says Trish. Sam, who's having trouble coming to terms with this change in events, asks again about the value of the jewellery that April and Trish now have. Martina repeats that it is of little value as all the really expensive items were in the safe and that the burglary has left the police confused. "Some really amateur stuff and some really professional. They think there was, like, a father and son maybe."

"Fuck me! You mean I spent half a night watching your father having the world's largest crap and scratching his bollocks for nothing?"

"Not for nothing! I'm going to get the money. I said I would. I owe you. I want to help Kate anyway."

"Oh yeah? How?" asks April.

"One of you has to be my mother."

"And go to the bank with you?"

"Yes and sign a form. That's all. I have a copy of my mother's signature." There is a burst of chatter as all the three give their reactions but Martina cuts into this, "That's not the only reason I called you." She has to say this several times. "That's not all. There's something else I want to tell you." Eventually she gets heard and there is a grumbling silence. "I cleared out the safe, as I said. Hid the stuff." April asks where. "In plain sight. In a folder in his study. Got it this morning." Martina is now up and pacing round the room. "I cleared out all the safe, everything in it, thinking if there were burglars, they would take everything. Anyway, this morning I'm sorting through and I come across this." She fishes under her jacket and takes out a large brown envelope with PRIVATE CONFIDENTIAL KEEP SAFE scrawled across it. "I knew it was my brother's handwriting, recognised it immediately. He came to the house a few months back, spent some time with my father. I opened it of course."

"Of course," says Trish as Martina takes a large bound report out of the envelope.

"It's, like, accounts." All the women shrug.

"So what?" says Trish. Martina looks hard at April.

"I think it's the accounts of that company Kate was sacked for. It's a large American bank, you've heard of it, The Dearing Brothers. I think this was what she was auditing when they dismissed her." April looks interested.

"So you think Kate went to America with your brother to audit this company, saw the figures were wrong, quarrelled with him about it, got back and was given the sack. You think there's something false in these accounts?"

"Exactly. Why else hide them? Maybe criminal even."

"Why would he hide them there? Away from his work at your home?" asks Trish.

"Well," says Martina, "this is where it gets interesting." Trish groans and puts her head in her hands, "I think they're a safety net for him. I think he's a lazy bugger and he's most probably facing the sack himself. But not if he has these."

"That's a bit of a jump," says Trish.

"Yeah, I know, but I think if Kate had these she could put the pressure on."

"Why aren't you in prison?" asks April. "First, you want us to steal. Now you want Kate to blackmail. Hold on, I know why you aren't in jail, it's because you get others to do your dirty work. Does it never stop?"

"Look April, believe me she needs to see these. She can decide what to do with them. I'm not doing anything."

"Only problem is we can't find her," says April.

"You have them," says Martina, giving them to April, "take them. When she comes back, you give them to her. See what she says." April flicks through the report that is quite thick and filled with pages of numbers. It means nothing to her. She puts it into her handbag with a slight mystified shake of her head.

"What about the money you owe us?" she asks.

"Someone has to be my mother. One of you."

There follows disbelief, an argument and a long talk with other ideas being suggested but none of them will get the cash by tomorrow, all of them have been discussed before and dismissed. They go around again but come up with no new ideas.

"I'll do it," says Sam out of nowhere. "I didn't play my part in the first bit."

"You would actually be my choice," says Martina, "you are the one that looks most like her, just change your make-up a bit and hide the hair."

"My mother was Greek, so I'm dark. I can forge any signature if I practice."

"You'll need to memorise stuff: date of birth, address, postcode."

"I can do that." There is an outcry from April and Trish but they cannot move her. "I'll do it whether you want me to or not," says Sam. "Come on, Martina, we're going back to my place to look at clothes and practice." She goes to the door, "Don't worry I'll keep a firm hold of the cash," she says as she passes Trish.

"Watch Martina. Watch her, watch her," warns Trish.

"I'm coming with you, Sam," says April.

After they leave Trish is throwing some old food remains into black rubbish sacks that are already overflowing when she hears the phone ring and stops to listen, dreading to hear the sound of her mother's voice saying she knows about the cheque. All week Trish has been cursing herself for putting it into an old building society rather than using a more unorthodox but quicker method to cash it in. Tomorrow it will be cleared. Only another 24 hours. She comforts herself with the fact that Stuart told her he did not write anything on the stub and made sure that the cheque came from the centre of the book. Anyway, it might all be useless if Martina can't get the money out of the bank. She hears the answerphone kick in.

"Patricia, Patricia," comes her father's voice, "is your mother with you? She's gone missing I can't find her anywhere. Please help me look for her? She said she was coming to see you, but she's not slept in the bed." Trish picks up the phone wearily. At least she is forewarned this time.

"Papa, it's me. Is there anybody there with you?"

"Nobody, she's gone. I woke up this morning and the bed hadn't been slept in."

"Can you look in your pockets? Do you have any notes there?" But her father says he doesn't have any notes in his pockets, only £20. She presumes that her mother has gone shopping, or is out for her walk, and probably has arrangements for someone to be with him, so she tells her father to wait for a moment and her mother will be back. Then, with some annoyance, she makes a phone call to her brother Anthony, telling him that their father is complaining again and saying that, as she has done her stint earlier that week, it is over to him.

She goes back to sorting out the kitchen, takes the bin bags out and loses interest in cleaning. She is dispirited, she thinks that Sam is walking into a trap but does not know how to stop her. She has to go to the pub soon anyway, she has no time for this. The phone goes again, and it is her father once more and she ignores him as he rambles on, repeating himself. She has officially handed the headache over to Anthony. She wonders about pulling the phone out but doesn't want to, in case April or Sam need help.

She is up in the bedroom getting dressed in a sexy outfit which usually makes her feel good. But after looking at herself in a mirror she changes out of the fishnet tights and short black skirt into jeans and a t shirt. The phone goes again. She stands at the top of the stairs and listens as Anthony leaves his message.

"There's a first time for everything I suppose. Thanks for your phone call."

"Nice to hear from you too," Trish replies sarcastically to the air.

"Well once bitten twice shy, thank God, at least you haven't called the fuzz out this time. No, Patricia, I've no idea where mummy is, most probably up in the attic tidying up from the mess left after your last visit. I'll get onto Geoffrey, see if he's back yet and knows anything about it. Best of love, sister dear. So nice we're back now in REGULAR touch." And he rings off. She chuckles, remembering that he was always her favourite brother and has just got back downstairs to make a coffee when the doorbell rings.

Noting that the time is about 11 she wonders if it is the postman with a package, Ricky has talked about ordering parts. She flings open the door to see her mother standing primly on the porch wearing her best casual angora jacket and a smug smile. She is holding a small jar of caviar and a packet of blini. On the driveway behind her sits her glossy red Mercedes.

"Don't look so pleased to see me." Her mother speaks as Trish takes a shocked step back. But Trish knows the determination behind that smile and so she opens the door, gesturing to her mother to step inside and walks ahead of her to the kitchen, asking her if she wants some coffee. As her mother enters her home, Trish can feel the hard breeze of her disapproval, but Trish is used to this. She does not need to apologise or explain how she lives; she's always known what her mother thinks about it and it has no weight with her, in fact it makes her walk more jauntily and regret her change of clothing.

"I have got a bottle of fizzy in the car, to go with the caviar." Her mother says, opening the fridge and depositing the caviar on a shelf, pointedly moving the half empty milk cartons, the remains of a pizza looking suspiciously hardened and tins that have been opened and dropping them into the half-filled bin bags.

"I'll make the coffee first," says Trish and boils the kettle. Virtually the only thing that Trish is particular about is coffee and she makes some fresh in a cafetière. Thanks to Sam's actions the kitchen is looking relatively clean and finding two mugs is easy. She directs her mother into the living room and towards one of the Lloyd Loom chairs whilst the conversation hardly sparkles.

"I hope you're getting better."

"Much better, really well in fact. I was out of the hospital that afternoon." Her mother removes a motor bike part from the chair and turns whilst holding it with two fingers.

"Good." Trish takes the part and throws it onto the sofa where it crashes against some others.

"It was keyhole surgery so only a very small scar." Her mother looks down and pointedly brushes the cushions vigorously before perching on the very edge.

"Great." Trish turns her own garden chair round but has to straighten one of its bent legs before sitting carefully in it. Silence drops into the room until Trish hears the kettle boiling and fetches the coffee from the kitchen.

"And virtually no aftereffects." Her mother continues, dusting the arms of the chair with hard swipes before clapping her hands together and sighing as Trish hands her the coffee mug, "Jolly good."

"I hardly feel anything at all." Her mother inspects the coffee mug and doesn't drink it but places it on her lap.

"Good-oh. I presume papa was alright?"

"Fine. Marjorie went there. The place is still a mess. The attic is a total shambles." Her mother is looking round with resignation. "So that's where you put Great Aunt Irene's desk. I did wonder."

"Papa phoned me this morning actually."

"I hope you didn't do anything silly again? Marjorie is on her way there."

"You could pay for a carer?"

"Thanks for your advice."

"Is the coffee OK?"

"Fine I'm sure," says her mother, moving an ashtray overflowing with butts, including a couple of roaches, off the nearby table and putting her mug down in its place. Trish watches her ignoring the coffee and knows from her cheerful demeanour that she is gloating.

"Mama, what are you doing here?"

"Well I thought I'd bring you the caviar you so despise."

"And?"

"Why does there have to be an 'and'? I wanted to see how you lived now."

"So?"

"So it is as I remembered. A bit better, if anything, for a council house, but still dreadful. You've made it worse of course. Shall I get the fizz and open the blinis and caviar?"

"What, forget the coffee?"

"Unless you need it this morning after getting drunk last night?"

"I've already had some. And yes, I was partying HARD last night. What did you expect?" Her mother steps away with a tut, carefully lifting her suede loafers delicately off the grimy floor and goes out to the car as Trish rolls a cigarette and snatches up her phone. She sends a text to April telling her to keep watching and to stop Sam from doing anything stupid. Also Vince at the pub to tell him she'll be a bit late. Her mother goes into the kitchen and busies herself there, occasionally calling out for things such as glasses, plates, a good cutting knife. Trish sits and smokes her roll-up, calling out answers and feeling irritated and wrong-footed by her mother's assured presence. Her mother returns to clear a space on a table and sets out the blinis which have been topped with crème fraiche, finely chopped boiled eggs and caviar. She opens the bottle of champagne and fills the glasses, then proceeds to help Trish and herself to the snacks.

"I'm not wonderfully smitten with caviar, as you know," says Trish, taking a sip of champagne. "But ta anyway. I do like champers." Her mother smiles graciously. "So what is this for? What are we celebrating?"

"I thought I should come and see you to soften the blow."

"What's happened?"

"I've stopped the cheque, that's what's happened," and she bites cheerfully into the blini. "And I have an offer for you."

Fifteen

Friday afternoon

April drives Sam and Martina to Sam's house whilst the jewellery rolls in the boot of the car, making them all snigger. Sam makes them coffee in the kitchen which they take up to her studio. Martina has been talking non-stop, complimenting Sam on her house, showing some knowledge of painting and now is wandering round her studio asking questions.

"What a cool room. Wow! Is that your sketchbook? Your mother was an artist too? How cool. Is this your stuff here? What are you making now? What an amazing drawing, a prototype for earrings? That's beautiful. How do you do enamelling? That's amazing. You do yoga? Did you paint this as well?"

Sam answers all these questions, and despite Trish's warnings is beginning to like Martina, she's so full of enthusiasm, so respectful of what Sam's doing. It's such a change to meet a person who is genuinely interested in her work.

"That knee looks a bit weird." Martina is scrutinizing a life sketch that Sam drew several decades ago.

"Yeah," says Sam, "I got the angle wrong; it was bent back." They both lean in to look at it more closely, "but I always seemed to get plants and insects, particularly butterflies, right, the natural world has always spoken to me." Martina nods, turning over the pages, and April speaks.

"Can I just stop this? Great that you're interested, Martina, but let's get on with the stuff, shall we?" They both step back and Martina digs into her jacket and comes out with a driving licence saying it's her mother's and she's only been in India a couple of years, but they can get the signature and the date of birth from this.

"You'll need to change your look a bit," she continues, and when April asks why, Martina says that her mother's passport was used to open the account, so they will have the same photo on the system. "I went with her everywhere," Martina continues, "she was in such a state that I did everything for her, got the flights, got her new passport, got her visa for India. She just wanted to get out, 'go home' as she put it. She lost her driving licence when she got there so I got this new copy but never sent it to her. She moved round relatives for a while then six months later she was in Rishikesh 'sitting at the foot of the master'. Like, got fed up of visiting all the extended family. Been quieter since then. Seems happy.

Annoying emails though, about me needing to find inner peace and worldly goods are nothing. I hope she's sending the same to my brother. It's well expensive. The master must be sitting on masses of worldly goods. Doesn't seem to interfere with his karma. About time I went to visit."

"Right," says Sam, "first the signature." She looks at it and is encouraged, saying it's not so hard, has a certain artistic style. She gets out a pen and paper and starts copying repeatedly, getting the flow. Meanwhile April and Martina consult over how they can change her look.

"It's the impression you want," says Martina.

"What? A sari?"

"No, that's gross! My mum hasn't worn a sari in the UK for ever! Certainly not to go to the bank."

"What then?"

"A business suit. She was, well is, a director of a few companies. I have some of her gear at home that should fit Sam. I have a whole suitcase of her stuff, ready for when she returns."

"What happened to the 'like'?"

"I'm learning." They all go down to Sam's bedroom to look in the wardrobe, they flick through her clothing as Sam continues practicing the signature.

"Is nothing here suitable?" asks April. Martina shakes her head.

"They're all too Sam." April can only nod her head in agreement. Nothing says 'businesswoman'. Every item says 'artist'. They flick through her sparse supply of mainly crushed linen clothing dismissively.

"Sam'll need some good high-heeled shoes or boots to go with the suit, her ethnic footwear is totally uncool. My mum def wouldn't wear those." She points at Sam's flat, hand-stitched footwear. "Hey Sam, what size feet do you have?" Sam turns and tells them she's a size five and Martina says she thinks her mother's will fit. The problem is finding a suitable executive cover for her hair. They fetch and examine a number of Sam's artistic hats and then scarves, but none is right.

"Ask me the questions now," begs Sam so they go through name, address, date and place of birth, and pin number repeatedly. Sam gets better with time and shows them the signature. They examine it and agree that it is good. But she needs to make it flow effortlessly. Martina says that she can come back tomorrow morning with the dresses and shoes and help Sam into them. April insists that she will drive them to the bank and wait, as she has to collect the cash from Philip Henderson's cheque anyway. She will park in the High Street and be there to pick them up.

A child's crying disturbs them. It is coming from downstairs.

"It's Helen," stammered Sam. "With Salome. You'll have to go down," she whispers. "Distract her, give me some time to hide things." April goes down to the kitchen where Helen is attempting to microwave a jar of organic mush for Salome who is hanging from one of Helen's arms, almost upside down.

"Hiya Helen, I'll do that," she says, and is passed Salome immediately. "I meant microwave the food," she blurts out, trying to grip Salome and make her sit upright. Salome flops, almost landing on the tiles, but April catches her just in time and puts her down where she melts into the floor and lies there on her back, singing tunelessly to herself.

"For God's sake," says Helen, "what is with you lot and the kitchen floor? Haven't you heard of a highchair or did all of your children grub about in the dirt?" April is about to make a restrained reply when Martina steps into the room.

"Bit rude," says Martina, "she seems happy down there to me." She turns to April, "Is this the kid that, like, won't stop crying? That is dumped on Sam, like, everyday?"

"Who are you?" asks Helen, "it's no business of yours what I do." She takes off her hat and throws back her head to see this stranger more clearly.

"Cool hat," says Martina, "just what your mother wants. A bit dressed up, aren't you? You must be going somewhere." There is a moment's silence as April looks at Helen and recognises the truth of this immediately: she is wearing a low-cut mauve top over tight

194

designer jeans and her lips are glossed. "Not really suitable for looking after a toddler," continues Martina, "more a meal out with someone. Ah, perfume! And do I smell fresh underwear?" There is a moment's stunned silence as Helen blushes and then she pushes past Martina and up the stairs, calling out for her mother. Martina looks innocently at April who can't help sniggering. Martina picks up the jar of home-made baby food, finds a spoon and sits down on the floor next to Salome and feeds her whilst the voices argue in the bedroom with Helen's being the loudest and longest. Eventually the mother and daughter descend to the kitchen, Helen still protesting, Sam still soothing.

"I've no idea what you're up to anymore. These so-called friends of yours..." Helen gestures round the room to where April is munching on some shortbread she's found and Martina is licking the spoon after feeding Salome.

"Would you like a cup of tea, dearest?"

"No I bloody wouldn't. I only came to let you spend some time with Salome."

"So, you're staying then?" asks April pointedly.

"No, actually, I need some time away. You wouldn't understand." April shrugs.

"So your mother is looking after your daughter for you?" states Martina, wiping Salome's mouth. "Again?" She adds at the last critical moment.

"It's got nothing whatsoever to do with you. I don't know you. I don't want to know you." She is working herself into a rage and Salome stops eating, looks at her mother and begins to cry. Sam makes a cooing sound and bends down and picks up Salome who struggles in her arms.

"I know you, though," says Martina, "used to go out with my

brother. William Chowdhury. Wanker William." Helen suddenly is bright red. "So, he's back in town then? Figures." She plucks Salome from Sam and hands her to Helen. "Look after your own daughter. Your kind and talented mother is busy. She has a life of her own. She won't babysit whilst you go out with wanker William."

Helen splutters, glares at Sam who is looking confused and, telling Sam to follow her, stalks out of the room. She turns to collect her hat, but Martina snatches it off the table, saying, "William hates women in hats," making Helen give a snort of anger.

"Oh dearest," protests Sam, following Helen out, glaring at Martina and snatching the hat back from her. They hear a conversation at the door and down the drive. April makes tea and then toast and they eat whilst talking.

"He always keeps his old girlfriends close," says Martina. "He has 'a tart in every town' as he puts it. Can't be bothered with taking time making new contacts. Just wants a fuck and off. Sam's daughter is a prize bitch, always was. Deserves him. Of course she wouldn't remember me, too up her own arse. What's her husband like?"

"Seems nice enough," says April.

"Boring eh? And Sam's husband?" April doesn't say anything, feeling that discussing Sam's choice with Martina would be disloyal. "Oh, the same?" April protests that he is a nice man and Martina laughs. Sam appears carrying Salome who has stopped crying.

"Well really, Martina, whatever got into you?" she puts Salome down on a chair. "Of course Helen isn't having an affair with your brother. She and Jeremy get on really well. She's going to meet an old schoolfriend. But she did give me the hat, said it suited me." She turns her head from side to side, showing off the hat.

"It does," says Martina. "We can push your hair under it and the peak should provide a bit of cover from the cameras in the bank."

She adjusts the cap on Sam's head, tucking bits of hair underneath but suddenly turns away as her phone makes a dinging sound. She reads and gives a chuckle.

"It's done," she turns to them both, "you are off the hook. The stuff in the safe has been handed in to the police." She smiles widely, the first time this week April has seen her happy. "You can relax now."

"So we're only small-time thieves," says April, wondering why she doesn't feel completely reassured. But Sam smiles back at Martina and laughs 'phew!' whilst going to make more coffee. Salome sucks her thumb, climbs off the chair and, putting her cheek on the floor, hums tunelessly.

"The benefits of underfloor heating," says April.

Outside her flat April looks round, noticing with relief that there are no black cars outside belonging to either the police or the gamblers. It's three p.m., so she can have a little doze before having a bath and preparing for tomorrow. She drops her keys on the kitchen table and turns with a sigh to ease her bra strap down one arm. As she starts the kettle, she hears a sound coming from the back of her flat and freezes. She tiptoes to pick up a knife, stalks carefully with her back to one wall and calls out,

"Who's there?" Kate is standing in her bedroom doorway, looking baggy-eyed and dishevelled as if she hasn't been sleeping well or at all. April runs towards her with a sob of relief, dropping the knife and hugs her, almost knocking her over in her rush.

"Kate, thank God, you're alright. Thank God. Thank God," she cries and feeling Kate's arms go around her, strokes her familiar flesh, breathes in her smell, kisses her neck, clutches her, touches her, home at last. She draws back for a moment, looks into Kate's eyes, sees the inward look of the defeated and kisses her forehead. "My best, my favourite daughter." Kate laughs wryly, her eyes still shadowed,

"Oh mum. I'm sorry, mum, I really am. I've done something terrible." She steps back for a second, "Whatever are you wearing?" April laughs and releases the other breast with a tug and throws the bra onto the table. Kate laughs as well. "Oh mum, I've missed you so much. But you're never going to forgive me. I've been such an idiot." But April shushes her and tells her she knows everything.

They sit down for a while and talk, April being selective in what she tells her, not wanting to trouble her further.

"I'm so sorry, mum," says Kate, standing up again. "I knew they'd come here but I just thought, stupidly, that they'd ask for me and then leave."

"They threatened me, two men, the smallest one broke all my crockery including gran's jubilee mug. They said that unless I gave them the money something would happen to you or me or the flat. They said if I didn't give them the money something terrible would happen, talked about fires and accidents. I was terrified they'd put you in hospital."

"Oh mum, I had no idea. Really. I should've come back sooner."

"You left your mobile. I had no way of contacting you. I didn't know where you were or whether you were safe. I phoned the hospitals almost daily, just checking."

"I'm sorry, I'm sorry. I'm so sorry."

"I was so frightened for you. I'm so glad you're OK." She stands up again, trying to quiet Kate, pats her shoulder, strokes her arm, then turns away for a moment. "It really hurt you know, not because of the job, but because you didn't tell me anything. Then you just left. I didn't know where you were or if you were OK."

"I'm back. I'm here. I'm so sorry. Will you forgive me, mum?" she asks. But April merely cries and can't speak, so they sit down beside each other on the sofa. April tells her what she's heard from Martina about Kate's dismissal.

"Oh mum. I had the best job ever. You know it's not the numbers that interest me, though that's always come easy, it's the people, the different companies, the atmosphere. I was working in London, the City, learning so much, I was mixing with such people, getting their experience. Managers took me seriously. Will finally took notice of me in a good way, he was a bigwig in the company, friends with the boss. We started going to clubs, restaurants, theatre, cinema. I was eating in the same place as Kate Moss, the Beckhams. Getting more responsibility, I could see my future. I saw how you could get out of this." She looks around the small rented flat with its second-hand furniture. "I was spending my time in a penthouse overlooking the Thames. At night we saw the lights of London set out for us, the curves along the river in the morning mist with the barges moving slowly. We went on weekend breaks, Rome, Prague, Florence, holidays in Rio, Moscow. I can't name them all. I'm sorry, mum, just so sorry I lost touch for a while. I was in love. I thought I was in love. I thought we were in love. I was so stupid."

"He pushed you off your bike," said April, "you forgot that."

"Oh mum, people change."

"Apparently not Wanker William."

"I'd forgotten! How could I forget? Anyway, I don't know how involved he is really."

"Martina gave me this for you, from her father's safe." April gets up and digs out the file from her bag and hands it to her. Kate takes it with a chuckle and puts it down without really looking at it.

"Typical Martina, raiding her father's safe. She's a good friend underneath it all. She's having a bit of a rough time at the moment." Kate then tells her story as April makes her tea, peels and chops vegetables to create a soup, makes her eat, cuts her bread and, watches her as she talks.

"I went to this firm in New York. Will was so excited; he loves New York. I was just there to learn, shouldn't really even have been there, I didn't go to the big meetings, stayed in the hotel, the most beautiful hotel, it was art nouveau, so gorgeous, Lady Di stayed there once. I just floated around.

Then one day I looked at the report the team was making. Will had left it there. I laid on the bed and read it, I took it downstairs and had a massage reading it. I noticed something. It's hard to explain. It was about how they classified their assets. It was wrong and if it was wrong then one of the most important banks in the world was in trouble. I didn't get it. I thought I must have misunderstood, and Will would set me right. After all I'd never audited such an important company, there must be a quirk somewhere, I'd only been learning for a couple of years. Maybe this was a permitted way of putting the figures. Maybe they had different rules in America. I knew some banks were in trouble, didn't know how bad it was getting. It was all just rumours." She stops and looks around, asks if April has any wine, April shakes her head, saying only tea or coffee, Kate continues with difficulty. "Will went berserk when he saw I'd been reading the report, shouted at me saying I was prying, I shouldn't have read it, it was draft. Then he laughed and said how silly he was to get so angry and kissed me, only he would be in trouble if they knew he'd kept a copy, the final version hadn't been agreed.

After we'd made love, I asked him a question. Then everything changed, he became cold, efficient, suspicious, accused me of spying, said he knew my mother was a communist. He knew the riff-raff I mixed with. He told me to pack and go. If I liked low life so much, I should go back to it." She stops and cries. April sits and cuddles her, wanting to rock away the pain as she used to do when she was four or five. "I flew back economy. When I got to work the next day my pass into the building didn't work, my assistant came downstairs in tears with my private things in a cardboard box. That was it. I'd lost everything. Everything I thought I'd built up vanished. Who would employ me now? I tried phoning colleagues, they didn't reply, the rumours were that I'd done something criminal. All the friends I thought I'd made, gone. Nobody even phoned to ask me about it. Not one. I went to my flat, got just the basic essentials and left.

I came back to you, but how could I tell you what had happened? What a mess I'd made of everything? I ruined it all. I had my chance and I'd lost it. If only I'd kept my mouth shut. I cried and cried. But what could I tell you? I didn't want to tell you how unhappy I was. How I'd screwed up. You all thought so much of me. I tried and tried to talk to Will. He blocked my texts and calls. That's it. I couldn't see any way out. I drank. I gambled. It all seemed a game. Still does. I lost as I we've always lost. I knew I'd lose."

"You don't lose. You've never lost. You've never lost anything of any importance. You're my golden girl who can and will do anything she wants." April gives Kate tiny shakes, trying to get across her point. "Don't let Wanker William win. Don't let them tell you what you can and can't do."

"I'm so ashamed, I lost my chance."

"You haven't lost your chance; you've lost your fight. You let them beat it out of you. Can you remember grampa saying the ones to watch were the ones in suits? You forgot that. You have to fight back, there must be a way."

"There's nothing I can do. I went to Grampa's grave."

"All the way to Leeds?" Kate nods.

"I hitched. I spent ages finding the place. Finally, I found the road where we used to live and then my feet took me to their church. I prayed, mum. I prayed, but nothing happened. I went to the graveyard, they were both there, but there was only silence, just their gravestones. I don't know what I expected. I loved them, they loved me, but I'd let them down."

"No, you haven't. He would've replied, so would she, maybe you're not hearing them. He would've said get up and get going. Can you remember him in the miner's strike?" Kate chuckles.

"He went out and joined the pickets. But they lost anyway, didn't they?"

"They went down fighting, that's what matters."

"He hit a policemen over the head with his walking stick!" and at last Kate laughed and April joined in.

"He was let off and came back next day with grandma. By God he made their lives difficult."

"They sweated. He ruffled them. I had forgotten." Kate swallowed. "I went to all the places I grew up in. It had all changed so much. I ended up in a hostel. It was awful. I realised how far I'd forgotten them and what they tried to give us.

When I was spending all that money, living the high life in London, I never thought of how they lived all their lives. Looking after us when your mother wouldn't. Never complaining. Going to chapel. Believing in the goodness of others. Helping where they could with what little they had. Holding to the truth, building up treasure in heaven. Giving to the poor when they had so little. Thanking God for every meal, no matter how small it was." She shakes her head and tears fall onto her hands. "I'd spent in a year more than they made in their whole lives. I'd eaten it, slept it, drank it, worn it. I'd not thought of anyone else. What a waste. I could have given you some luxury."

"This is luxury," says April, "having you here with me, safe, eating with you. This is luxury. This is all I need."

"But I so wanted to make you proud."

"I was always proud of you."

"I wanted to make life easier for you."

"Well you've certainly failed in that one!" and April laughs. "But I never expected you to make my life easier. Who has a child thinking their life will be easier?" She leans over and tucks Kate's hair behind her ears, "I know I haven't been a good role model for you," and she hushes Kate who is shaking her head and protesting, "I so wanted you to have what I never had, a continual loving mother. But I stopped being brave. I was frightened of taking chances and maybe I passed that on to you. But this week has taught me that I have the strength to do unexpected things. And so do you. You are part of me and if I can take risks then so can you." She pauses, watching Kate cry and leans back a little. "You need a bath and a rest I think. I have your mobile somewhere, I couldn't find a charger." Kate says she's looked for it and April must have it in the dreaded handbag and leans over and hauling the monstrosity down from the table roots in it, finds her mobile and takes it into her bedroom. April switches on the water heater. Kate reappears in a minute looking anxious, asking about the deadline, what the plans are. She knows the seven days are up tomorrow, she knows the men and is not convinced April is taking the threat seriously. April reassures her that everything is in hand, with a little help from Trish, Sam and her mother. Kate looks doubtful but is tired. At that point her landline rings and April picks it up.

"Oh April darlin'," Trish's voice comes over the phone clearly and can be heard in the room. "Fuck it!"

"What's happened?"

"My fucking mother has found out and stopped the fucking

cheque, apparently the bank fucking phoned her."

"Oh no!" April sits down on the sofa and tries not to meet Kate's questioning glance.

"I'm so fucking sorry. What can I do? Nada."

"You tried, Trish, you tried, that means a lot. And tomorrow we'll be able to get a large amount. We'll be able to give them most of it."

"I'm so fucking furious. I asked her to give it to me as a loan, but she won't. Look darlin', I'm coming tomorrow as back-up for Sam. That Martina is trouble."

"Of course. But Trish, Kate's back! Kate's here. Safe and well."

"Really? At last! Bloody hell. What's she been doing? I hope she knows what she's put you through. Has she got the money?" April shushes her, telling Trish not to make a fuss that she's OK, she's fine. She is forced to spell out for Trish that Kate hasn't got the money and hears Trish's moan of disappointment in response. Eventually, Trish phones off and April faces Kate.

"So there are problems?" asks Kate and April has to nod. She stops herself from telling the whole story to Kate. The week has been unbelievable and if Kate is suffering a crisis of conscience now, hearing that her mother has been forced into taking part in a jewel robbery would be unbearable.

"I'm sure we can sort it out, now that you're back," she says as Kate picks up the envelope that Martina has left and idly turns it over. Kate makes a squeak, exclaiming that the writing belongs to Will and opens it and sits for a moment flicking through the papers, then says coldly and calmly that it is THE report, Will must've taken it. She reads it for a while then suddenly puts it down and stands up, saying she knows how she can get the money.

She has been taken for a ride. Her mother was right. This is Will and the company's fault. She's going to face them; they've behaved disgracefully, and they tricked her. "Grampa was right, men in suits, I should've remembered. He was always right."

She says she's going to shower and change. Disappearing into the bathroom, she re-appears shortly looking clean and smart but still tired. She's washed and dried her hair, put on some make-up, and is sporting the glamorous clothes she used to wear in London that she's kept here untouched: an elegant woollen trouser suit, high-heeled boots, a full-length leather coat. Her shoulders are back and her eyes, though dark-rimmed, are brighter. She speaks firmly, saying she's taking her mobile and charger this time, to enable her to keep in contact with April but needs a few pounds. April scrabbles round and gives her £100 from her pawn proceeds and offers to go with her, but Kate says she must do this on her own. She's going to make these people sweat, make her grampa and April proud, not give up.

They hug, April holding her tightly before consciously opening her fingers and letting her go, holding her away and telling her she is brave. In the next second, asking April not to worry and reassuring her that she'll be fine, Kate sets out and the door shuts firmly behind her, leaving only a cold breeze in the still room.

Sixteen

Saturday morning

April dreams of Kate alone on a rock facing away from her, the waves writhing over her feet and tries to reach her, shouting and calling, warning her, terrified. A black smog rises up and rears over Kate, making April squirm and shout in terror. She reaches out but overstretches and rushes towards a dark sea, twisting, turning, dropping, falling, falling and then the phone. She wakes in a pool of sweat feeling as if she hasn't slept at all and moves sluggishly, hearing the answerphone and her mother's voice calling her name. She speeds up, every ache from Thursday making its presence felt, as she crosses to the living area and picks up the phone.

"Mum, what is it? Are you OK? It's …" she catches sight of the clock, "SEVEN o'clock!"

"You're gonna hev t' come and get me," her mother's voice sounds tearful and flat, defeated.

"For God's sake ma! What's going on? What's happened?"

"I've bin thrown owt!" she pauses and April hears her swallow, "Just come t' get me, will you?"

"OK ma but where are you going to stay?"

"God knows. Get here quick."

"OK, OK I'm on my way."

April has just thrown on a long red cotton gathered skirt and an orange jumper when the phone rings again, she runs to answer it and picking up hears a muffled argument as if someone has their hands over the receiver. But, finally, her mother's voice comes through this time with determination, "Philip is comin' too."

"Oh mum, why is he coming as well? Where will I take you both? How will you both get in? You know my car. It's got stuff everywhere. It barely goes at the moment."

"He's comin'. He mun get away! He has a right, after all he's bin through fer you and Kate." The phone goes down. April sighs.

As April turns into the road where the home is, she sees a crowd of people ahead spilling into the road. They all look old and some of them are still dressed in nightwear and slippers. She has difficulty manoeuvring to the car park as it is filled with people, moving slowly, most, apparently, the residents of the home.

April gets out, searching for her mother amongst them. Everyone is carrying belongings in either proper suitcases or carrier bags. Every type of walking aide is on display: sticks, wheelchairs, crutches, zimmer frames. Staff members have laid blankets round some people's shoulders and are putting coats on others and begging the residents to go inside. There is a central hub which consists of her mother and a small huddled man in a wheelchair with a group of more able-minded residents talking to them. Her mother is acting outraged: looking perky and brisk, and enjoying the attention. She spots April and comes towards her with that characteristic limp, half carrying just one suitcase that is dragging along the ground. April takes the surprisingly light suitcase from her and puts it in the car asking if that is all her mother wants to take. Her mother replies that she has collected the most important stuff and will return for the remainder later. Then she tells April firmly that they must get Philip.

Her mother moves back through the crowd, shaking hands with people and exchanging comments. One old man in a wheelchair is holding a handmade sign "BEYOND THE AGE OF CONSENT". An elderly woman, shaking badly, is holding up another sign "NO SEX PLEASE WE'RE INCARCERATED!"

"What's going on here?" asks April.

"They used paper from art classes. She does crosswords."

"Why's everyone outside? I thought it was just you. Have they all been thrown out?"

"It's a protest," smiles her mother. "One out all out. Get Philip. He needs lifting." April walks to the centre of the group of elderly people where staff members are talking to them, telling them they will get cold, they need to go inside. Philip is in a folding wheelchair, a frail old man, curled in a tight shaking ball, wearing a large scarf round his neck and chin, leaving wrinkled cheeks and a tuft of grey hair on show. Her mother introduces him to April and a smile brightens his pallid eyes and he murmurs something and raises a hand that shakes badly.

"This is ridiculous!" says April, "we can't possibly move him!" But Philip makes a noise, a rushing stream of quiet words that she leans forward to hear.

"I wanna come I must come I won't stay here get me up let me out I've had enough wanna go let's go." He tries to sit up as he speaks and her mother rushes to him, helping him uncurl, stroking his back. "Thanks thanks ta stand I wanna stand." He freezes suddenly with a judder, looking blankly at them.

"This is ridiculous," says April. "He should be left here. What's going to happen at home with him?"

"Tek him," says her mother fiercely, "this is because o' you. You owe him." Guilt-stricken April looks at Philip and decides her mother is correct: £5,000 gives you some rights though she still can't understand why he should be thrown out. Nevertheless, she decides to take him and wheels him to the car, opens the door and stands still for a moment.

She always used to regard herself as strong; she has wrestled wardrobes up fire escapes, lifted bags of manure, hefted old settees into position. In the past she would have had no doubts about lifting such a small man, he cannot weigh more than seven stone. She's older now, weaker and has stopped challenging herself physically. But only a couple of nights ago she took part in a jewel heist, ran up and down stairs, so maybe she is stronger than she thinks. She leans forward, takes hold of his back, pulls him towards her and swivels. He is heavier than she had anticipated, but still manageable; she drops him back into the car. April is surprised to see Philip smile and hears him say "good girl, good girl good girl well done", feeling his old gnarled hands reach out and stroke her back before the shuddering overcomes him once more. He is sitting sideways along the rear seat, so she goes to the other side and pulls him backwards, moving him into the car. She is pleased with herself and is about to close the door when three old people press round her and pass her several full carrier bags that must belong to him. Someone else leans inside and covers him with a blanket, whilst his wheelchair is folded and placed into the boot. She helps seat her mother, who's still talking to the residents telling them to "Stick to yer guns, one out, all out, we'll be back you see. We are adults. We are not children." There is a crowd of old people round the car, banging on the windows cheerfully and waving. One is holding a card that says, 'NO

FUCKING LIFE.' Her mother tuts, "He nivver had any manners, that one."

Driving away, April asks her mother, who is waving to her followers, what it was all about. "I were found in Philip's room this mornin!" April experiences a recurrence of feeling that she remembers from her childhood when her mother announced another marriage, another divorce, another new permanent love; it can best be described as a familiar shock.

"Well why not?" says her mother "it's not as if we're below the age of consent." She goes on to explain that last night she felt better and so crept downstairs and talked to Philip and then they fell asleep together. It was cosy and they both slept really well. The problem started when the carers came in very early to give Philip his meds and they were discovered. There was an almighty rumpus, a lot of shouting and running around, the blame falling on her. They called the manager, the manager called Philip's son, he didn't answer the phone, so Mrs Weekes left a message. Her mother went upstairs to pack, they told her to leave and anyway she didn't want to be in any home that treated them like kids still at school. She told her room sharer who woke the others and suddenly all the residents were protesting. When she got back to Philip to say goodbye, he said he wanted to come too. "He doesn't see what it's got to do with anyone who they sleep with, nobody is a child, nobody is being exploited. He's very happy, he wants to stay with me, and I want to be with him. What's the problem?"

"The problem, Philip," April tells them, "is your son."

"We'll deal with him," says her mother firmly and leans back to pat Philip.

There is no choice, they have to come to April's flat and into her bedroom which is the only one with a bed that can sleep two. Getting the couple into this back room is a lengthy process, with April lifting, pulling, carrying, pushing, putting down and every muscle being tested. Afterwards she massages her shoulders and makes them a cup of tea and sits on the sofa arm, drinking hers as she watches them settling onto her bed. Philip is propped up against the corner wall padded round with cushions and pillows, he looks remarkably comfortable and happy. His gnarled hands reach round to touch her mother and he dozes. All the bags are piled in an untidy heap in the corner. April will not be able to get into her wardrobe for days, if ever. And her mother has inveigled herself into her home.

They couldn't have come at a worse time. She knows that Sergeant Henderson will come to her flat, this is the first place he'll look, on the very morning when the gamblers are coming too. But there is nothing she can do about it now; she just hopes that he'll think she's a late riser. She carefully circles the flat, drawing all the curtains and closing and securing every window. Looking through the bedroom door she sees Philip smile and raise a shaking hand to Dotty, as he calls her mother, which she grasps and to April's astonishment, kisses and lays down and holds for a moment in beaming silence. There are the unmistakeable signs of people in love, universal whatever the age, only Philip looks so old and disabled, an unlikely lover. April has never seen her mother be so tender with anyone, herself included. Then she remembers many years ago, she must've been eight or nine, her mother, in one of her rare visits, bathing her, wrapping her up in a towel and sitting her on her knee and singing a lullaby to her. It is one of very few loving memories she has of her, smothered by following events, but now resurfacing. Philip nods his head in agreement to what Dotty has said, they smile at the same time.

"My life my life only my life I'll do what I want give my money to who I want no business of anyone my son means well but needs to let go …he's not in charge it's my life my life." April stands at the doorway as her mother picks her way through the contents of the carrier bags, taking out medicines, incontinence pads. Asking for towels, water, soap, slippers, a cardigan and blankets. She seems remarkably improved and alive, her limp and dropped mouth less noticeable: bossing April around, getting things organised. April looks at her watch and realises that she is late to pick up Sam.

April informs them both that the sergeant will come to look for them here but that she is leaving. She instructs them fiercely not to answer the door or open a curtain and to stay in her room as much as possible, warning them both repeatedly for God's sake not to open the front door or look out, but just to rest. They must ring her if they need anything, her mobile number is by the phone.

She will be back soon. Her mother says they will be fine and adds that she is not so daft as April thinks she is and can manage by herself. April, who remembers the years of trying to look after her mother and hold down a job, restrains her desire to make an irritated response, recalling the last stroke that left her mother slumped beside the fridge for a couple of days.

April leaves, worrying about them and hoping they will be OK. She walks round the outside of the flat, checking that nothing can be seen, and then gets into her car and drives off in a flurry of exhaust fumes to pick up Sam and Martina.

*

Sam is wandering round the house, unable to settle, waiting for Hugh to leave for work. He is reading a paper and resting back in his chair in the kitchen whereas usually he is up and off, whatever the day is. She clears the breakfast things off the table and wipes it down, pointedly asking him to lift his elbows so she can clean beneath. He looks up in some surprise.

"I have things I want to do," she explains, "I thought you were going to work today."

"I'm not stopping you. I thought you would want a quiet day; you seem to have been dashing around all week. You were really drunk and late on Thursday night. This whole week you have been different, not like you at all." He listens for a moment and Sam, inwardly cursing, hears the sound of a car drawing up on the gravel and knows it Helen's. She slams the cloth into the sink and turns to face the usual sight, Helen, carrying a crying Salome, standing in the kitchen doorway. She cannot help but grimace. Hugh stands up and kisses Helen and then they stand together, and Sam realises as they form a wall of concern that this has been pre-arranged. Helen has always got on better with Hugh, taking his work seriously, getting a degree in business studies, becoming one of the directors of his company.

"We're worried about you," says Helen, struggling with Salome who is dropping from one arm, moaning and eager to get down. Sam feels like screaming. How did she get this life? What is she doing with these people who are strangers to her? Who don't understand her? How has she let this happen? Nevertheless, she hopes that she can avoid the sort of emotionally loaded scene that she was exposed to so often in her childhood. She says there's nothing wrong, nothing to worry about and turns to dry her hands and mop the work surface.

"It's those other two," says Hugh, "Trish and April. You've been seeing too much of them and we think they're a bad influence, making you behave badly.

You were so late on Thursday and came back drunk and smelling of dope. I hope that's not starting up again." It is true that on Thursday night after the heist and pub, they all went to Trish's and she rolled a spliff and for the first time in ages Sam got ripped and they all celebrated their daring. She crept home early in the morning and sneaked into bed beside Hugh, giggling, saying she was drunk.

"They are making you act strangely," continues Helen, giving up the struggle with Salome who crawls along the kitchen floor towards Sam and then lies across her feet. "You're not putting your family first," continues Helen. "And that rude girl yesterday was the pits. Whatever was she doing here? Will told me stuff about his sister and April's daughter, they're friends. They're really bad news. Communists. Anarchists. Out to destroy society." Sam turns around.

"So you did go to meet him! She was right, wasn't she? About you and Wanker William? You've just said it. You went to lunch with him yesterday, maybe more?" Helen looks guilty, realising she's given herself away. "So you lied to me," continues Sam, "you dumped Salome on me, so that you could go off and have a lunchtime fuck." Hugh looks shocked and tries to speak to Helen, but she steps away from him.

"Really mum," protests Helen, "Think of Salome, watch your language!"

"Forget me, what about you? You dare to stand there throwing accusations at me, about my friends, about me not putting my family first. You hypocrite! You take every opportunity to leave me with your daughter whilst you go off to have fun with your friends! You don't think about me. Neither of you think about me. I have things I want to do."

"Oh. Your art..." mocks Helen, "making jewellery..." her contempt rings in the air, she glances sideways at Hugh who is looking increasingly confused.

"You've never looked at it," says Sam to them both.

"Yes, I have," replies Helen quickly, "just last week."

"You've not really seen it. Like you've not seen me. Or yourself."

She bends down to where Salome is now sleeping curled up round Sam's feet, "Or your daughter," she adds straightening up. "She should be your gift. You should love her and want to be with her. Why is she always crying? Why are you going off rather than staying with her? What's wrong?"

"Just bugger off, mum. I don't answer to you anymore. You go and play with your little friends. I thought you'd be glad to have a grandchild. I thought you'd want to spend time with her. I thought you'd want to help me have a rest."

"Well I don't," says Sam with relief, "not any day any time. I'll have her once a week and that's it."

"You're not having her at all. I'm never speaking to you again." Helen snatches up Salome who predictably grizzles and squirms. Turning to go, Helen gives Hugh a kiss on his cheek as she passes.

"Poor dad, I see exactly what you have to deal with. I'll phone you later." There is the sound of doors slamming and a car driving away. Hugh stands alone and silent, his hands hanging.

"Did you really phone her?" asks Sam.

"She phoned me, but I was worried about you, dear."

"Not enough to really spend time asking me. Not enough to listen to my answers. Not enough to put me first over making money. When was the last time we had a really good laugh together?"

"Well we're older now. More responsible."

"I don't want to be responsible anymore. I'm fed up of being responsible." Especially, she thinks, if it means a nice quiet night in with just him for company.

"Oh dear one, you don't mean that. We all rely on you," he comes towards her for a conciliatory hug, but Sam sidesteps him. Words fall out of her mouth, hateful loud words that she never expected, saying how bored she is of him, how boring he's become, how he never talks of anything except his work or money.

How mean he is in every way, how she can't remember the last time they had a really good fun time or did anything interesting together. How they have nothing in common anymore. Hugh recoils in horror, he's never seen her so upset and struggles for a reply, finally suggesting that she lie down and get a rest as she's obviously ill, she's hysterical. Sam tells him to get stuffed, just to get stuffed, to go to work, leave her alone. She is rigid with anger and shouting in a way she has always avoided. Hugh, shocked, bewildered and in a sulk, picks up his case and goes whilst making a remark about how his work pays for her, and has always paid for her. Sam, feeling a surge of powerful rage in her voice, screams after him at the door to fuck off, watching him slouch away she slams the door behind him. The house is silent as if taking an in-breath and her head rattles with things she could've said, should've said. She makes herself a coffee and sits down to calm her shaking nerves, she's never let go of her anger before; she didn't know she was so furious. Yet there is something here she wants to keep, some feeling of honesty, of fire, of clarity. But almost immediately the doorbell rings and it is Martina with a rucksack saying that she waited until everyone had gone. Sam offers her a coffee but Martina declines this, just helping herself to a glass of water instead and saying that they'd better get on with it and then looks at Sam who is sitting still with her hands clasped and shaking.

"I've just had a terrible quarrel with Hugh and told my daughter I'm not going to look after Salome again," blurts out Sam, realising suddenly how bad Hugh must be feeling. She's behaved badly, she's never sworn at him before.

"Good for you," replies Martina, "get it all out in the open."

"I feel awful. I must phone and apologise."

"They can wait. Let them think a bit. Anyway, we have things to do, come on."

In Sam's bedroom Martina unpacks her rucksack and throws everything unceremoniously on the bed, saying that the choice of wall-colourings and hangings are amazing and asking which of the paintings Sam likes best. Sam points to an abstract which Martina inspects closely but is called away from it at Sam's exclamation of dismay. She is holding up a short-skirted mauve suit which is obviously too small for her and picks up a pink crepe outfit with her nose wrinkling.

"It's the sort of thing Hugh would like me to wear," she says, pulling the skirt on with difficulty and pushing her arms into the jacket. "I hate powder pink." It fits, and seeing her in it make Martina snigger, who advises her that she'll have to wear tights and 'proper' shoes. Sam finds some tights and then forces her feet into the high heels which are about half a size too small. And so is the skirt which hugs her thighs and seems tighter round her knees. She regards herself in the mirror, turns sideways and cannot stop herself from giggling but says that she needs to do something with her hair. Martina, with a flourish, produces some hair gel and proceeds to plaster Sam's hair down and back and place Helen's hat to complete the disguise. Sam puts on some make-up, choosing a little-used lipstick and sits back.

"It would be nice if you had some earrings," says Martina and immediately Sam raises a finger and walks carefully to her studio, returning with something wrapped in tissue paper. She opens it to reveal enamelled drop earrings in turquoise that spin and reflect the light as she puts them on. Martina unwraps some glass bracelets to provide a jangle of colour at Sam's wrists, and they both examine the outfit in the mirror and are satisfied.

"You look horrible," says Martina, "not your usual self at all. But those earrings are so cool."

"I haven't got a coat; won't they think it a bit odd in October?"

"Just stepped out of the jag."

"April'd better not park nearby, the exhaust fumes will give the game away. My bloody feet are killing me already. Where is she? She should be here by now." Martina suggests they go downstairs to wait, and she'll text April. They sit in the kitchen with Sam drinking coffee as she practices the signature and answers the questions.

"No reply," says Martina, looking at her phone, "but maybe she's on her way."

"I'm getting really nervous," says Sam. "I just want to get this over with."

"You look great," says Martina, "nobody would know it was you. Let me," and she leans forward to adjust an earring and then, to the loud rattling sound of April's approaching car, she bends and kisses Sam squarely on the lips. Sam freezes, the doorbell rings and Martina trots off to answer it. Sam gets up as April rushes through the door and laughs disbelievingly at first then becomes enthusiastic, saying how fantastic Sam looks, truly different. She gives Sam a hug and then steps away.

"Sorry I'm late. Trouble with my mother. I won't tell you now. Let's get going." She turns to go then looks back, "I'm sorry Sam. You look sort of frozen. Nerves I suppose. Have you practiced? Do you want me to test you some more?" Sam stands up and shakes her head, doesn't look at Martina, fiddles in her bag and produces a wad of cash and gives it to April saying that it's £1,500, she's taken money out of the cashpoint each day. April hugs her again, thanks her wholeheartedly and puts the money at the bottom of her bag, remarking that hopefully they won't need it.

April parks in the high street immediately outside the bank

building, and lets them out, watching them go inside with trepidation. Going to her own building society to collect the money Philip gave her earlier in the week, she is surprised that there are no questions asked and takes the deceivingly small bundle of notes, pushing them to the bottom of her bag, adding them to Sam's money. When she returns, a traffic warden is hovering near her car so she is forced to drive slowly round the block, parking up eventually on the opposite side of the road and keeping an eye on the bank.

The road is busy with Saturday morning shoppers, many going into the usual chain stores, Woolworths, British Home Stores, Marks and Sparks and the many restaurants. The pedestrian area is off to one side and people are streaming along it from the station in loitering groups, greeting friends, catching hold of children or walking determinedly. In this confusion it is difficult to see the door of the bank or to keep an eye out for the traffic warden. It is an irony that she knows most of them by name, but that won't stop them giving her a ticket.

Inside the bank Sam and Martina perch nervously in the public area on the soft chairs, with Sam keeping her eyes down and not looking at Martina, her bracelets jingling as she clasps her hands tightly together. Martina has made an appointment apparently; they have been told to wait and a specific booth is being opened for them. It's very quiet in here, nobody is speaking loudly, the counter is in front of them, the clerks sitting raised behind it. There is a small queue of people waiting their turn, they all get dealt with, and the clerks have a moment of rest and a chat behind their glass wall. Finally, Sam sees someone come out from behind the tellers and go to the far booth on the right, a tubby middle-aged woman with an air of importance and a wall eye. She logs onto the computer system and reads the screen. She glances at them. There is no escape. Sam looks down, says the passcode under her breath, puts her hand into her handbag and clutches the credit card given to her by Martina, shifts on the seat.

The woman calls a name and Sam looks up confused, and it is only when Martina puts her hand under her elbow that she realises that it is of course her assumed name. She stands and goes towards the counter with Martina beside her.

"Sorry to keep you waiting," says the woman, smiling politely at them, she looks directly at Sam, "Ah Mrs Chowdhury. Namaste." Sam smiles and nods her head, feeling a sudden tautness in the small figure beside her. "I spent some time in India, myself," continues the woman, "volunteered out there near your hometown Shimla?" Sam nods and smiles, Martina butts in.

"My mother has had a bit of a cough and a cold, so she is trying to save her voice." Sam feels in her bag for a tissue, finds one and pretend-wipes her nose.

She stares, wondering what to do whilst the teller is chattering about India and Shimla, The Mall, the monkey temple, the people, the bazaar, and smiling at her. In between this, she asks Sam to put the card into the slot and key in the pin code and apologises for her wittering, saying that India is her passion. There is no outcry. Sam has remembered the pin code correctly.

"Well let's get on with it," says the woman, "£25,000 you want? In fifties?"

She passes a piece of paper through the glass and asks Sam to sign it and produces a pile of cellophane-wrapped notes saying there is £1,000 in each and asking if Sam wants them counting out. Sam shakes her head; she is looking at the form in front of her which only requires her signature. The woman suddenly leans forward confidentially.

"Can I just say, how much I absolutely love your earrings. I can't take my eyes off them; they are just so beautiful." Sam can't help smiling and turns her head to show them better whilst the woman continues with a storm of admiration. Sam passes the form back and as it reaches the other side of the glass suddenly realises that, distracted by the compliments, she has thoughtlessly signed her own name. She reaches out instinctively to snatch the note back and all the alarms go off.

The result of this is immediate. Martina grabs Sam's hand and runs out of the door. She is through it first with Sam following automatically. Metal barriers close behind them. Sam is running, trying to dodge past people who are carrying bags or holding small children by the hand or worse, just standing and staring.

Her heels are making her ankles twist and turn. The bank alarm has caused chaos in the high street and everyone is going towards the sound. Except Sam. An elderly man looks as if he wants to challenge her. There is the sound of a police siren near at hand and Sam, panting, her feet askew in the high-heeled shoes and unable to stride out because of the too-tight skirt, tries to speed up. She can see April's car over the other side of the road and is just going to stumble across when a police car draws up outside the bank. As she hesitates, a young fit police officer gets out, clutching a walkie talkie and talking into it while looking in her direction. Martina has run off and is lost amongst the crowds, but Sam's a sitting target. She's going to be arrested and sent to prison.

April calls out of her car's open window and Sam crosses to the middle of the road towards her, but the police officer is running at Sam, shouting, and her feet have lost their direction. Then there's a roar coming from behind the policeman, and Trish overtakes him on her Harley, saying, "Get on for fuck's sake and hold tight." Sam jumps up and lands sideways and has barely clutched Trish before they glide off and away, her hat flying off her head, the cold air hitting her face and arms. Trish turns down a side street and Sam clings on fiercely, feeling the force of the backward pull as they rumble forward, gaining speed.

Seventeen

Saturday afternoon

Driving towards her flat, hearing police sirens ahead of her, then behind her, then ahead again, April cannot work out where they are going to or coming from. She only knows that her two best friends are in deep trouble. All for her. All for Kate. She feels sick with worry, she knows they will be caught, perhaps that would be better than the alternative: she dreads hearing the sound of an ambulance. It would've been easier and safer if she'd just refused to pay the gamblers the money and gone to the police. The whole week has been a disaster, lurching from bad to worse. And she has endangered her two best friends in the process.

The car is on its last legs, spluttering and throwing out thick clouds of smoke. She dares not approach her flat directly because if Philip's son is watching then he will demand that the door be opened, and she cannot face another scene with a police officer near the time when the gamblers will be coming. But it is about 11 now and she wonders about whether her mother and Philip are coping inside. If anything happened to them, it would be terrible. She has always known that she cared for her mother, despite her apparent disregard for April and it has annoyed her, she has seen it as a weakness, a curse, something to be denied, yet now she openly worries about her mother. With the gamblers lurking, April has put her mother's life at risk. She catches her bottom lip in her teeth. This chaos is all her fault. Then she corrects herself. No, it is all Kate's fault. But why is everything going wrong?

She suddenly remembers that there might be a way of getting into her flat round the back, through a gate that leads from the block of council flats. Soon having avoided the front route, she is parked up in the council flats' car park and is looking at the back of her flat through an iron gate. Unfortunately, a padlock has been put on the low-level spiked gate, but for someone who is a jewel thief and has lifted a man into a car it looks a doddle. However, at a critical point, balanced at the top of the gate, her hefty bag rotates round and pulls her backwards, making her fall. But it is not too bad, merely a landing on her buttocks and some bruises, torn tights and a dirtied skirt, though the concrete path is hard. She sits up and rubs her bum, unknots and pulls her skirt down to her ankles again and allows herself a moment of victory. Easy peasy.

But getting up is not so easy, her ankle has been twisted, making her limp as she proceeds slowly to the back window where her bedroom is located, noticing with relief that the window is closed and the curtains are drawn. She taps on it gently and calls her mother but there is no reply. She has told them not to open the door or window but surely they should be able to hear it is her? She speaks more loudly.

"Mum, mum, it's me, April, for goodness sake open the bloody window. Are you OK?"

"I can't tell you how many calls we've received about you," comes a familiar male voice from behind her, and turning, April sees

Sergeant Henderson and a young woman police officer, both in full uniform, both looking severe. "Breaking and entering?"

"Of course not," says April, "this is my flat. As you know."

"How would I know that? And why would anyone climb over a back gate and try to creep up on their own flat? Just about to break the window, I suppose?"

'No! Why would I do that? Of course, it's my flat, and if I want to get into it in a strange manner, then I can."

"Prove it's your flat, then?"

"Well, my name is on the buzzer for a start. You came to it a few nights ago. And here's my keys," and she produces the clinking bundle from her handbag, realising too late the inevitability of the next step.

"I'll take those," says Sergeant Henderson, twitching them from her fingers and marching round towards the front door with April protesting and the PC following. The PC offers her some help which April ungraciously refuses. He unlocks the door, flings it wide and strides into her flat. The curtains are still drawn and the flat is dark and silent with no sign of either her mother or Philip. Her bedroom door is closed. Sergeant Henderson switches on a light and looks keenly round the room, which is a mess, many things that should've been in April's room have been taken out and dumped on any available space.

"See," says April, "this is my home, now please give me my keys back and go," but her voice sounds feeble and unconvincing. The Sergeant opens the door to Kate's room, the bathroom and the store cupboard in quick succession and then April's bedroom. In this small back room the light is on and April's mother sits on one side of the bed in a rather revealing nightie, brushing her hair, whilst Philip's father is lying looking comfortable and relaxed propped up against the corner that the double bed is pushed against, neither seem surprised to see the Sergeant.

Philip attempts to raise himself and his lips shiver as he stares at his son and tries to speak. Dorothy leans over to help him.

"Leave him alone," says the Sergeant "He's my father I'll make sure he's OK. It's alright, dad, I've spoken to the home, they've got everything ready for you, so I can just take you and everything will be fine. Don't worry." Philip struggles backwards as his son reaches for him.

"I think you'll find," says April, finally finding her voice, "that he wants to stay with mum. That's what he wants."

"I think you'll find that he has been defrauded of large amounts of money by your 'mum' and you. Con artists, battening off a poor old defenceless man!"

"He says he wanted to give the money to her."

"I'm sure. After you and your mother persuaded him! I'm going to charge you both with fraud and abduction. You obviously want to keep him and milk him of every penny he has." And he leans over to reach his father. "Come on now, dad, I'll have you home in no time." But his father still writhes away from him, his mouth locked and shaking.

"I think you should listen to him," says April, and it is true that Philip is trying to talk, though so softly and quickly that it is hard to hear, but he holds tight to Dorothy's hand and finally looks at her and shakes her hand.

"Tell him tell him," he says.

"I'll speak for him," says Dorothy, she is using her posh voice, the one she uses for interviews or dealing with officials.

"Oh no you won't," says the Sergeant, trying to get over the bed to his father who shrinks backwards again as he approaches. "I hope you haven't been brainwashing or coercing him. You have absolutely no rights over him at all. I'm his son and I have power of attorney." There is a silence and Philip once again grips Dorothy's hand as if trying to get through to her.

"Well I'm his wife," says Dorothy and everything stops.

"That's ridiculous."

"No, it isn't. We're married."

"Of course, you aren't. You can't be."

"Well we are."

"Don't be stupid, that's untrue. He never left the home," says the Sergeant. "How long have you been married for? If you did manage it, I'll get it annulled."

"45 years or so," says Dorothy calmly. The shock ripples round the room, bounces across the walls and cascades into the flat.

"That's impossible," is all the Sergeant can say.

"Well, I think you'll find the original marriage certificate in your father's possession. And I have a copy in my bag here," says Dorothy calmly, "and now take your hands off my husband. He doesn't want to go back to the home unless I go with him."

"That's just an unbelievable lie!" snorts the Sergeant.

"That can't be true," whispers April, but then begins to laugh, sitting down on a corner of the bed. The policewoman walks over to the small suitcase April's mother is pointing at and opens it up to reveal pills, a bag of makeup, a false teeth holder and a folder containing a set of papers. She takes the latter out, sorts through it, and hands the top certificate to the Sergeant who takes it, reads, and is confused.

"I've never seen this before. I don't understand, dad," he says, "you married Dorothy Roberts, widow, in 1962. Is this really you? But this isn't my mother's name." Philip nods his head and shifts uneasily.

"That's mine," says Dorothy, "my copy of my marriage certificate, my second marriage, after my first husband died. To your father."

"So why aren't you Mrs Henderson now? If you were married to my dad?"

"I kept my stage name," says Dorothy, "after my first husband died." The Sergeant leans against the door jamb and looks at the certificate with shock.

"I don't understand," he says and stares at his father, "so when did you marry mum? This must be before you married mum? Right? I don't understand. No, it doesn't work out. I was born in January 1963." The hand holding the certificate has dropped and he looks dazed. April waits, knowing something is going to be revealed about her mother's past and that it will not be good news. It never is. "Did you get this annulled or something? To marry my mother?" He shakes his head and peers at his father who is frozen with only his jaw twitching. "Or maybe you weren't married to my mother after all?" His father is shaking his head and looking at his son fixedly, unable to speak.

"You might be a police Sergeant but you're pretty daft," chirps in Dorothy, making April wince: she thinks she might have the answer, but can't quite believe it.

'But..." and the Sergeant stops as the PC plucks at his elbow and passes another piece of paper to him.

"What are you doing with my birth certificate?" he shouts at April's mother. "What's this?"

"Born on January 5th 1963," stutters her mother and then sits down holding Philip's hand tightly, she looks fearful, all bravado has now gone from her.

"I don't understand. Is this some joke?" April leans over and takes the papers from the Sergeant's hand and reads them "You're Mrs

Henderson here on his birth certificate," she says and feels some answers click into place. "Another child, you had another child. Oh God of course. It was a difficult birth." She looks at her mother who nods briefly but keeps her eyes on the Sergeant who is speaking to his father.

"But my mother's dead, dad, you said she was dead. You told us all she was dead, grandma said she was dead. You said she was called Sugden before you got married."

"My mother's maiden name," says April, "she was a Sugden once." Philip shakes his head feebly, trembles and clutches Dorothy's hand more tightly whilst looking anxiously at his son.

"No, this isn't possible," says the Sergeant, looking in disgust at Dorothy.

"Why, mum? Oh. Why didn't you tell me? Why didn't you tell anyone?" asks April. Her mother shrugs and shakes her head. "And why did you leave your son? How could you? Why didn't you bring him back to Leeds?" Philip shakes his head and tries to speak but Dorothy slurs her answer.

"His son. He wanted him and he could care for him. I'm no good as a mother. I know that. I never wanted to be good as a mother," and then she slurs words that only April can understand.

"My Fair Bloody Lady," April states. She stands up and looks at the Sergeant, "As she seems to be your mother and she definitely is mine, you should know she's worked in theatre and films, bit parts most of her life. If the theatre or film called, then everything else went down the tubes. She must've been offered a part in the film of My Fair Lady. She must've left you to Philip. If it's any consolation she left me as well. All the time. Mainly with my grandparents, you would've liked them, good honest, mining, chapel-going Yorkshire stock." April turns, brushes past everyone to get into the main room and begins drawing back the curtains and tidying up the mugs, limping badly before suddenly sitting down on the sofa and bursting into tears. Her heart is broken, but she does not know why. Behind her in the bedroom a conversation is going on, but April no longer cares about what is being said. A hand comes into view as April wipes her eyes on her sleeve, it belongs to the female PC who is silently offering her a cup of tea and gratefully April takes it and sips as she looks across the room at the Sergeant who is now sitting in the armchair and studying her.

"I think you drew the long straw," says April, "your father is obviously a really nice kind man who has dedicated himself to you and your family. You can be proud of him," and she sobs again. "I wish I'd known; I just wish I'd known." She understands now why she is crying so hard; she has been robbed; robbed of a family, robbed of a brother. But more than that, there is an element of relief, she wasn't the only one haphazardly abandoned.

"This makes you my half-sister," says the Sergeant. "But you're much older."

'OK, OK, rub it in. She must've had you when she was nearing 30, I can't do the sums now I'm too upset. She had me when she was 17. I never knew my father, he died." There is a silence as each looks at the other, seeing some similarities in face, the same bushy hair, the shape of the eyebrows. April reaches over and opens a drawer and takes out an album and flicks to a page of black and white photos of her grandparents and herself outside Filey holiday camp. She is wearing a knitted wool bathing suit and they are fully dressed in smart clothes, each holding one of her hands, all three of them stare unsmiling at the camera, behind them a group of people play table tennis. "This must've been about the time you were born," she says, "you look like him. I noticed it the first time I saw you," and she hands him the photo album. "It doesn't look as if we're exactly having a ball. But they were lovely people. Stout Christians. Both dead now of course." The Sergeant looks at the pictures and turns the pages with some bemusement, he is obviously in shock and accepts the tea from the PC placidly.

"I believe in cases like this we should be falling on each other's necks and sobbing," says April, "but I don't even know your first name."

"It's George," he says and watches with some surprise as April's eyes fill with tears that she angrily brushes away.

"It's grandad's name," she says, and he puts his cup of tea down and picks up the album again, turning the pages and returning to the small black and white photos of April's grandparents and larger glossy publicity shots of 'their' mother.

"Can I borrow this?" he asks. April nods, there are several incriminating photos of her in there, but he might as well know the worst; she drinks and smokes weed and behaves disgracefully at festivals, it could be worse. She gestures to the graduation photo of Kate that is on the table beside her and, trying to even the respectability score, says that it is her daughter.

"I'm not sure now what's going to happen to those two in there. Do you have any ideas?" she asks.

"I don't know. This changes things, doesn't it? Why didn't he tell me the truth?" and George's voice rises in fury, "He lied to me. He led me to believe a fantasy about my mother. He told me she was a lovely, warm, funny, caring woman who drowned suddenly after being swept off Brighton pier in a storm."

"Now that's one of my mother's tales, I can recognise the hand there."

"We went every year and threw flowers in the sea!"

"Gosh! And sometimes she might've been appearing in a show in Brighton at the same time. Do you think they met?"

"I don't bloody care. Why did he lie? Grannie never liked her though, she never said anything directly, only had this look in her eyes when my mother's name was mentioned. I've often wondered about that, but I thought it might be jealousy, she and my father were very close."

"Mum does have some good points."

"I don't care. She left me. That's all I need to know. She's never been a part of my life and never will. Worse, he lied to me! And I don't care what happens as far as his accommodation goes. When I think of all the time and energy and worry we put in." He twists his hands, what'll I tell Sally? And the children? It's such a shock. They adore him."

"Maybe not tell your children anything for the moment? Your father and my mother seem well settled in here for now," says April. "Oh God. It should be 'our' mother, shouldn't it? I'll most probably move into the care home; they seem to be taking over here." She stands up and looks round at the PC who has removed her hat to reveal sleek red hair and who has been washing up and speaking into her walkie talkie, now calls out,

"Sarge, there's things going on in town, we need to be moving." George stands up and walks to the front door, putting on his cap as he goes.

"I'll come back after I finish my shift," he says, adding "maybe". It is only after he leaves that April worries about him and the gamblers meeting. But right now, she has no emotion left for anything, she just wants to sit in a quiet room and digest everything that has happened. The sound of police sirens pass round the town and a helicopter flies overhead.

*

Trish is desperate, she knows that once the call has gone out that the police like nothing better than a lovely chase, it's their idea of a good time, what most of them joined the police for: speeding after criminals. She knows the town well, the lanes and one-way streets, the wide and narrow roads, the paths with bollards that will stop cars passing through. But her geography is disorientated and, at this juncture with Sam behind her not wearing a helmet and perched sideways, she is terrified. At least Sam is clinging tight and knows enough to lean with the bends, but she is in real danger of slipping off. Trish cannot focus. She is not clear where she's going. Any possible route has left her mind. She only knows she has to evade the police. She cannot go to hers, April's or Sam's home. She has no idea where she can be safe. The police sirens are gathering round the town.

Surely all of them cannot be for her? She needs cover and to get Sam seated properly, somewhere to think, lay up for a while, get her mind clear, fix a story with Sam. She only needs a few minutes, but there is a flash of blue lights ahead and behind her. She will soon be on a dual carriageway, but two police cars block the way ahead.

She swerves left into a no-through road that leads to public toilets and a small recreation area. The road is packed with people resting from their shopping and waiting outside the loos. She goes past them and across the grass, coming out on a pedestrian area teaming with people who will not move out of her way. She stops for a moment and shouts at Sam to get off and get on again properly. Sam hitches her pink skirt well up over her knickers and gets astride and immediately Trish sounds the horn and continues slowly along the street. The sirens wail and she knows the police have now gone around and will be trying to cut her off at the other end. She veers down a pedestrian lane that crosses between parallel pedestrian streets and revs up and beeps, holding steady and seeing people ahead of her jumping into doorways and cursing her. She comes slowly out, crosses the next pedestrianised street, shouting at everyone to get the fuck out of the way and goes into a path between houses that takes her away from the centre of town towards the station. The only problem here is that she is also going away from anything she knows, but if she gets onto the by-pass, she can pick up some speed. She may have remembered a place where they can lay up for a while. She's finally got her bearings. She must be quick. This path is wider and seems less populated, few people are using it except those who live on the houses on either side. She manages to accelerate a little and makes an acceptable speed uphill, still taking care, looking for anyone on foot and opening doors.

Arriving at the top she swerves to the left onto a dead-end street that leads to the station car park. There are two ways out she recalls, one with a short barrier that allows her bike to go through but doesn't leave enough space for a car. She wonders if any police officers are aware of this discrepancy. She waits at the entrance barrier, hearing the sound of police cars behind, takes her ticket and goes into the car park. Two police cars enter the car park and attempt to cut her off as she weaves through the parked cars and Sam, sighting them, squeaks and clutches her more tightly. But Trish sees her escape, makes a turn and is round the other barrier leading down into a tunnel that finally takes them up and onto the by-pass. She turns onto it with gratitude, heading away from town in the direction of London. She speeds up. Everything now relies on her losing the police.

Sam is shivering with the cold and bends her head down, clutching Trish convulsively, tucking her freezing hands under Trish's jacket, not looking where they are going. A strobe of lampposts and trees and now open fields flash past her, Trish is undertaking as well as overtaking, the speed they are making seems phenomenal, everything blurs, vans and cars almost seem to be reversing. There are police sirens, but they sound some distance away now. Then Trish brakes suddenly and they are going up a steep path that leads to a cattle bridge over the road and they cruise down the other side and head back into town. The police sirens pass them, going in the opposite direction very fast. Trish rides along the dual carriageway and takes a sudden side turning near the edge of town and they swerve twice and are crossing a school playing field and aiming for the main school building. There is a large, transparent curved covering over picnic tables and chairs at the front that Trish pushes the bike beneath, moving some chairs to one side. They both dismount and Trish starts rolling a cigarette whilst Sam massages her thighs and stretches her back and legs. She cannot speak for a moment, the thrum of the engine is still in her bones, her buttocks ache, she is cold. A helicopter flies slowly overhead, they keep still until it passes. Trish lights up, takes a deep inhale and then addresses Sam,

"So, what happened?"

"It was my fault," says Sam, "we waited some time for the bank clerk and when she came, she burbled on a lot about India and Shimla, where I was meant to have been born, and said something nice about my earrings. I signed my own name! My own bloody name! I'm such an idiot!"

"So, she found you out?"

"No, worse! I reached over to grab it back. All the alarms went off."

"Bloody hell!"

"Martina just grabbed me, and we ran. The police came so quickly. God knows what would've happened if you hadn't been there!"

"Lucky I decided to come! I knew there would be trouble!"

"Oh Trish, I'm sorry, it's all my fault."

"Quite frankly, darlin', you did fuck up, let's face it. You're not the best person under stress as we all know. Neither is April actually. But you tried. Did you actually say anything?"

"I never got a chance. But I put in the pin code. God I'm cold! How long will we be here for?"

"Not very long. I just need to think where we can go."

Trish meanwhile sends some texts, one to April from them both saying they're OK at the moment and not in police custody. They hear the police cars returning fast down the dual carriageway, passing the school. They swap tops, "just to make a different impression" so Sam is wearing Trish's leather jacket and Trish is wearing Sam's pink jacket, they can do little about the most distinctive thing: the Harley. The helicopter flies slowly back and takes some time circling, it stays hovering overhead.

"I think we've been spotted, maybe the caretaker saw us," says Trish. "Well let's make a run for it, we'll try for the pub, perhaps Vince can help. I know a back way."

"I don't want to be Thelma or Louise," says Sam, getting on the pillion, "though Susan Sarandon is more my style."

"Darlin', neither of us have any style left at the moment." She starts up and they leave the school grounds the way they came in, across the playing field with the helicopter tracking every move. They return to the dual carriageway and Trish accelerates round a lorry and they take off at an unforgiving speed past cars, lorries and vans. A police car joins the carriageway behind them, its blue light flashing and siren sounding. Another one joins at the next entrance, ahead seems to be traffic lights, on red. Trish slows slightly, going through them, narrowly missing a cyclist, swerves right, crosses a roundabout, makes a U-turn and they are going along a footpath beside a river.

Parallel to them is a main road and a police car sounds on the carriageway as it matches them, Trish pulls Sam forwards as she ducks under a low bridge, they splash and bump over the rough ground and after that the main road is 50 feet or so away, the path turns inwards away from the river, but the main road is now lost in a complex of houses, roundabouts, one-way streets. Ahead is the pub beer garden. Trish pulls up on the grass outside, parks up, grabs Sam and they run into the back bar and Trish pulls Sam into the men's loos. Trish pulls off her helmet and looks around, there is one person in here, washing his hands rather thoroughly. The sound of sirens gets louder, the helicopter is rumbling overhead.

"For fucks sake," says Trish, "where can we hide?" The man washing his hands turns.

"Gosh, your life is an adventure!" says Dr McGiveney, "always wanted to do this! Saw it in a film." He shepherds them into the only toilet cubicle, locks the door, and gallantly helps them to stand on the seat, then apologizing, he turns, plants his feet firmly in front of the loo and lets his trousers fall to the floor. Sam grabs onto the top of his head to stop herself from falling off the edge of the seatless toilet, Dr McGiveney stands as solid as a rock, wearing batman underpants, Trish notices. There is the sound of feet and lots of knockings and door slammings and shouting, the word "Police!" features a lot and so does "Come Out We Know You're In There." Finally, someone bounds into the men's toilet and a voice shouts "Police! Come out!"

"Can't at the moment!" calls back the doctor amiably, "just in the middle of something, if you know what I mean. Please feel free to wait. Shouldn't be too long." There is the sound of scuffling, whilst someone obviously looks under the door and then the noise of feet going out. Dr McGiveney holds up a finger as Sam puts some weight on his shoulder preparatory to getting down, they hear someone taking a pee and then the door opens and closes again. Dr McGiveney pulls up his trousers and grins at them both. "Always wanted to do that," he says, "evading the police! Marvellous! Speeding I suppose?" He opens the door, there are three police officers waiting silently across the exit, "They've obviously seen the same film," he sighs.

*

Sitting in her front room April hears her phone ping and looks at it: a text from Kate. She's on her way but is late, she might get there in about an hour if she's quick. Delay them, if they arrive. It pings again and it is Trish, they are safe, not in police custody as yet. She stands up with a blast of joy and does a small hop across the room on her good leg. She feels like crying again, but sends a text saying thank God and another saying take care. She wonders when the gamblers will be here. She has hardly anything of the £35,000 to give them. She is totally at their mercy with no one to help her and now she has both her mother and Philip to protect.

She limps into the back bedroom where her mother is putting what looks like incontinence pads into one of the carrier bags. Philip looks asleep. Her mother gazes at her for a moment and speaks but continues fussing with pads and bags.

"I want to say ah'm sorry," she says. April is flabbergasted. "I were no good as a mother. No good at all. I should a just left yer to mam and dad. But I hated that house they were in. A dead-end place. That street. The Chapel. The mine." She shakes her head in dismay and pushes something down hard into a carrier and glances briefly at April. But April cannot respond, she feels emotionally battered. "I want yer to know you'll always be my daughter." Dorothy stands up with some difficulty and speaks more briskly, glancing at April as if she's unsure how her words went down. "Black bags, we need black bags. Tek these away." She gestures at the carrier bags filled with what look like laden incontinence pads, the smell is acrid in the small room and April nods and picks them up. She struggles out with them and seeing that her kitchen bin is full, empties them into the bin outside, looking out for any strange black cars. She sees no-one and wonders what to do, maybe she should get her car and put her mother and Philip into it and drive them somewhere else until Kate gets here. It might be useful to have the car nearby anyway; she might need it to collect Sam or Trish.

She returns to the flat briskly, grabs her bag, and, scrabbling in it for her keys and mobile, walks quickly round to collect her car and drives to the front of her flat where she sits for a second, looking at her mobile, checking if she has any more messages from Trish or Kate. There is nothing. She curses and sends a text to them both asking if they are ok. She drops her keys, bends down to pick them up from the floor of the car and when she looks up the gamblers' limousine has parked across the door to her flat and the two men are standing at her doorway as the younger man rings her bell. The sleek black car with its blacked-out rear windows blocks the space between her and the front door.

"I'm over here!" She jumps out, calling loudly and waving in order to draw their attention so if her mother does answer the door they won't notice. Both of them turn to face her and walk round their car and stand directly in front of her. This time they are dressed in jeans and bomber jackets, looking more casual, but also, more ready for action, dressed in their work clothes, ones they can get 'dirty'. They both have a spring in their step, a liveliness, as if they are doing what they enjoy; out for a pint, getting pissed, having a fight.

"There's a bit of a problem," she says, "you see the thing is..."

"You ain't got the money!" says the older man.

"No," says April carefully, "I have got the money."

"So where is it?"

"Well there's a bit of a hold up, you see."

"You ain't got the money."

"No," repeats April, "I HAVE got the money, just not here at the moment."

"So you ain't got the money," he gestures to the younger man who reaches into the black car and comes towards April, casually carrying a baseball bat. "I have! I have! Honestly I have!"

"So git it." April backs towards her car and reaches inside for her handbag and feels for all the money she has acquired during the week. Philip's £5,000, Sam's £1,500 and the remains of her pawning her jewellery, about £300. She empties into this the coins from her purse. She's only about £28,000 short. She turns back to them again, and hands the money to the Enforcer, her hands shaking. Behind them she sees her front door opening and her mother looking out.

"Kate's on her way," she says as the Enforcer looks at the money with disgust.

"What's this? What do you call this?" he is looking into the envelopes and has let the coins drop to the ground where they roll along the tarmac.

"About £7,000," says April, moving a little further round the other side of the car, "but there is more coming, any minute now!" The Enforcer nods to the younger man who raises his bat and takes a step back, rotating his shoulders for a practiced baseball swing. April wants to run away but can only half crouch behind her car. The bat lands on the glass of the front windscreen with a thud.

The noise is surprisingly small as the toughened glass cracks and splinters rather than shatters. But he rises up onto his toes, stares at her, hefts the bat behind his head and arcs it down viciously and this time it lands squarely, spattering the glass across the car park. April makes a small sound in her throat and steps away, keeping her eyes on him as he smiles and struts towards her, bouncing the bat loosely on an open palm before throwing it backwards and forcing it through the driver's window with a sideswipe that twists him round. Shards of glass spray into and out of the car, the crash echoes round the car park. April looks up at her block, expecting to see faces appearing at the windows, but nobody is looking out, or they've taken English non-interference to an incredible degree. He walks round the boot of the car and towards April who backs away as he lifts the wooden bat, glaring at her. She scrunches up with her hands over her head, as he seems to be aiming at her rather than the car. His feet in white trainers with fluorescent heels make a light movement and she knows he is getting ready to strike again.

A tiny dark figure sprints across the car park and catches him on the hip and throws him to the ground, the baseball bat skitters under the gambler's car and towards April's front door.

"Sit on him! Sit on him," says Martina, who is lying across him as he curses into the glass-flecked tarmac. April drops onto his back and hears him groan, she remembers now, it was judo that was Martina's sport, she got a black belt in it, almost made the Olympic team. Martina stands up and then laughs. The Enforcer is dashing towards them and Martina is ready for a fight: dancing lightly from foot to foot she moves in and throws the Enforcer easily to the ground and bounces away again. The Enforcer jumps up and clenches his fists, adopts a boxing stance and sidesteps towards her, fists raised. But behind him, limping, comes April's mother holding the baseball bat. She is swinging it loosely in front of her in a simulation of what April recognises as the Indian Club keep-fit routines of her youth. The Enforcer is looking at Martina and so is taken by surprise when he gets hit on the thigh from behind and his knees buckle with the pain. Dorothy drops the bat as it recoils in her hand and Martina jumps forward, steps behind him, hooks one leg and tips him over backwards with ease and grabs the baseball bat. Both of the men are swearing, the one beneath April is squirming and is making her seated position difficult so she bounces up and down on him until he is quieter. "Get inside," April calls to her mother, who goes back and waits and watches with the front door slightly open. The Enforcer is obviously hurt and has difficulty standing; he swears as he gets up, slowly grasping his stomach and muttering about his hernia.

The whole game changes when the Enforcer, leaning on the car and at the limit of his patience and in pain, reaches into the glove compartment and produces a gun. It's a small black flat-looking object whose purpose is clearly death. He points it at the women, telling Martina to drop the bat and April to get up and his accomplice to get in the fucking car. "A bad decision," he says to April as she slowly stands up, releasing the younger man, "stupid. Like your fuckin' daughter. You had your chance! I warned you!" The gun waves around whilst April and Martina stiffen and watch.

There is a voice from the back of the car. One blacked-out window oozes open, revealing a man who speaks sharply to The Enforcer telling him to put the gun away. "Now! And better be quick about it!" He turns towards the women, revealing a wrinkled face, flashing white teeth and a stubble of grey hair. His red tie is knotted firmly beneath a shiny grey suit and when he points his hand his white shirt sleeve shows gold cufflinks and a Rolex. The Enforcer stands up straight and pushes the gun out of sight. The younger man jumps up and brushes himself down.

"Geddin! Bof of yer!" The voice is clear, a London accent, clipped, commanding: he is talking to his henchmen. He turns towards April and Martina. "Idiots!" and he points his chin sharply at the two men now scrambling into the car. "Can't get decent staff. Know what I mean? Beaten by women? Well I ask yer! Wavin' a bloody gun around fer all to see? Gawd 'elp us!" He beckons to both the women confidingly and they go towards the limousine and see him more clearly; he must be almost 80, his faced tanned and crossed with deep lines. He sits straight and alert, dwarfed by the cavern that is the black leather seating area. "I like yer," he continues, his pale grey eyes contradicting his words, "not rollin' over, puttin' up a bit of a fight. Good on yer!" His false teeth flash as he assesses the women, taking his time looking them over, so they both shift back a little. He strokes his chin, "but I gotta be careful. You and yer daughter gotta pay up. Or pay fer it in other ways. My blokes 'ave spoken to yer. You know what'll 'appen now."

He sits back, tells the men in front to move off and the window rises up, blocking him from sight. It all happens so quickly that April has little time to react, but Martina jumps forward and knocks on the window of the moving car, crying out,

"Double or quits!" April looks at her aghast.

"You can't do this…"

"Yes I can." She turns to April and speaks quietly, "If they go now you have, like, no idea when they'll be back. But they will be back. Sometime. Soon. Do you want that? Here or when you're, like, out walking somewhere? Him with the gun?"

"I just want this to stop now…"

"Double or quits," Martina calls again. The limousine stops, the men in front are talking to each other and half-turned as if discussing with the boss behind them. April is torn between hoping she can delay them further and the disastrous possibility of doubling the debt. But Martina is standing boldly in front of her and April catches her daring. She raps on the window and challenges the boss. "Come on now!" she bellows, "It's a fifty-fifty chance. Half and half. Why shouldn't you win?" The back window lowers, revealing the old man who is chuckling as the Enforcer gets out of the car.

"I like yer style, girl. But," he pauses and draws on a cigar that he has just lit, "I want yer to know. This is THEIR bet. Not mine. I niver gamble. They are tekkin the risk, not me! If you win, they lose. If you lose, I win. Easy innit?" He blows a cloud of smoke out of the window, grins and shakes his head.

"Right," says the Enforcer, getting out of the car, bending down and picking up one of the twopenny pieces that he let fall earlier. "I'll throw, and you call." April reflects that after all she has an even chance, surely it would come down on her side? If she wins, she can make up for all the chaos she's caused, give the money back she's borrowed, get on with her life again. A car is drawing into the car park as she makes her decision.

"I'm ready," says April. "Double or quits!" He throws the coin. April steps in closer, very close.

"Heads!" she calls out. Heads for hope, heads for victory. It flashes upwards as time slows, and it turns as she exhales, her breath clouding the coin's face as it passes: heads, tails, heads, tails, heads, tails, heads, tails, heads, and it is coming down, heads, tails, heads, slower now, heads, heads, tails, tails, tails, tails, tails …..

Kate's hand reaches out and catches it before it lands on the Enforcer's palm and grips the coin, hiding it in her grasp.

"Not doing that again," she says, putting her hand into her pocket and pulling out a wedge of £50 notes. "Only a fifty-fifty chance. Really mum!"

Eighteen

Saturday evening

Trish, Sam and April sit in a huddle on April's sofa scoffing pizza and drinking champagne. Kate sits opposite them, laughing, and Martina is perched beside her, legs swinging, on the arm of the chair. The door to April's bedroom is open and inside Philip lies propped up whilst Dorothy is feeding him small pieces of pizza and giving him sips from her glass, both of them are enjoying themselves hugely, feeling part of the younger life happening in their sight.

The three women have been telling Kate the story of the week and she finds it hilarious. After April describes her ordeal behind the bath in Martina's house, Kate asks about the jewellery from the dressing room.

"So where is it now?"

"In the boot of my car," says April, "I can't bring it in here, every cupboard is crammed. Martina has said she can make sure it's all returned later in the week. Should I get it in?"

"Later!" choruses Trish and Sam, both swigging the champagne, "More!" calls Trish so Kate gets up and opens another bottle.

"Martina," says Trish, "Stu sent me a news clip stating the news that they've 'found' the jewels you half-inched from the safe. At least we're off that major hook then."

"They've, like, called off the big guys. Gave the case back to the local police."

"A lot for them to work on," says April, "what with you two..."

"Dr McGiveney was an angel," pipes up Sam, "tried to hide us then gets his wife on the phone, she's a solicitor. She saved the day. Told me that if Martina's mother had authorized it, I could be OK."

"Why didn't you just ask your mum before all this?" Trish storms at Martina.

"I didn't know she could do that," says Martina, calmly looking at Sam. "Anyway, I got through to her, fast, today when I got back and she sent something to the bank immediately saying Sam was acting as her agent, spoke to them for some time. Said I was confused and so was Sam and she might've given us the wrong instructions. They absolutely don't want to lose my mother's custom."

"The police let me go, once the bank explained it was a misunderstanding and they were not prosecuting," says Sam.

"I'm going to India next week. Got to sort out my mother."

"I'll read the news from India with interest," says April. "Any major upheavals will have your name on them."

"I'll be convicted of speeding," says Trish, "and maybe more driving offences. I said I picked up Sam outside the bank, didn't know anything was going on then took her for a spin. It's a bit of a bind, if I get too many points I can't ride my lovely Betty. They gave me the old Breathalyzer, proved I wasn't blotto, so no drink-driving charge."

"I'll pay your fine," says Sam, "The ride was worth every penny. It was so exciting. Like being in a film. Apart from being cold, the world flashing past and the power! Amazing! I've never gone so fast."

"It was far more dangerous than you realise, darlin', especially you with no helmet and dressed in that stupid outfit!" She shivers. "But Kate, darlin', you do know that we've all done appalling things for you this week, but these two in particular. The one good thing is that April's old wreck of a car has been well and truly put out of action. Maybe she can claim for it on the insurance and she might even get a few quid for the old banger." Kate sits forward in her chair.

"I can't thank you enough, all of you. I have said it before tonight, and I will keep saying it forever. I can't believe what you've done this week: a burglary, an attempted bank robbery, a police chase, a fight. You fought the gamblers, mum.

My grandmother attacked a thug with a baseball bat! It's so brave of you all. You've all been so clever, so resourceful, so daring, put yourselves at risk. For mum. For me. I'm blown away!" She goes forward to the sofa and is pulled in and hugged by three pairs of arms. "I'm so sorry I put you through all that. I wish I'd had the gumption sooner. I could have sorted it all out earlier." She gives her mother a particularly long hug then goes back to the chair. "I went to my old boss, I rooted him out in his place in the Cotswolds. Will and I had gone there for a weekend once." She pauses for a moment, clearly choosing her words carefully. "They agreed to give me a proper severance package and compensation in return for the report and my silence. I've got loads of money. I made them give me the thirty-five grand in cash, that's what took the time. The rest is in my bank. They are also going to give me good references, so I can start applying for jobs I really want to do. I should have done this first off, stood up for myself, but I was just so shocked. It needed my mother to set me straight."

"So, we can give Philip back his five grand," says April, "and Sam, your money can go back to you. And I can reclaim my jewellery that I pawned. Whooppee!"

"I can do more than that, mum, I can buy you a new car. We can go on holiday."

"Oh brilliant! Can you pay off my debts?"

"I'll do my best; I just dread to think what they are!"

"Not as much as your gambling!" There is a general kerfuffle and a round of healthy insults and they all are laughing when the doorbell rings and looking towards the front door, April sees a flash of blue light and says it must be the police. Everyone goes quiet. But Martina jumps up, heads for April's bedroom, opens the window and is out and gone in a flash. April gets up to close the window and sees her lightly vaulting the gate and then running away, she shakes her head and asks Kate to open the front door.

It is the Sergeant, who shows surprise at seeing so many people, hesitating by the door, he looks keenly at them all. April asks him if he would like a cup of tea or is he off duty? He strides thoughtfully into the middle of the room and is clearly uncomfortable. Kate asks him to sit on the armchair, but he refuses a seat and she makes him a cup of tea even though he has not answered April's question. After looking into April's bedroom, he returns to stand near the window where April joins him, but he does not smile or acknowledge her. He is struggling.

"It's been a strange day," he finally says, "very strange. I am still on duty. Sort of. We got a phone call some time ago about a fight going on in the car park here. Car windows being smashed, a scuffle, but this was after the event and she said it was all quiet now and no-one seemed hurt, so we put it down our priority list a bit. But as we were finishing for the day and handing over to the next shift, I recognised the address, I knew it was where you lived, so I came to have a look. I've been outside for a while and it's your car that's clearly been vandalised, so I just wondered if you want to report anything?" He stares at April who looks back innocently.

"Hoodlums!" she says, "they ran away before I could get to them, goodness knows why they chose my car! I was waiting until morning to report it. Nothing I can do, I'm a bit tied up with Mum and Philip as you know, and a couple of friends called round and Kate's home now."

"She said an old woman was wielding a baseball bat."

"Unbelievable!" says April, "why was she doing that?"

"Fighting them, apparently."

"Gosh that's some feisty old lady! Did she give a description of anyone else?"

"Not clearly, two men apparently, a young dark girl fighting them and another woman walking around, but she wasn't clear at all. The witness is in a flat at the top of the block."

"Well do let me know how your investigation goes," says April politely.

The Sergeant who has been shifting from foot to foot suddenly walks into April's bedroom with April following out of curiosity. He looks at his father and doesn't smile, glares at his mother and his gaze goes around the bedroom and comes to rest on the baseball bat propped up in one corner. He looks at his mother again, who straightens her shoulders and pats her hair. There is the sound of a whispered conversation in the main room behind and quiet laughing. He turns back into it and speaks quietly to April.

"The police database," he says, "your fingerprints were on there after you were arrested."

"For Flyposting. I'm amazed they kept them on there it was so long ago."

"The big jewel robbery that's happened in town. They match to that. I saw them. On the door to the dressing room."

"Well Kate and Martina were best friends at school; I've visited Martina a couple of times. She secretly showed me round the house."

"Now they're looking for Martina and want to question her, something also to do with a possible bank fraud."

"Gosh! I thought she had loads of money."

"And your two friends over there are somehow involved."

"Really? Trish and Sam? Do you think so?" He looks at her, looks back into the bedroom at his father who is smiling and struggling to speak, but the Sergeant turns away and the light goes out in Philip's eyes. Dorothy rolls over and snuggles into him and his shaking arm covers her and then relaxes. April suddenly remembers and points to an envelope on her windowsill. "Five thousand pounds," she says, "I've thanked Philip for the loan and I've given it back. Do you want it?" The Sergeant looks up briefly and shakes his head.

"You keep it, they'll need it. The home won't have them back. No married accommodation apparently."

"You have asked then?" says April. He nods his head briefly but looks defiantly uninterested.

"They phoned me, asking when he was coming back, I told them they were married. The home's in an uproar, apparently your mother has got everyone up in arms, they've only just managed to get them all back inside. There's been a formal complaint as well."

"Bloody hell, they'll both have to stay here for a while, what'll I do with them?"

"As you reap, so shall you sow," says the Sergeant and watches with incomprehension as April's expression changes.

"It was one of grandad's favourite biblical quotes," says April, wiping her eyes, "you just looked so like him, he spoke that way, with a broad Yorkshire accent of course. He was a good man but bloody hard to live with." She walks towards the door, still limping. Sam and

Trish are chuckling on the sofa quietly. Kate is openly inspecting the Sergeant who pointedly ignores her, pulls the door back, straightens his shoulders and leaves without a backward glance.

Later, the three friends sit on the sofa, Kate has gone to bed and April's bedroom door is closed. She's going to sleep on the sofa tonight and for quite a few nights ahead. They are now drinking tea, as Trish has to sober up a bit before taking Sam home.

"It won't be the fun trip you're used to, darlin', but I have got a helmet for you this time. I think I'll take a long drive tomorrow, make the most of it whilst I can."

"I'm so sorry, Trish. All this mess is my fault."

"Martina, she made the whole thing worse. Landed us in it well and truly!"

"She kissed me!" pipes up Sam.

"Tongues?" asks April.

"No," says Sam, smiling, knowing it isn't a real question, "but I like her: she is young and vibrant, shows an interest and is informed. It makes a difference."

"So?" asks April, "are you leaving Hugh for her? Turning gay?"

"I think I might be leaving Hugh." There is a silence as both Trish and April struggle as to what to say without showing their joy which they don't want to influence her decision. "But first I'm going to learn to drive and I'm going to take back control of our finances."

"About bloody time! Not that we two are role models as far as financial management goes."

"I realise how much I've let others run my life, how much I've danced to Hugh and Helen's tune. I'm going to get my life back. Get a mobile. I'm going to take my work seriously."

"That's fabulous news, Sam, well done! Your mother would be proud of you."

"I've loved it!" she continues, "this whole week. I've really enjoyed it, being with you both, taking risks, behaving badly. It was fun. Uncomfortable, frightening, but fun. AND I didn't feel ill, I mean, I forgot I was ill."

"I've got what I wanted," says April, "I've got Kate back and I've got paid time off work. I can't say I've loved it as I spent most of my time worrying about Kate. But she's come through and is now tucked up here. But I was bored before! God I was bored. It's got me out of a rut. Made me think."

"So?" asks Sam.

"After this I'll get a different job. I can't waste more time in a job I hate. Maybe I could do something around cooking?"

"That's fab, darlin'. We all love your food. What about your brother?"

"I certainly don't want more family, especially not a police Sergeant who disapproves of me! But it has made me feel better, knowing I wasn't the only child mum abandoned. I also have to admit that she really pulled out all the stops for us this week. Got the money for Kate. Actually attacked the gamblers! And seeing her come out fighting for me, has made a difference."

"Forgiven her?" asks Sam.

"For the moment."

"Mama made me an offer when she came to visit," says Trish softly.

"When she told you she'd stopped the cheque?" asks April.

"Yes. She said she would pay for any qualification that I wanted, however long it took and if it was fulltime she would help support the family financially," she pauses, looking doubtful. "She said that I've spent my life running and that any offer from her I refuse because it is from her. She's right about that, I don't want to be a notch on her Wife-Of-The-Aristocrat belt. But I wonder now if there's something I want to do; I wonder if I need a challenge. What do you think?" Sam and April think for a moment, both careful to tread delicately in this difficult area.

"You could think about it," says April eventually, "seriously think about it I mean. But you have to bear in mind that she will want to be more in your life, it's an offer with strings, so only take it if you want those strings as well."

"Your mother's right though," says Sam, "you have so much talent."

"You think I've not done myself justice?"

"We none of us have," says April, "to be frank. Maybe we should all take time to look at our lives? Think again."

"This crap about realising one's potential, darlin's. Who does that? Who ever does themselves justice? Really?"

"Well I think this week we've all done ourselves justice," says April, "and more than that."

"I've certainly surprised myself!" says Sam.

April struggles with something she wants to say. "There is another thing though," she confides, "Sergeant, sorry, George, Henderson doesn't know that my mother was married twce before Philip. I remember my grandparents telling me. She was supposedly widowed from the first, my father, but I don't think she ever got a divorce from the second one. And I also know she was married again in the 90s to another chap who committed suicide. So …"

"But that means…" begins Sam as Trish starts laughing.

"It's bloody typical of her!" says April. "I just hope no-one finds out. Especially not Sergeant Henderson!"

They giggle a lot and swap moments from the week for a while, then further back in the past, hands touching, shoulders nestling, comfortable, at ease, laughing, contented. Taylor's Three at peace.

ABOUT THE AUTHOR

I have no pets.

I do not live in a farmhouse in the Cotswolds.

I have never received any writing awards.

I do not teach creative writing or history or anything at any University.

I love watching birds, dancing and reading.

My partner of 24 yrs and I live separately and so the relationship prospers.

My female friends keep me sane.

I am busy writing another book featuring Taylor's Three.

Rosie Chapple, 2020

Printed in Great Britain
by Amazon